The Exec[...]
to put the hunt club out of business

Bolan hadn't planned much beyond the act of turning the tables on his enemies. They were expecting him to play the game by their rules, start to finish, cowed by fears of what might happen to Chelsea Rawlings if he missed his cue.

Unfortunately for the home team, there had been no opportunity for them to study Bolan's background, analyze his mind-set, as they went into the game. They couldn't know that he had killed more men than all of them combined, that he had lost more colleagues, friends and loved ones in the long years of his private war than they could even contemplate.

For all of that, the soldier's choice to break the rules wasn't a rash, impulsive act.

But to pull it off he had to stay ahead of the hunters—he had to survive.

Other titles available in this series:

Stony Man Doctrine
Terminal Velocity
Resurrection Day
Dirty War
Flight 741
Dead Easy
Sudden Death
Rogue Force
Tropic Heat
Fire in the Sky
Anvil of Hell
Flash Point
Flesh and Blood
Moving Target
Tightrope
Blowout
Blood Fever
Knockdown
Assault
Backlash
Siege
Blockade
Evil Kingdom
Counterblow
Hardline
Firepower
Storm Burst
Intercept
Lethal Impact
Deadfall
Onslaught
Battle Force
Rampage
Takedown
Death's Head
Hellground
Inferno
Ambush
Blood Strike
Killpoint
Vendetta
Stalk Line
Omega Game
Shock Tactic
Showdown
Precision Kill
Jungle Law
Dead Center
Tooth and Claw
Thermal Strike
Day of the Vulture
Flames of Wrath
High Aggression
Code of Bushido
Terror Spin
Judgment in Stone
Rage for Justice
Rebels and Hostiles
Ultimate Game
Blood Feud
Renegade Force
Retribution
Initiation
Cloud of Death
Termination Point
Hellfire Strike
Code of Conflict
Vengeance
Executive Action

DON PENDLETON's

MACK BOLAN®

A GOLD EAGLE BOOK FROM
WORLDWIDE®

TORONTO • NEW YORK • LONDON
AMSTERDAM • PARIS • SYDNEY • HAMBURG
STOCKHOLM • ATHENS • TOKYO • MILAN
MADRID • WARSAW • BUDAPEST • AUCKLAND

First edition March 2000

ISBN 0-373-61471-3

Special thanks and acknowledgment to
Mike Newton for his contribution to this work.

KILLSPORT

Printed in U.S.A.

There is a passion for hunting something deeply implanted in the human breast.

—Charles Dickens

It is very strange, and very melancholy, that the paucity of human pleasures should persuade us ever to call hunting one of them.

—Samuel Johnson

Sometimes a game gets out of hand, and when it does, you need a referee. I'm shutting this one down. Nobody wins.

—Mack Bolan

To Nelson Mandela, former president of South Africa,
and to his nation's courageous
Truth and Reconciliation Commission.

PROLOGUE

The lone guerrilla knew that he was being hunted. He had picked up on it more than an hour earlier, more premonition than verifiable knowledge, but he had learned to trust his instincts in the jungle. Those instincts—and his skill with the weapons he carried—were all that had kept him alive through the long years of war.

The young man knew that he was being tracked because he knew the jungle and because he had hunted men himself. Some of those men were dead now; others—but a very few, he told himself with pardonable pride—had managed to escape. He had been hunted, too, in cities and in jungle, since he joined the Rwandan Patriotic Front as a teenager four years earlier.

Four years was a long time to survive in the slaughterhouse his native country had become. Five hundred thousand had been killed in 1994 alone, victims of tribal massacres between the Hutu and Tutsi, after the great "peace accord" fell apart. It had required another four years of genocidal bloodletting before the United Nations established a peacekeeping mission in 1998, and close to one million war refugees—mostly Hutus, once the rulers, now displaced by victorious Tutsi rebels—had returned to Rwanda from their meager sanctuaries in Zaire and Tanzania.

And almost as soon as they arrived, the killing had begun once more.

It was payback time in Rwanda, the once persecuted Tutsis settling old scores with any tools at their disposal, the arsenal ranging from rockets and machine guns to hoes and machetes. Once the hunted, nearly killed a score of times by government forces or hostile civilians, the young Tutsi rebel had become a hunter in his turn, and he had gloried in it.

Until, this afternoon, he had become the prey again.

The truly strange part of it, in the Tutsi's mind, was simply timing. He was going home on leave, to visit his family at his home village, in the Ruhengeri district, near the border with Uganda. He could only take the train so far, conditions being what they were, and then he had to walk the final twenty miles or so to his village through lush, virgin forest.

He had covered perhaps one-third of the distance before he realized that he was being stalked.

His first thought was a leopard, seeking easy meat. The cat would be surprised, he told himself, and smiled, because even off duty, he still carried the old AK-47 assault rifle he had been issued to replace his rusty M-1 carbine two days after RPF troops had driven the ruling Hutus out of Kigali, the Rwandan capital. The AK-47 would make short work of a leopard, though the hide would be ruined as trophy material. For serious cat-hunting, he favored a bolt-action rifle, like his late father's Mauser Gewehr 1898. Designed more than a hundred years earlier, it would still drop a charging leopard or a gorilla with a single shot.

But, then again, it hadn't saved his father's life.

The Kalashnikov would have to do, and he was glad to have it when he realized that no animal was stalking him. No four-legged animal, at least.

If asked, the young man couldn't have explained how he knew his pursuers were men, or how he knew that there were several of them following the trail he had blazed through the jungle. Some of his people would claim that a spirit guide had warned him, before any human sense could pick up sound or smell from the stalkers, but he was largely divorced from the old ways, having seen and done too much in his short life to hold much faith in gods.

As for devils, the young man thought, *they* were real enough.

Some of them wore uniforms, with shiny silver emblems on the epaulets.

Once he had decided that his pursuers were human, the young man used a process of elimination to identify them, sight unseen. There were no pygmies in the Ruhengeri district, and the few who survived in Rwanda at large were mostly battle-scarred supporters of the Tutsi rebellion, persecuted in their own ways by the former Hutu regime in Kigali. That left only Hutu or Tutsi, and while he should have been emboldened by the fifty-fifty odds, the young man knew that many of his own tribesmen had gone bad in the long years of war, others grown drunk on blood and vengeance since the Hutu government was overthrown.

Instead of simply killing Hutus—which, after all, was both expected and encouraged by the new lords of Rwanda—certain rogue Tutsis had learned to rape, rob and kill indiscriminately, preying on anyone who crossed their path, regardless of blood or tribal allegiance. Some of them formed outlaw bands, terrorizing whole districts, and they were stalked without mercy by their fellow Tutsis in uniform, shot on sight, without trial, as a service to the people. Others—still a very few, but doubtless growing in numbers—had gone off on their own, abandoning any vestige of community and reverting to virtual savagery.

It had been said that some of them grew fat on human flesh.

If there were truly three or four trackers behind him, the young man counted it a mixed blessing. Multiple hunters meant his faceless enemies were probably simple mercenary cutthroats, rather than sadistic cannibals intent on roasting him alive. At the same time, however, it tripled or quadrupled the odds against him. Against survival.

But he had dealt with deadly odds before, and he was still alive, going home, in fact, to visit the surviving members of his family. No bandits were going to stand in his way.

The soldier pledged that to himself and picked up his pace, looking for a spot to stage an ambush.

KARL SHUKER OFTEN WONDERED if it was the hunt that he enjoyed more, or the kill itself. It was a fact that he had done more hunting in his life than killing—though his body count was edging toward the triple digits—but that was only to be expected. Unless your chosen target waited on a street corner in broad daylight, exposing himself to a drive-by killing, it stood to reason that there would be stalking involved.

Anticipation heightened satisfaction, as the saying went.

The jungle was a somewhat different proposition, though, and Shuker had begun to wish that they could get the sweaty business done—particularly since he wouldn't be allowed to make the kill himself.

He had been paid for his sweat, however, and very handsomely at that. It helped to keep him from complaining when another insect bit him, drawing blood, but even money couldn't wipe the grimace from his face.

It had been very different when he was Sergeant Karl Shuker, of the West German security force, tracking left-wing terrorists who robbed banks in the name of liberty and murdered wealthy businessmen they deemed symbols of "the fascist juggernaut." Those hunts were mostly urban, though they sometimes took him to the countryside—Bavaria, ironically, had been a favored hiding place for certain ragtag holdouts from the Baader-Meinhof gang. Sometimes the hunt had ended with arrests instead of silent bodies stretched out on the ground at Shuker's feet. Not often, granted, but enough to make him think he could do better elsewhere if he tried his luck.

The final break hadn't been his idea, at least not consciously. It might have crossed his mind, before he pulled the trigger on an unarmed fugitive in Wuppertal, but he had done the same thing on prior occasions, without any comebacks from the brass.

But this time, apparently, it was a special case. The target was a neo-Nazi skinhead, distantly related to a legislator with some muscle, and the recent rush toward reunification had placed public relations in the forefront of political minds. Sergeant Shuker had been cashiered out, stripped of his pension and reminded on his way out the door that he was lucky to avoid criminal prosecution for manslaughter.

So much for uniforms and official sanctions.

He hunted for himself now, and for pay. Or, to be strictly accurate, he served as general aide-de-camp and troubleshooter for the man in charge...which meant that he rarely got to do any real shooting. If there was trouble—if they found themselves outnumbered, for example—Shuker had a chance to do what he did best. On most trips, though, he served as pointman, tracker, guide and general "dogsbody"—a British term that he had never understood but that fairly described his feelings in the midst of the steaming Rwandan rain forest.

He was itching like a dog with fleas, in fact, but couldn't scratch himself for fear of giving the game away, alerting their target. The mark was a black man, of course. Shooting a white man in Rwanda these days meant taking out a UN peacekeeper or some stodgy diplomat, and Phelan would never countenance that, due to the shit storm of trouble it would bring down on their heads.

Besides, where would be the sport?

This black was young, dressed almost casually in what might have been a poor-fitting uniform, or perhaps some clothing purchased from an army-surplus shop. There was nothing casual about his AK-47, though, or the cartridge belt he wore around his waist, supporting the weight of spare magazines and a thick-bladed machete.

The quarry was certainly armed well enough to defend himself against attack. Whether he had the skill and the necessary killer instinct to survive remained to be seen.

Shuker caught himself hoping the client would blow it somehow: miss cleanly, perhaps, or else wound the prey and fail to make a quick kill, lose his nerve at the sight of blood and the symphony of screams. It had happened more than once with the clients who hired Phelan's services—fat-cat Americans and Euro-trash, most of them, with the rare Japanese tossed in for seasoning.

When the client missed his shot and couldn't follow through—or when he made a shot of sorts, and couldn't bring himself to finish off the prey—then it was Shuker's job to do the honors. It wasn't satisfying as a solitary hunt, but when you paired the killing moment with his paycheck, it was damned near good enough.

They had come in from Uganda, having greased the proper palms in that benighted realm, and found a likely place in which to watch and wait. The quarry had obliged them after barely seven hours in the stand, stepping from a dusty, World War II–vintage train onto a platform with no station, no porters, no shade.

The client had been predisposed to shoot him then and there, wait for the train to puff and wheeze away, then drop his quarry on the tracks and head back to the relative comfort of a hotel room in Kampala. Phelan had discouraged him, reminding his fat-cat American of the price tag—nonrefundable, of course—and asking if he really wanted to spend so much money on seven hours of waiting and ten seconds of marksmanship.

The clincher, Phelan judging his client astutely, had come when he slipped in the needle. "If you wanted to drop a brother that way," he remarked to the American, "you could've stayed at home. Drive into Bed-Stuy or the Bronx and pop him from your Lexus."

Shuker didn't know what Bed-Stuy was, but he had visited the Bronx, a stewing pot of crime and moral lassitude that left him wishing he could call down an air strike and cleanse the place with fire. Of course, he had a penchant for extreme solutions.

Final solutions, as it were.

Three hours, now, to walk four miles, and the quarry was bending to drink from a fast-flowing stream in the forest when he stiffened, sensing them behind him. Shuker couldn't have explained how the prey found them out, but there it was.

The young man didn't run, nor did he spin and rake the jungle with his AK-47. To the undiscerning eye, in fact, he seemed completely unconcerned, oblivious to danger and the fact that he was being stalked.

Appearances could be deceiving, though.

Appearances could get a careless hunter killed.

Shuker smiled, ignored the green fly biting at his neck and thought the hunt might prove to be a rather special outing after all.

IT WAS A LONG WAY from Manhattan to the Ruhengeri district of Rwanda, and while Leonard Coulter didn't have a clue what district he was in, he felt the distance in his bones. He felt it in his queasy stomach and sweat-scalded armpits, in the feet that chafed his hiking boots from L.L. Bean. He felt it in the clammy palms that gripped his rifle, a pump-action Remington Gamemaster .30-06 he had bought for himself as a thirty-fifth birthday present, three years back, which he had only fired twice in the field.

He had one white-tailed buck to show for it, and one clean miss. Of course, his prissy wife, Lucille, had turned her nose up at the venison, and she wouldn't let him hang his trophy antlers in the house, because she said it made her feel as if they were living on Tobacco Road.

This hunt was different, though. It was an exercise in attitude.

Coulter's fabled killer instinct in the boardroom had landed him very close to the top of the heap in Manhattan, which meant he was very near the top of the heap in the whole frigging world. His yearly salary as CEO of Enerdyne Unlimited was in the very comfy seven-figure range, with stock options, a benefit package to die for and a twenty-year-old personal assistant who was gorgeous even with her mouth full, kneeling in the hidey-hole beneath his desk while Coulter talked shop with his peers in Washington, L.A. or Tokyo.

And still, he felt he needed something more.

Not recognition, mind you. There would be no record of this hunt, no trophy for Lucille to roll her eyes at while she slugged another gin and tonic down the hatch. This thing was personal, a chance for him to find out if he really had the balls, the killer instinct, after all.

Hostile takeovers were one thing. Scoping out some bastard armed with a machine gun and splattering his brains was a whole other ball game.

And now, to his dismay, Coulter had begun to fear that he would choke when his turn came at bat.

He wasn't positive about that. He hadn't frozen yet, or started throwing up the salted meat and warm, flat beer that passed for lunch when a person was sitting in this godforsaken jungle, waiting for a train to come along and drop somebody in your lap. Coulter still reckoned he could shoot. He *hoped* he could...but what if, finally, he screwed the pooch?

No refunds. That was first and foremost, right up front. You miss your shots—or even miss your flight, cold feet and all—it meant a million dollars down the crapper. Lost and gone forever.

The money wasn't Coulter's problem, though. He wouldn't miss a million, most particularly since the cash had come from his special, very private account in the Cayman Islands. And there was always lots of money going his way.

No, it was the thought of failure—worse, of failure in the eyes of *men*—that made Coulter sweat now, out of all proportion to the cloying African heat. He thought his camouflage fatigues had to be approaching kelly green by now, drenched through with perspiration, but he couldn't turn the nervous faucets off.

What would the others think of him if he fell short?

More to the point, if he froze up and weaseled out, would they even allow him to live? Would they trust a spineless wimp to keep their secret when he got back home to air-conditioning, prime rib, clean sheets and telephones, the FBI?

It would be easy, Coulter thought, for them to take him out. Just kill him where he stood and leave him for the animals and insects. In a few days, maybe less, his bones would be picked clean, and who in Rwanda would be interested enough—much less qualified—to identify his scattered remains and launch a competent investigation?

Meanwhile, at that very moment, a ringer who fit Leonard Coulter's description was living it up on his plastic, building a clean paper trail in Vancouver, Canada, where Lucille believed he had gone to a last-minute business meeting. The boys at the office, meanwhile, thought he was on a long-delayed vacation, yachting in the South Pacific, beyond reach of telephones or fax machines.

It was perfect...unless Phelan wanted him dead.

So, he had to make the shot. When the time came, he had to take what he paid for and suck it up. If he didn't like the feeling afterward, he would learn to live with it, the same way he had learned to live with insider trading, income-tax evasion and artful embezzlement. It was easy, once you got the hang of it. And practice made perfect.

Besides, he thought, who would miss one black man in this fucked-up country, where they killed one another like it was going out of style?

That was the beauty of the plan, as Phelan had explained it to him. No comebacks, because the hunts were carried out only in active combat zones, or else in regions where civil unrest and general mayhem would cover the kill. That pretty much left the whole Third World and certain parts of Europe up for grabs, at least according to the nightly network news.

Something like half the planet's land mass was a free-fire zone at any given time.

Perfect.

All Leonard Coulter had to do was keep the sweat out of his eyes and not freeze up when it was time to do his thing. The Remington's trigger had a four-pound pull, and the scope was zeroed in at one hundred yards, though he would be firing from half that distance or less.

No sweat.

He had ruined men in his time—whole families, in fact, when he thought about the trickle-down effect. What difference would one more possibly make?

Almost without noticing it, they had overtaken the German scout. Coulter didn't like the man's shaved head and oily smile, but he could live with it. The German seemed to know his business, and any personal feelings he held toward Coulter were irrelevant.

He watched as Phelan huddled with the man, lips moving, their voices so muted that Coulter couldn't catch even the barest suggestion of audible speech. Finally, when they were done, Phelan moved to stand beside him, leaning in until his lips were kissing-close to Coulter's ear.

"With me," he said. "It's time."

ADAM PHELAN'S FIRST RULE of doing business was to *always* look a gift horse in the mouth. He counted himself a fair judge of character after so many years of dealing with people of various races and backgrounds in life-or-death situations. He knew beyond a shadow of a doubt that few men were exactly as they seemed in brief, casual meetings. Some telegraphed their personalities with loudmouthed stunts, of course, but even then, there was generally something else behind the facade: a latent trace of childhood insecurity, perhaps, or even primal fear.

Phelan could use that when the chips were down.

His latest client was a scorched-earth CEO five days a week, a little skimming on the side, and he was bogged down in a marriage that had started to unravel. The hunt was clearly Leonard Coulter's way of winning something back, convincing himself that he still had the heart and balls of a lion.

As motivations went, in Phelan's line of work, that was fairly routine. Most of his clients were on the brink of what was loosely termed middle age and some were already over the hill. A few of them were stone-cold psychopaths, living a late-life fantasy of blood and pain, but for most, the hunt was more about *them* than their targets, more about regeneration than sudden death.

Phelan watched Coulter and wondered whether this guy had the stones to pull it off. He didn't give a damn if Coulter found emotional fulfillment or a brand-new lease on life; that was some pansified shrink's job, not Phelan's.

At the moment, he was simply wondering if Coulter had the guts to make his kill.

For most of Phelan's clients, fronting a seven-figure payment in full was the easy part of the deal. Beyond that point, there first came drudgery—the preparations, looking after every detail of the trip, the alibi, what-have-you—followed by the stalk, which could be arduous and grueling or a simple bore.

And then there was the kill.

Some twenty percent of his clients froze up when it came to pulling the trigger. A roughly equal number were so keyed up or downright clumsy that they muffed it, putting both themselves and Phelan at risk. He knew what to do in such cases, but mop-ups were still a pain in the ass.

With Leonard Coulter, he couldn't be sure. Not yet.

Shuker reckoned their quarry had made them, and while he resisted the notion, wanting everything to run like clockwork through the kill and their evacuation, Phelan couldn't deny that the prey had gone cagey on them, glancing frequently over his shoulder, unslinging the old Kalashnikov when he crossed open ground, seeking paths that would make their pursuit just a trifle more taxing.

Dammit!

If they got into a firefight, he would take down the target—unless Shuker got there first, of course—and Coulter would have the option of extending his trip, trying again another day or else going home empty-handed. It made no difference to Phelan one way or another, since he took his money in advance and gave no refunds.

When it came to hunting humans, he would guarantee a body on the ground. As far as client satisfaction went, there simply were no guarantees.

Their quarry had covered the best part of six miles, by Phelan's estimate, when he came to a deep, rugged gorge slashed out of the jungle by some prehistoric upheaval. Phelan heard the faint sounds of a waterfall somewhere away to his right, and the gush of a river far below his quarry's feet. A solid-looking bridge of rope and pale wood planking spanned the gorge, secured to heavy wooden posts on either side.

Perfect.

It didn't get any better than this: the target isolated, with nowhere to hide, clearly outlined for the killing shot. If Coulter moved a few yards to the north, he would have a clean shot at the quarry's back, with no need to lead a moving target on the bridge. And when the job was done, whether the prey fell of his own accord or needed help, the river below would clean up after them, carry the stiff downstream to assume its new place in the food chain.

"This is it," Phelan said, leaning close to Coulter and whispering, despite his conviction that the sound of rushing water from the gorge would effectively deafen their quarry.

"On the bridge?" Coulter asked him, sounding uncertain.

"You'll never have a better shot," Phelan advised him. "Plus, he's acted spooky for a while, now. If he gets across and lies up in the trees to find out if anybody's following, he'll catch us in the open with his AK when we try to cross."

"I'd better do it now, then," Coulter said, as if the thought had sprung full blown into his mind that very instant, a product of divine inspiration.

"I would," Phelan told him, and flashed an encouraging smile.

Coulter lined up his shot through the Gamemaster's Bausch & Lomb scope, hardly needing it for the distance involved. No more than fifty yards, by Phelan's estimate. The prey's face had to have seemed life-size in the eyepiece of Coulter's telescopic sight.

And still, he muffed the shot.

Phelan was watching the target when Coulter let go, so there was no way for him to judge what had gone wrong. The shot wasn't a clean miss, of course: a blind man could have winged the kid from that range. Still, Coulter hit him low, an inch or so above the bulky cartridge belt, and well right of center.

It was more than a flesh wound, far short of a kill. The prey stumbled, throwing out a hand to catch himself, and clutched the guide rope to his left, using the momentum of impact to help him pivot on one heel, swinging the AK around toward his rear.

Not half-bad.

"Again!" Phelan snapped, not bothering to whisper now, with the sound of the rifle shot still ringing in his ears.

Coulter pumped the Remington's slide, ejecting spent brass and chambering a live round, but he lifted his eye from the scope as he did it, staring at the wounded man who faced them now, halfway across the swinging bridge.

And Coulter froze.

He was still standing there, gawking at his wounded quarry, when the AK opened up and bullets started snapping through the air around them, spraying bark from tree trunks, clipping leaves. The quarry hadn't spotted them, but he was coming close enough to make Coulter lurch backward, trip on a root and go down hard on his backside, his second shot wasted on the canopy above.

To hell with this.

Phelan shouldered his AUG assault rifle, making split-second target acquisition through the built-on optical sight, and stroked the trigger to release a burst of 5.56 mm tumblers. Even as he fired, he heard Shuker cut loose with his Benelli semiauto shotgun, cranking off three rounds in rapid fire.

The squall of incoming fire ripped their target apart, spun the quarry like a dancer on speed and punched him over the waist-high guide rope on his left. Already dead before he took the dive, he made no sound other than the flutter-flapping of his camou clothing as he fell.

Coulter was on all fours and giving up his lunch when Phelan turned to face him. Shuker sneered and turned his back, a gesture of contempt. Phelan, for his part, wasn't disappointed by his client's poor performance. It didn't reflect on *him* in any way, and he had Leonard Coulter's money safely in the bank.

Nor was he worried that Coulter might report their little hunting trip to the authorities. For starters, he wouldn't be out of Phelan's company again until they reached New York. Few people in the States cared anything about another death in Africa, and those who did had no authority to make arrests for crimes committed on another continent. If Coulter blew the whistle, he would have to prove a shooting had occurred—without the victim's name or body to support his tale—and furthermore, that Adam Phelan had been party to the crime, which meant producing nonexistent records of a secret cash transaction.

More to the point, if through some chain of miracles he managed to achieve all that, Coulter would simply be informing on himself. *He* was the man who had commissioned Adam Phelan to arrange an African safari, while arranging for a ringer to provide him with an alibi in Canada. Phelan and Shuker would, of course, express dismay at Coulter's obvious psychotic break—the stunning moment when he sighted on a human being, in lieu of the big cat they were stalking. Once the stranger had been wounded and returned fire with an automatic weapon, self-defense was automatic and instinctive.

But it would never come to that, Phelan knew, and for one simple reason.

Leonard Coulter still wanted to live, and the Manhattan CEO was well aware of what would happen to him if he went to the authorities. No matter who reached him first—be it Phelan, Shuker or some unknown hitter—Coulter would be dead within a week, at the outside.

And thus, no problem.

"When you're finished there," Phelan said, "we should go. You'll have to do without the Polaroid photo...unless you want to find another stand and try again?"

"Nuh...uh-uh...no."

"Well, then—" the master of the hunt was smiling as he spoke "—what do you say we hit the road?"

CHAPTER ONE

Nightfall had always been Mack Bolan's friend. From childhood, he had always felt at home in darkness, never fearing it the way some others did. Years later, when he chose a warrior's path, he learned that sometimes there were dangers in the night.

And he was one of them.

He had deliberately dawdled on the drive from Washington, through Arlington and Alexandria and something like a dozen smaller towns. At times it was a test of patience waiting for the perfect moment to arrive, but waiting was the first thing they had taught him in the U.S. Army sniper's course.

It had been dark for several hours when he made his move. More waiting, but he never rushed this kind of operation if he had a choice. Sometimes the point was simple hit-and-run, but this time he would also need to verify the target before he struck, and that might well involve more than simply peeping through a window or staring over distance through a telescopic sight.

The target was a renovated farmhouse, located just over a mile outside Stafford, Virginia, on nine acres of mostly wooded land. There was a rustic wood-rail fence along the road that seemed to be more decoration than defense, though he would have to watch his step the whole way in, if even half of what he heard about the mark was accurate.

There was no view of the Potomac River from the house, or even from the acreage out back, but anyone with decent stamina could reach the water if he wanted to, an easy two-mile run on fairly level ground. At night, the trees would be a hazard, but a runner familiar with the land could be standing on the riverbank within half an hour of leaving the house, day or night.

Bolan kept the escape hatch in mind in case something went wrong and the mark slipped away.

It was supposed to be a soft probe, and he kept the hardware to a minimum. The combat blacksuit with its hidden pockets let him carry a stiletto, a garrote, lock picks, a penlight and a handful of incendiary sticks. The selective-fire Beretta 93-R was in its customary place beneath Bolan's left armpit, custom sound suppressor attached, two extra 20-round magazines dangling in pouches on the other side. And just in case the silent approach didn't work for some reason, a .44 Magnum Desert Eagle pistol rode his hip on military webbing, spare clips slotted into pouches on the belt.

He came equipped with infrared night-vision goggles, but left them in the car as he prepared to make his entry, trusting the light of a three-quarter moon. The goggles penetrated shadows well enough, but he preferred to do without them when he could, especially when he was creeping residential property. One unexpected flash of light—from outdoor floods, even a good-sized flashlight—and the goggles backfired, blinding the wearer for thirty seconds minimum, with an agonizing whiteout.

Thirty seconds was a lifetime when your enemies could see, and you couldn't.

Bolan had driven past the property on his approach and kept on going for another mile before he killed his lights and made a U-turn in the middle of the two-lane road. There was no traffic, and the target's nearest neighbor seemed to live three-quarters of a mile due south. The sound of gunfire would be audible that far away.

It was a chance he was prepared to take.

Parking was easy. Little access roads between the blocks of property led Bolan from the two-lane blacktop and any casual sighting by passing motorists. When he was suited up and hands and face darkened with combat cosmetics, he locked the car and slipped the solitary key into another pocket of his blacksuit. One more glance toward the highway, a nod to the watchful moon and Bolan started moving toward the house.

It was spring, which meant rattlesnake season, and Bolan watched his step without being unduly concerned. He would have watched it regardless, had he been in snake-free Ireland or Hawaii, since the greater danger lay in traps or sensors that his target might have planted to secure the property. A Claymore mine or trip-wired fragmentation grenade was deadlier than any serpent, and if the soldier stumbled into one, there would be no time to react before it exploded.

Of course, explosive traps—or any other kind that

left a victim screaming, maybe dead and rotting in such close proximity to farmland and neighbors—would rebound against the trapper, too. One midnight blast would bring a crowd of uniforms to investigate, while one or two gunshots might pass unremarked in the sticks. Silent traps were less reliable, and they would require daily checkups, with a potential for full-daylight corpse retrieval.

On balance, Bolan decided, his target was more likely to defend his outer perimeter with eyes than with fangs.

Security devices—be they motion sensors or fiber-optic cameras—posed a different kind of threat. They wouldn't kill him where he stood, but they might well alert his target, and the man he had come to see was, by all accounts, quite lethal in his own right. Forewarned was forearmed, and if Bolan lost the precious advantage of surprise, he could easily become the hunted, walking into another sniper's sights.

He took his time. If the mark was even home this night, he wasn't going anywhere...except, perhaps, to bed.

That would be fine with Bolan. He preferred a dragon to be dozing when he poked his head inside its lair.

His first glimpse of the house confirmed his impression from aerial photos, examined and incinerated earlier that day. The photo shoot had been a relatively risk-free operation; Stafford was planted squarely between Richmond and Washington, its residents long accustomed to air traffic of all kinds, from Piper Cubs to Harriers and *Air Force One.*

The house was midsize, and nothing flashy—slate shingles on top and an attached two-car garage. He spotted floodlights mounted at the corners he could see, beneath the eaves, but they weren't illuminated at the moment. There were no lights showing from the house at all, in fact, although that didn't mean the solitary occupant was gone.

He could be sleeping. Maybe sitting in a lounger, in the darkened living room, sipping single-malt whiskey and counting all that money in his offshore bank account.

Then again, he could be thinking of the last time he went out to kill.

Bolan was poised to move when something caught his eye off to his right. He swung his head in that direction just in time to see another black-clad form detach itself from the tree line and creep toward the house.

Hunched over, that way, it was difficult to judge the prowler's size, but Bolan was more interested in what he carried; the slim barrel of a rifle or shotgun glinted darkly in the moonlight as his competition closed the gap.

The Executioner was nothing if not flexible. Within the space of two heartbeats, he had revised his plan and changed directions, moving silently and blending with the darkness.

Following the prowler like a shadow.

HATRED WAS THERMIC. It generated a fierce heat of its own, sometimes enough to fuel a lifetime of pursuit, in quest of revenge.

The night was warm, even for spring in Dixie,

and the prowler was uncomfortable in her clinging turtleneck and jeans, her hiking boots, the woolen ski mask that was rough against her face and made her itch. In fact, she had begun to itch all over, as if ants had found their way inside her clothing, scuttling busily across her skin. She longed to strip off the garments and scratch until she bled, but there was no time to indulge herself.

At one point, she had actually considered leaving all except the boots behind, painting her body black from head to ankles, every inch, and simply tying back her raven hair. The thought had a certain atavistic appeal—the night air on her naked body, a soothing caress—and she had even considered the impact of her nudity on the man she intended to kill, wondering if the sight would startle him enough to give her an edge, let her take the first shot.

She had finally rejected the notion, based on two considerations. First, her enemy was by all accounts a consummate professional, as cold-blooded as they came, and she couldn't count on him to be unnerved by a little T and A, with or without body paint. Second, and more critical in making her decision, was her yearning to succeed—and to survive.

What good was vengeance, after all, if she was dead and buried, unable to enjoy it? Where was the cosmic justice in that?

She needed extra ammunition for the rifle she had chosen, a belt and sheath for the knife, someplace to put the flashlight, minicrowbar, as well as other odds and ends she had determined she couldn't do without. That all meant pockets and pouches, and too bad if the outfit made her itch.

The mask had been her last addition to the costume. She wanted her target to know who she was—she'd count the trip at least a partial failure, in fact, if he died without knowing who had killed him and why—but she couldn't count on his being alone, and she had no desire to kill anyone else.

Unless, of course, it was absolutely necessary.

In her old life, what she still regarded as *before*, it would have been unthinkable for her to contemplate a single murder, much less the assassination of assorted inconvenient witnesses and bystanders. But hatred's flame had cauterized her conscience to the point that one man's death seemed critical to life itself, and no one who associated with him voluntarily could be regarded as a total innocent.

His taint was so malignant, so obvious, that it had to necessarily rub off on anything and anyone he touched.

The rifle was a lever-action Winchester—a .30-30, whatever that meant. She didn't have to understand the nomenclature, anyway, as long as she could load and fire the weapon, hitting what she aimed at with sufficient force to knock down a man-size target.

She had originally thought of purchasing a handgun, but was put off by the waiting period and background check imposed by law. That left rifles and shotguns, the latter too noisy, with too much recoil for her taste. There had been numerous rifles to choose from, including the sanitized paramilitary models, no longer assault weapons thanks to some minor cosmetic corrections. In the end, she chose the Winchester because it was simple to operate and because it reminded her of classic Western movies from her childhood, the ones boasting stars like John Wayne and Clint Eastwood, rugged souls who stood up for themselves and meted out vengeance alone, without recourse to courts and police.

If there was killing to be done, the Winchester would do the job. She didn't have to crawl around in the dark, picking up the spent cartridges, either. Detective novels had taught her the way around that problem, wearing latex gloves whenever she handled the ammo to avoid leaving fingerprints. She was wearing them now, as a matter of fact, double gloved to prevent any rips, snags or tears in the heat of the moment.

The hunter was convinced that she had thought of everything.

The car she drove that night had been rented in Washington, using a passable fake driver's license and matching credit card, the plastic having cost a cool five hundred dollars in New York. She would have paid ten times that much to see the bloody business through. The money was a part of her inheritance, in any case. One way of looking at it was that she could afford the extravagance thanks to the man she intended to kill.

It was strange, about hatred. Aside from the raw heat and energy it provided, she was surprised to find that it also served as a kind of natural anesthetic—first dulling, then entirely replacing the grief of her loss at a time when she feared that the pain would consume her. Hating, she found, was a vast improvement over simple grieving. It gave her direction, a goal, and the drive to pursue it. Instead of nursing her pain in a great empty house, with the blinds drawn tight against daylight, she had discarded the hurt, surrendered to rage and set off on the path to revenge.

Which led her to Stafford, Virginia, and a late-night trek through the woods with a Winchester rifle in her hands.

The rifle could kill from a distance, she understood. The clerk who sold it to her had thrown out some numbers—a hundred yards, two hundred, more?—but she wasn't concerned with that. For one thing, she couldn't have recognized her target from that distance, much less in the dark. She couldn't have been certain that her bullet found a vital spot and finished him.

More critically, however, shooting from a distance would have meant the bastard never knew what hit him, much less who had pulled the trigger.

And she wanted him to know. She *needed* him to know.

That, in turn, meant she would have to penetrate the house itself, unless she found some way to lure him outside. This late, a man who lived alone and was a professional assassin would be no easy task. She didn't have her plan worked out in that detail, since there had been no opportunity to scrutinize his home. The better way, she thought, would be to catch him napping, slip inside the house and let him wake up staring down the muzzle of her Winchester.

Or maybe, if her nerve began to fail, not let him wake at all.

Tracing her enemy had been more difficult than picking out a weapon or acquiring false ID. She had been left a name and nothing more, amazed when she discovered it wasn't, in fact, a pseudonym. An ex-policeman turned PI had found out that much, after only two days on the job. It took another seven days and fifteen hundred dollars to acquire the man's home address, but even then, the file was almost totally devoid of background information.

No problem. She was more concerned, at the moment, with making him dead.

Reluctantly, feeling the first true pangs of nervousness now, she left the shelter of the tree line and moved toward the house. She kept her index finger on the rifle's trigger, her thumb on the hammer, ready to cock it and fire at the first sign of movement, the first hint of danger.

"I'm coming, you bastard," she whispered. "Get ready to die."

BOLAN'S CHOICE WAS SIMPLE. He could watch and wait to see what happened with the prowler—maybe nothing, if his target wasn't home—or he could take the necessary steps to intervene. Both choices came with risks, and either way he broke it down, his prospects for a quiet probe were shot to hell.

If he hung back and watched, the drama could play out in any one of three ways. The prowler might discover that their apparently mutual target was out for the evening, in which case both he and Bolan would have wasted their time. Assuming the mark *was* at home, that left two possible scenarios: the rifleman would either take out Bolan's prey or he would die. The first scenario left Bolan hanging in a void of doubt. The second, in turn, would require him to strike—thus silencing the target himself—or to withdraw to try again some other night.

Intervention was the other way to go, but it was also fraught with peril. In the first place, short of using the Beretta, he couldn't expect to stop the prowler without some kind of scuffle—and that, in turn, meant a risk of rousing anyone inside the house. Deadly force was one way to go, if all else failed, but it would also permanently silence a potential, unexpected secondary source of information. Short of killing, though—if he only disarmed the prowler, or even rendered him unconscious—Bolan would have to break off his probe and withdraw, either covering his hostage all the way or carrying deadweight.

Decisions.

Bolan watched as the prowler approached the house on a diagonal from the tree line toward the southwest corner of the building. Dark, curtained windows offered no suggestion that his advance was being observed. A few more yards...

He made his choice when it was almost too late, the gunman nearly equidistant between trees and house. He drew no weapon, leaving both hands free and hoping that he wouldn't have to kill this total stranger—at least, not yet. He wanted some answers first, before it came to that.

The prowler heard or felt him coming. Bolan was never sure which, and it made no difference to the end result. Whipping around on a dime, the slight figure raised his weapon—was that a lever-action rifle, for God's sake?—and swung the muzzle toward Bolan.

He was close enough to bat the weapon aside with his left hand, reaching out with his right, but the gunman was quick, skipping backward and fending him off with a kick that missed Bolan's groin, glancing instead off his thigh. It hurt, a solid hit, but not enough to slow him.

Instead of firing while he had the chance, the gunman swung his rifle around, aiming a butt stroke at Bolan's face. He ducked and shot an arm up to deflect the blow, pain flaring as the stock connected with his elbow. Another desperate swing came right behind the first one, hammering his shoulder, dropping Bolan to one knee.

To hell with stealth. His hand was closer to the Desert Eagle, and he clawed it free, locked on to target acquisition even as the rifleman drew a bead on his face. Still, Bolan hesitated, without knowing why. Some hesitancy in the gunner's attitude, perhaps? A sixth-sense kind of feeling that the prowler didn't want to rouse the house by squeezing off a shot?

Whatever, Bolan's hairbreadth judgment was rewarded when the rifleman stepped back a pace, then turned and bolted for the trees. In that instant, Bolan knew that he was dealing with an amateur, albeit one who could defend himself when fighting hand-to-hand. No pro—or hard-core amateur, for that matter—would turn his back on a hostile weapon without first disabling the shooter. The move telegraphed panic, or else something less than a total commitment to kill.

Once again, Bolan had a split second to make up his mind. He glanced back toward the house—no sudden lights or signs of life behind him—and lunged to his feet, taking off in hot pursuit of the runaway gunman. As he ran, he slipped the Desert Eagle back into its holster, fairly certain now that he could settle this part of the game without a kill.

Unless the gunman managed to outrun him in the dark.

He picked up the pace, following the sound of hurried progress through the trees. At one point, his quarry collided with something and cursed at the pain.

He saw the Winchester lying where its owner had dropped it, passed by at a run without trying to retrieve the weapon. His adversary might not be disarmed, but his losing the rifle surely swung the odds in Bolan's favor.

It took another hundred yards or so for Bolan to overtake his prey. The ski-masked prowler heard him coming and gave up the chase, turning at bay with a quick glint of moonlight betraying the knife in his fist.

Bolan slowed to a walk, then halted entirely, standing just outside the circle of the small man's reach. "You didn't shoot me when you had the chance," he said. "You want to gut me now?"

Instead of answering, the prowler started edging backward. Bolan recognized the signs, was ready when the smaller man broke and turned to run. He used the moment to lunge forward, taking advantage of the stranger's self-distraction, going for the knife.

He almost got it as the lithe figure whipped back around with a lunge and thrust toward Bolan's face, hissing another curse through a slit in the ski mask.

The soldier dodged the thrust with half an inch to spare and grabbed the wrist in one hand, twisting while he threw himself against the other in a stunning body block.

They fell together, Bolan on top, but he was nearly unseated as the smaller man bucked against him, the free hand lashing up to rake Bolan's face. He saved his eyes by fractions of an inch by rolling away and felt rubber-sheathed fingertips claw at his cheek. Both hands were scrabbling at him, meaning that the knife had fallen clear, but his opponent was all knees and elbows, striking anywhere and everywhere that a target presented itself.

The second knee to Bolan's groin connected well enough to stagger him, without the disabling misery of a direct hit to the crotch. He fired back with a forearm to his assailant's head, releasing one wrist in the process, rewarded with a solid hit that put the other on his knees.

Bolan wasted no time, in the circumstances. Quickly stepping behind his opponent, he went for a choke hold but missed it. His adversary nearly wriggled clear before he found the right grip for a solid bear hug.

Something...

In the instant that he recognized what was amiss, he nearly lost his grip, recoiling this time more from force of habit and childhood training than anything else. The impression of firm, round breasts still hot in his palms, he snagged the ski mask from behind with one hand, ripped it free, shoving with the other hand to put some distance between them.

Long dark hair spilled from under the hat as it

came away. The woman spun to face him, darting a glance toward the ground in search of her knife. Not finding it.

"Okay," she said, out of breath. "You got your feel. What's next? You want to prove your manhood? Is that the deal?"

Bolan tossed the ski mask to her, watching it land at her feet. He frowned and answered, "Chelsea Rawlings, I presume?"

CHAPTER TWO

Washington, D.C.

"Let's watch a movie," Hal Brognola had suggested one day earlier. A gesture with his left hand set the minicam that dangled from a slender wrist strap spinning in the breeze.

Bolan and the big Fed were strolling through the Constitution Gardens, headed in the general direction of the Vietnam Memorial and the giant Lincoln on his marble throne. Away to their left, the Reflecting Pool was a bright slash of sunlight glinting on water, two middle-aged men in gray uniforms sweeping the surface with nets, as if fishing for minnows.

"That's it?" Bolan asked him, not touching the minicam yet.

"That it is."

Even now, when he visited Washington, Bolan couldn't help recalling the old days when he had been hunted by Brognola and the whole team at Justice, the most wanted man in America. There had been a time, not so long ago, when the mere rumor of Mack Bolan's presence in D.C. would have emptied the FBI Building faster than a bomb threat, hungry agents spilling into the streets as they grappled with Kevlar and weapons. Times changed, of course. Today, a sighting of the Executioner outside the White House at high noon would prompt derisive laughter, maybe curt directions to the nearest exit.

It was handy, that way, being officially dead.

"What's on the tape?" Bolan asked, stalling for no good reason he could put his finger on. The warm sunshine was part of it, but underneath, he felt the makings of a chill. If Brognola had brought a tape for him to watch, he knew it wouldn't be home movies from a pleasant holiday.

"It's strictly PG," the big Fed replied, alluding to the standard movie-rating system. "Nothing wet."

A bench was coming up, complete with shade, and Bolan veered in that direction, leaving his old friend to trail behind him. Settling in with a body's width between them, Brognola passed him the minicam and talked him through the simple steps required to view a tape, instead of recording one.

"You'll want the earplug," the big Fed suggested, fishing a plastic-wrapped bundle out of one pocket and ripping it open, handing Bolan the brand-new earplug with its coil of slender wire attached.

He found the socket, plugged it in and stroked a thumb across the play button, adjusting the volume control as a burst of static hissed in his ear. Some kind of leader rolled across the tiny screen in front of him, familiar from copies of other tapes dubbed by the FBI and filed as evidence. Ten seconds into it, the camera found a man and focused on his upper body as he leaned forward, elbows resting on a massive wooden desk.

Bolan tapped the pause button before the man started to speak, examining this stranger and the setting he had chosen. The room—what Bolan could see of it—looked like money, with leather-bound books filling the visible wall, the mahogany desk polished almost to a spit shine. The man's suit was Armani, top of the line. His salt-and-pepper hair was neatly trimmed in a style that left you guessing as to whether his last haircut had been that morning or two weeks earlier.

The cultivated look of class.

"Name's Quentin Rawlings," Brognola remarked. "He doesn't introduce himself." He hesitated, then added, "You recognize the name?"

"Should I?"

Brognola shrugged and shook his head. "No reason I can think of," he replied. "He was second vice-president of a petrochemical company based in Houston. Old oil money in the family, and he was taking home twenty-some million a year, on top of stock options and whatnot."

Bolan noted the big Fed's use of the past tense. It told him he was looking at a dead man captured in freeze-frame, about to hear him speak across the void.

"Okay," he said, and tapped the pause button again to roll tape.

"I don't know where to start," Quentin Rawlings said. "Apologies would be in order, I suppose. Chelsea, I'll miss you. I had plans to watch you growing up. You're grown up *now*, of course—I know that, honestly I do—but you know what I mean. Big wedding, grandkids, all that stuff. You'll have to carry on without me, princess. And I know you'll do just fine.

"I hope you can forgive me for what I'm about to do, but in the end, that's your decision. Yours alone. Whatever you decide is for the best, I know. You have to understand, though, why I'm doing it. I've thought about it every waking moment for sixteen months, and dreamed about it every night. If there's another way to go, I don't know what it is, and I've been fretting over this too long to care.

"I guess I should begin at the beginning, like they always say. My problem is I'm not quite sure where the beginning is. My part of it, I mean. The thing that made me go along."

Quentin Rawlings hesitated for a moment, eyes downcast, before he lifted them again to meet the camera's impassive gaze.

"No," he continued, "that's not right. I didn't 'go along' with anything. That makes it sound like someone came to me and whispered in my ear and led me down the garden path. It's not like that. First thing I should admit, right here, would be my own responsibility."

Another hesitation, long enough for Rawlings to swallow, clear his throat.

"It was my idea, no two ways about it. Phelan provides the service, but he doesn't advertise or go looking for clients. The clients go to him. I went to him. You need to know that, Chelsea, for the record. It's the truth. You have to judge me based on who and what I am.

"I'm getting ahead of myself," Rawlings told the camera, frowning and squaring his shoulders before he continued. "I first heard of the hunt club about two years ago, from one of the guys at...well, let's just say a competing petrochem outfit, and let it go at that. We were having drinks, maybe had a few too many, and he started talking about this great safari to Angola or Uganda—someplace in Africa, I don't remember. Kind of worked his way around to it, the way a drunk will when he's still got wits enough to know he's walking on thin ice. Anyway, he told me about the hunt club.

"That's not a name," Quentin Rawlings explained. "You won't find it listed anywhere, in any directory I ever heard of. Adam Phelan runs the show. That may or may not be his name. I haven't tried to get in touch with him or track him down since...well, since the last time we spoke.

"Long story short, this fellow gentleman from one of our competitors described the hunt club to me. He made it sound like the getaway adventure of a lifetime for the man who's been everywhere, seen everything. Not selling it, you understand. He didn't have to do that. If you're in the proper frame of mind, the hunt club sells itself."

Another pause, while Rawlings collected his thoughts, chewing on a bitter pill. "I'm stalling," he said at last. "You can see that, right? No point in beating around the bush at this stage of the game. So, here it is—the hunt club arranges special safaris for clients with money to burn. It's strictly one-on-one, no crowds, no witnesses. I've heard about these deals before, some joker charges you six figures for a shot at a Komodo dragon or a Bengal tiger, some endangered species. Phelan's service is different. He charges seven figures—a cool million dollars, no refunds—and there's nothing rare or endangered about the game.

"Adam Phelan hunts people."

Rawlings paused once again, more to catch his breath than for any dramatic affect. When he resumed speaking, his tone of voice had changed, becoming almost leaden. Bolan recognized it as the voice of a beaten man.

"The way it works," he said, "at any given time there must be twenty, thirty countries with some kind of civil war or revolution going on, unrest between the local tribes, drug wars, your basic ethnic cleansing—call it what you want. It all comes down to killing people by the hundreds, maybe thousands, so that one or two aren't even missed.

"Phelan makes all the arrangements—visas, bribes, whatever—and takes each client to a different place. There's no pattern that way, no reason for anyone to get suspicious. One trip may take him to Bosnia, the next one to Peru, the one after that to Algeria or Sri Lanka.

"Mine went to Chiapas, in Mexico."

The speech had taken something out of Quentin Rawlings. His face had lost most of its color, and he was hunched farther forward, most of his weight on his elbows and forearms. In front of him, his hands were clenched, the fingers interlocked as if in prayer, his knuckles blanched.

"I can't explain what made me want to get in touch with Phelan. Looking back, I can hardly believe it myself. But it happened. My friend was nervous—scared, I think—when I called him back a few weeks later. Had to think about it, so he said, and make some calls. Eventually, I was provided with a number in New York—area code 212, 555-3735. Before you bother trying it, it's disconnected now, no forwarding number available. I tried it myself yesterday."

Rawlings leaned back in his chair and opened a drawer of his desk, to his right. He rummaged around inside it for a moment, then seemed to forget what he was looking for and left the drawer open, returning his hands to the desktop, fingers interlaced.

"The number didn't put me through to Phelan, anyway. It was a cutout, I believe they call it. A machine picked up after four rings, and I could hear all kinds of clicks and hissing on the line, before it rang again, somewhere else. The second time, I got an answering machine, with a generic male voice on the tape. I left my number, waited for a week or so, then I got a call.

"It wasn't Phelan on the line, of course. He's not a stupid man. No walking into traps for him. Some flunky, I imagine it was, hired by the hour to screen out kooks and make appointments. I repeated my name and enough personal information to let Phelan verify my position with the company, and the go-between promised a callback.

"It came six days later, at the office. I was heading out to lunch when a voice I didn't recognize instructed me to go downstairs and wait on the corner for my ride. A limousine came by five minutes later, and I met Adam Phelan for the first time.

"He had a sidekick—called him Karl, no last name used in front of me—who frisked me in the car before Phelan would talk to me. At first, I thought he was looking for weapons, but then I understood he was afraid of being taped, some kind of sting operation. When they were satisfied I wasn't packing any microphones, Phelan introduced himself and we got down to business.

"We spent the first half hour talking about me, repeating how I heard about the hunt club and why, assuming such a service was available, I'd want to take advantage of it. I didn't have a decent explanation for Phelan then, any more than I have one to offer you now, Chelsea, but he didn't really seem to care. The bottom line was money, and before we ever met, Phelan had already confirmed that I could meet his price.

"One million dollars," Rawlings said, announcing the sum as if it had no particular significance, as if the price he paid to kill a man for sport couldn't have fed and sheltered a dozen large families for the next decade. "There was no negotiation on the price, no question of a refund. Phelan guaranteed an opportunity to make the kill. As far as any client satisfaction was concerned, well, that was up to me. My conscience and my quirks, whatever. I could either celebrate the kill or simply learn to live with it. And if I couldn't manage that...well, here I am."

Rawlings spent another moment staring at or past the stationary camera, as if consulting cue cards to find his next line. A tremor seemed to ripple through him, but it could have been imagination, Bolan thought, perhaps some glitch in dubbing off the tape.

"I wasn't told where we'd be going, in advance," Rawlings continued, "but an alibi was set up, just in case. You might remember, Chelsea, when I went to spend the week in San Diego—on a business trip, you thought it was. In fact, I booked the airline tickets and hotel, but I was never on the flight. Phelan arranged for someone else to take my place, run up a tab on my American Express card, laying down a bogus paper trail.

"The morning I supposedly took off for California, Phelan and Karl met me at Hobby Airport, for a charter flight to Guatemala. We landed in Guatemala City, unloaded our gear and Phelan greased our way through immigration. From the capital, we traveled overland into the sticks, and wound up hiking across the border into Mexico—specifically, Chiapas.

"How can I describe it, Chelsea? In one sense, it was almost like being a kid again, playing war, only this time with real guns and bullets, in an honest-to-God foreign jungle. It was an adventure. Hell, it was exciting. I didn't really think about the ultimate objective all that much, until our second day out in the field."

Rawlings shifted uneasily in his chair, frowning at the effort, as if one of his legs had gone to sleep. In fact, Bolan guessed, the man was simply buying time, aware that he had precious little left to spare.

"You know about the trouble in Chiapas, I imagine," he went on. "The Zapatista rebels—native Indians—have been fighting the government for years. Neither side will give an inch, and it plays hell with business, but it's just the sort of atmosphere Phelan looks for when he's setting up a hunt. So many people getting killed all the time, day in and day out, who'll miss one peasant? Or one soldier, for that matter?

"I'll give Phelan this much—he tries to keep it sporting. Told me up front, first thing, that he didn't book outings for psychos, wouldn't take anyone gunning for women or children. The quarry on a Phelan hunt is able-bodied, male and has a fighting chance—to hear him tell it, anyway.

"What separates his paying clients from the psychos is beyond me at the moment. I thought I saw the difference then, but I can't see it anymore. Not even when I look in the mirror."

Rawlings shook his head, clearly disgusted with himself, but he was committed to the narrative now, forging doggedly ahead. "There's no point going into great detail. What happened in Chiapas is no crime in the United States, and I'd lay odds that you'll never convince the Mexican government to prosecute. Why should they, when we did a bit of their dirty work for them?

"Suffice it to say that we found a Zapatista village, or so Phelan claimed. We staked it out overnight, waited for the rebels to send out a two-man 'patrol,' and tracked them through the jungle. When we were far enough from the village to avoid any surprise reinforcements, Phelan gave me my shot...and I took it.

"The 'man' I killed was sixteen, maybe seventeen years old. I shot him in the back, dead center, and I doubt he ever knew what hit him. His companion started to return fire, and I froze. I don't know whether Karl or Phelan did the honors, but one of them dropped him. I passed on the optional Polaroid shots, and we hiked back to Guatemala, free and clear. I've been living with it ever since...until today.

"You'll wonder, Chelsea, why I chose this way to go, instead of calling the police. I've mentioned the jurisdictional problem already, but that's not the whole reason. There's a kicker to the deal, you see. Phelan's personal insurance for the hunt club. If a client talks, the client dies. I wouldn't mind, except the client doesn't die alone. His family goes with him. They go first, so he can think about it, on his way to Hell."

Reaching back into the open drawer beside him, Rawlings produced a short-barreled revolver. It was stainless steel, with black rubber grips, a Smith & Wesson Model 49, the Bodyguard, with a hammer shroud to prevent any snags on a quick draw from hiding. Rawlings placed the pistol on the desk in front of him and covered it with his hand, as if hiding a shameful secret.

"I'm taking out the middleman," he said. "This way, Phelan can't hurt me. He's got no incentive to come after you. I've left detailed descriptions of Phelan and Karl in my safe-deposit box, at Houston National. If you have any problem with police protection, Chelsea, call Sheriff Doolan direct. He's done well with our stock through the years—better than the voters might suspect, in fact. Mention his blind account in the Bahamas as a last resort. I think he'll see the wisdom of providing you with any help you need."

There was a hitch in his voice as Rawlings said, "It's time to go, now.

"Chelsea, the life insurance won't pay off on suicide, I understand, but you won't need it. Talk to Arnie Beck at Childers, Beck and Gold. He'll sort the whole thing out. I trust him with my life—and yours. I'm sorry, princess, but there's really nothing more to say. I have to go, now. Please remember that I love you. Chelsea, and forgive me if you can."

He took the pistol with him as he rose and walked around the desk, his torso blotting out the picture for a moment, before the tape ended. Bolan tapped the stop button, removed his earplug and handed the minicam to Brognola.

"You've checked on this Phelan, I take it?" he asked.

"Yes, indeed. The amazing thing is, he used his real name. Adam Phelan, no middle name on record. Born September 16, 1956, in Fresno, California. He missed the draft and Vietnam, but volunteered for the Army straight out of high school. Tried for the Rangers and made it with honors. He was nine years into making it a career when he went to Grenada, in 1983. Something went sour for him during the invasion. Records from the Pentagon are spotty—one might say deliberately incomplete, if one were so inclined. Phelan wound up with an early discharge and half pension, with nearly three years left to run on his third tour of duty. What's that sound like to you?"

"Could be anything," Bolan answered, picturing his brother Johnny in Grenada, facing the same Cuban guns. "Could be medical, even mental. If it was disciplinary, that should be reflected on his discharge papers."

"Should be, right," Brognola said.

"What's he been up to since the discharge?" Bolan asked.

"Security consulting's what he calls it on his tax returns to Uncle Sam. Also, he's got a Class 3 firearms dealer's license, with all the necessary paperwork for doing business overseas in military hardware. Pays his taxes on time and files all the right paperwork with ATF, so I'm told. They have no reason to suspect he's broken any laws or dealt with any nations on the no-no list."

"In other words, he's clean."

"You'd think so, wouldn't you?" Brognola smiled.

"Except for that," said Bolan, nodding at the minicam.

"Except for that, and certain scuttlebutt that's found its way to Stony Man by hook or crook."

"Such as?"

"The word is, Adam Phelan's done some mercenary work—a lot of mercenary work, in fact—in Africa and South America. It's been suggested that he might have done some contract work—the wet kind—but I couldn't give you dates or names. Hell, Phelan might have made the stories up himself for advertising purposes."

"But you don't think so," Bolan said.

"You're right. I don't."

"How long ago did Rawlings bite the bullet?"

"Going on three weeks," Brognola said. "It's

taken us that long to run basic background on Phelan."

"You found him, I take it?"

"He's right down the road," Hal replied, "in Virginia. A little town called Stafford, forty miles due south. Can't miss it, if you were taking I-95 in that direction."

"Is that his residence?"

"And an office, too, according to his tax returns," Brognola said. "Of course, I couldn't swear he lives there. The arms business operates out of a small office in Fredericksburg. The last ATF spot inspection found the files in order and the necessary license prominently posted, as required by law. No hardware on the premises, which lets him skate on any inventory tax, along with dodging special insurance requirements. Of course, as a Class 3 dealer, Phelan's authorized to possess a full range of samples—anything from full-auto weapons and silencers to grenades, LAW rockets, the whole wide world of what ATF labels 'destructive devices.'"

"That's handy," Bolan said.

"You know it. He can tool around with half a dozen Uzis in his ride, all silencer equipped and loaded up with armor-piercing ammo, damned near anything he wants to pack. If he gets stopped, he's taking samples to a business meet with a potential buyer, and the ATF will back him up."

A question had been nagging Bolan. He decided it was time to ask. "This doesn't sound like something that would go through Justice," he remarked. "If anything, State should be looking at him for a violation of neutrality laws, assuming they can make a case.''

''Like that'll happen,'' Brognola replied sarcastically. ''You're right, though. This is more than business—for me, anyway.''

''Want to share?'' Bolan asked.

''Quentin Rawlings was…aw, hell, I was about to say 'a friend,' but that would be a stretch. I mean, we were friends in college, and we've kept in touch, more or less. His lawyer—this Arnie Beck, from Houston—gave me a call after watching the tape with Quentin's daughter. She wants some action taken against the man she refers to as her father's murderer. Can't blame her, but there's next to nothing I can do.''

''Officially,'' Bolan said.

''Right. Officially.''

''You want him taken out?''

Brognola blinked at that, frowning as he considered the question. ''If he's dirty,'' the big Fed replied, ''nothing would make me happier. That's not what I'm asking, though, because the fact is that I just don't know. I mean, I see no reason for Rawlings to lie—much less an explanation for the details of his story, why he'd target Phelan for that kind of parting shot, if Phelan was clean—but I still want to know. If Phelan *is* running this hunt club, we're talking multiple conspiracies to commit murder, tax evasion on a grand scale, endangerment of U.S. international relations with God knows how many European and Third World nations. If it's true, it has frigging nightmare potential, on top of the smell.''

The smell of death, that would be, Bolan thought. How many million-dollar hunting trips in the past ten or fifteen years? How many victims shot for sport, by fat cats who could hire a human predator to iron out the details?

The answer that came back to Bolan was: not many, in the scheme of things. If Rawlings and Phelan had killed two young rebels in Chiapas, the Mexican government had killed thousands, with hundreds of soldiers lost in the process. Ditto any man-hunting safaris into Bosnia, Algeria, Angola or any other hot spot on the global fever chart.

Assuming he was guilty, Adam Phelan was also dead right. No one would quibble over—if they even noticed—one or two additions to the standing body count.

No one except the dead, that was, and those they left behind to grieve.

"Stafford, you said. Due south on 95?"

"About an hour, give or take," Brognola told him, visibly relieved.

"It might be worth a look," the Executioner advised his old friend. "It just might be at that."

CHAPTER THREE

Virginia

"You know my name?" the startled woman asked.

Bingo! Bolan had recognized her from Brognola's photos, even in the darkness, but the confirmation helped. "I'll take that as a yes," he said.

"You're not—"

"The man you came to see?" he interrupted her. "No, Chelsea, you'd be dead by now if I was Adam Phelan. We might both be dead, unless we find another place to have this talk, and soon."

"I don't know what—"

"We need to talk," he said, cutting her off again, relieved that she had the good sense to keep her voice down. "About the man you came to kill."

She stiffened at that and took half a step backward. "I never said—"

"I'm going," Bolan told her. "We should really talk, but if you'd rather not, that's fine. Whatever you decide, you need to make your mind up in a hurry, just in case there's someone home, back there."

"My rifle?"

"Over there somewhere." Bolan nodded vaguely toward the dark trees and the house beyond, invisible from where they stood. "You have a flashlight, maybe you can find it, but it wouldn't be the best idea you've had today."

"Goddammit!"

"See ya." Bolan turned away, had taken three full strides before she stopped him.

"Wait!" Instead of shouting it, Rawlings was smart enough keep her voice low. Bolan paused and turned to face her. "Where are you going?" she asked him.

"Depends," he replied. "If you're hanging out here, then you don't need to know. If you're coming with me, we'll find someplace to talk."

"All right," she muttered. "I'm coming, dammit!"

Bolan led the way, alert for any sounds of pursuit, hearing none as he angled toward his waiting vehicle. Rawlings followed him for something like a hundred yards before she spoke again.

"My car's in the other direction," she told him.

"You want to split up?"

"I'm just saying—"

"We'll take mine," Bolan said. "I'll drop you at yours. You can follow or not, as you like."

"Follow where?" There was suspicion in her tone, and Bolan didn't blame her for it.

"We'll find someplace," he told her, thinking of an all-night coffee shop or drive-in, someplace where the help was bored, maybe a little rude and didn't hover.

"We could go... I mean, I have a room in Hartwood."

Ten miles west of Stafford, give or take. He smiled and said, "I barely know you."

"Smart-ass! If you want to joke about it—"

"Your place would be fine," he said, turning away from her once more and proceeding through the trees.

Arriving at the rental car, he checked it out from force of habit. He didn't mind if the woman memorized the license number, since a survey of the Avis paperwork would lead her nowhere. He had used a phony driver's license and a matching credit card. The latter was legitimate, at least to the extent that any charges Bolan ran up on the card were paid in full, thus helping to support his cover. Anyone who ran a credit check on Michael Belasko would discover that his ratings were solid.

Bolan unlocked the driver's door and hit the power switch that opened Rawlings's side. She hesitated, with one hand on the door, well after he was settled behind the steering wheel.

"Time's wasting," Bolan told her. "If you want to jog along behind, just point me toward your ride. It might get dusty, but I'll try to keep it down."

"No dome light," she observed. "Why's that?"

"I disconnected it," he replied. "It helps, sometimes, if you don't want the other guy to see you coming."

"Oh. Okay."

She settled in and closed the door behind her, keeping one hand on the inside handle, ready to bail out if Bolan made a sudden move. He put the car in gear and cranked it through a three-point turn, headed back toward the two-lane country highway. A right-hand turn would take them in the general direction where Rawlings had said her car was parked.

"Say when," he told her after they had driven close to half a mile.

"It's not much farther. On the left side there, ahead. Among those trees." Bolan was slowing for the left turn when she said again, "You know my name."

"That's right."

"Okay. So, shouldn't I know yours?"

"Belasko," Bolan told her. "Mike Belasko."

"And you were—"

"This must be it," he said, stopping behind a blue Ford Taurus. No rental stickers were visible from where Bolan sat, and he wondered if the woman had been foolish enough to come gunning for Phelan in her own private car. "We can talk about the rest of it at your place."

"Right. The cryptic type. Terrific."

It was a twenty-minute drive to Hartwood, minding posted limits all the way, with Rawlings leading in her vehicle. Bolan had no fear of being led into an ambush. It was obvious to him that Chelsea Rawlings was alone in her pursuit of vengeance, and there had been no chance for her to arrange a trap in any case. If there was backup waiting for her, she wouldn't have gone to Phelan's house alone, with nothing but a lever-action Winchester to do the job.

Bolan wasn't anticipating much in terms of lavish lodgings, and the Rustic Pines Motel was pretty much what he expected: a one-story structure, built in a truncated L-shape and showing its age. The manager's office was dark, but he drove around in back to park the rental, just in case. He took a chance and left the web belt with the Desert Eagle in the car, shoved underneath the driver's seat. A light windbreaker covered the Beretta 93-R's shoulder rig. Moistened towlettes stripped the war paint from his face and hands. He stepped into a pair of faded blue jeans, cinched the belt around his waist and went in search of Chelsea Rawlings.

She was waiting for him in the open doorway of room 9, at the inside angle of the L, light spilling onto the pavement around her. She blinked at Bolan, taking in the changes. "Thought I lost you for a minute there," she said. "You didn't have to go all formal on me."

"This old thing?" He brushed past the woman, leaving her standing in the doorway as he checked the motel room, then moved on to scout the bathroom.

"We're alone," she told him, sounding none too happy at the prospect, as she closed and double locked the door. "I don't have anything to drink, unless you count the coffeemaker."

"That's all right."

She took the only chair in sight, leaving Bolan to stand or sit on the bed. He took the corner of the mattress nearest to the door and sat.

"So, do I have to guess, or would you tell me how you know my name?"

He thought the truth—or part of it, at least—would serve him better than a lie. "I've seen your photograph," he said. "I've seen your father's tape."

The second statement hit her like an openhanded slap across the face. She flinched, hands closing into small, white-knuckled fists, her spine stiffening. It wasn't the right place or time, Bolan thought, to notice her breasts, rising beneath the clingy fabric of her turtleneck, but he noticed them anyway, remembering the way they filled his palms when he was wrestling with her in the dark.

"How'd that happen?" she asked, when she could trust her voice. "And just who *are* you, anyway?"

"You pressed for an investigation of your father's claims against Adam Phelan," he said.

"You're damned right I did," she replied, "and got nowhere for my trouble. Brush-offs from Houston PD and the Rangers, a polite 'no-can-do' from the great FBI. Nobody gives a damn."

He let that go and said, "You found him, anyway."

"Yeah, well, what can I tell you? Money talks, and thanks to Phelan's little hunt club, I've got cash to spare."

"He didn't pull the trigger, Chelsea."

"No," she said, "my father beat him to it. Tell me, Mike—you don't mind if I use your first name, right? I mean, us being such close friends, and all—when was the last time you tried living with a ghost?"

"You'd be surprised."

She frowned. "Okay, you're made of sterner stuff. Congratulations. Anyway, he couldn't take it.

And you don't need to remind me that he put himself in that position to begin with, okay? Phelan's a murderer, no matter how you slice it."

It was Bolan's turn to frown. "Forgive my saying this—"

"Wait, let me guess," she said, cutting him off. "You only have my father's word for that. Is that about the size of it?"

He nodded.

"And since no one's doing anything at all to check it out, that's how it stays, right? Phelan walks."

"I wouldn't go that far."

"Oh, no? Then tell me, has anybody from the Bureau spoken to him yet? Has anyone from any-fucking-where so much as called him on the telephone?"

"Not yet," he said.

"So, there you have it, friends and neighbors. Looks like someone put the famous wheels of justice up on blocks."

"And that leaves you to settle up?" he asked.

"Who else?"

He shrugged. "It just seems odd...or maybe I should say ironic. After what your dad went through, I mean, to find you stalking Phelan with a rifle."

"There's a difference," she assured him, and he felt the sharp edge of her voice. "My father killed an innocent man—at least, that is, a man who never did him any harm—and now he's paid for it. The ultimate price, by his own hand. You should recognize the difference between payback and cold-blooded murder."

"Recognizing the difference is one thing," Bolan said. "Living with the result is another."

"I can handle it," she said.

"You couldn't handle me," Bolan reminded her. "You had me cold and couldn't pull the trigger."

"Didn't pull it, not couldn't."

"When you're dead, it's all the same."

"You took me by surprise," she said defensively.

"And you think Phelan won't?"

"You're not my bodyguard!" she snapped. "And while we're on the subject, you still haven't said what you were doing out at Phelan's house tonight, all painted up like Rambo."

"I was checking out the set," he said.

"Whatever that's supposed to mean."

"The plan was to find out if Phelan was at home, and if he was, discuss your father's allegations with him one-on-one."

"The Bureau didn't send you," Rawlings said. "Those guys all wear Brooks Brothers suits and carry warrants."

"No, the Bureau didn't send me," he agreed.

"So, what's the deal? You're not with Phelan, and you're not with Uncle Sam. I know damn well I didn't hire you. What's that leave?"

"Suppose your fathers allegations—"

"Facts. They're facts, as far as I'm concerned."

"Suppose they couldn't be pursued officially," Bolan said. "Say, for instance, that the man he named is squeaky-clean as far as public records go. No evidence at all of any criminal activity in the United States."

"Of course not! He—"

"Suppose the Bureau only has a dead man's word—the word of a self-admitted murderer, at that—"

"You bastard!"

"—to suggest a crime committed several thousand miles outside of U.S. jurisdiction. What are they supposed to do?"

"I don't know, dammit!" There were bright, angry tears in her eyes. "How about asking him if it's true? They could do that much, right? Ask a straightforward question? I mean, it is the Federal Bureau of Investigation, right?"

"And when Phelan denies it, laughs the whole thing off, what then?"

She glared at him in silence for a moment, then responded, "So, you're out there with your guns and war paint for a reason, yes? What's your idea?"

"The first thing," Bolan said, "is for you to stand down and not get yourself killed. One thing we know for sure about Phelan is his military training. He's top of the line, combat tested. You don't stand a chance."

"And you do?"

"Let's say I speak his language, and leave it at that."

"So, you're a killer, too?" When Bolan didn't answer that, Chelsea Rawlings averted her eyes, the pink stain of a blush rising into her cheeks. "Look, I'm sorry for that. I mean, unless it's true. The fact is, I don't much care who or what you are. I just want Phelan punished for my father's death."

"His suicide."

"I thought we'd covered that."

"Sometimes there's a difference between punishment and death," Bolan reminded her.

"Oh, right," she fired back. "Let me guess. Our government can't prosecute him—or it won't—but if I'm a good girl and I wait a few more years, there's a one-in-a-thousand chance he'll be sent to some other country where he's already bribed all the cops. Is that about the size of it?"

"I don't do deportations," Bolan said.

"Well, hey, as long as I can list the things you don't do, I suppose I should be satisfied." She hesitated, then went on. "My father's dead. He blew his brains out in his den, because he couldn't live with what he did, what he found out about himself, from Adam Phelan. I don't know if you've lost anyone you cared about, in circumstances that were even vaguely similar—"

"I have," he told her, seeing no need to elaborate.

"What did you do about it?"

"Settled out of court," he said.

"Well, there you go."

"Two problems with your plan," the Executioner replied. "First up, you haven't verified your target. Hate might help you pull the trigger, but it won't confirm an enemy ID."

"I've told you that I trust my father's word. He didn't make that awful tape just so he'd have another chance to lie before he died."

"And second," Bolan said, as if she hadn't spoken, "you don't have the proper training for the job you've got in mind. I'm not convinced you have the nerve."

"Is that a challenge?"

"My professional opinion," Bolan said.

"Professional? Is that supposed to mean you're—"

"Qualified in areas where you aren't."

She sniffed at that and told him, "I'll do better next time."

"There won't be a next time, Chelsea."

"Don't bet anything you can't afford to lose on that one, Mike."

"One phone call, and you're off the street. Stalking, attempted murder, pick your felony."

"You said you're not a cop."

"Call it a citizen's arrest," he said. "I'll do the paperwork and pull the necessary strings to see you charged."

"An inconvenience," she retorted. "I'd make bail."

"And while you're out on bond awaiting trial, with a restraining order that can put you back inside, you'll be under surveillance, day and night."

"You can't do that!"

"Is that a challenge?"

"Look...just wait a sec, okay? You're throwing ultimatums at me, and I still don't have the foggiest idea of who you are, or what you plan to do about this whole damned thing. You want me to cooperate, it's time to share."

"There's not much I can tell you," Bolan answered. "And the truth is, Chelsea, you'll be safer if you don't know anything at all."

"Not good enough," she told him flatly. "It was not your father on that videocassette. It's not your father in the ground. You can't just tell me to forget about it and have faith that justice will be done. I've gone that route, remember? Every door I knocked on wound up slamming in my face."

"It could be that you've found the right door this time."

"Oh, well, hey! That clears it up, right? How could I have doubted you?" Her bitter smile stopped just short of being a sneer. "Jesus, give me a break!"

Bolan watched her for a moment, considering what he could safely tell her without compromising himself, his support or the mission at hand—without, in fact, compromising the woman herself.

"Your father had a friend," he said at last, "well placed in government. The name and office are irrelevant. This friend isn't in a position to do anything officially, but he's determined not to let it slide. He has the necessary pull to get things done, but he insists on being positive before he takes a leap. Fewer mistakes, that way. No mess to clean up afterward."

"This friend—"

"I've told you all I can," he said.

She waved his words away. "It isn't that. I need to know, does he believe my father's story?"

"As of now, pending complete investigation, yes, he does."

A tear spilled over from her left eye, leaving a moist, bright track across her cheek. "Thank God for that, at least." She blinked at him, as if to hold the tears at bay. "That's why you're here?"

"Friend of a friend," he said. "It's worth a closer look."

The frown was back on Rawlings's face, but it was different, somehow. "So," she said, "I guess I screwed things up tonight."

"It had FUBAR potential," he acknowledged, "but we might have pulled it off. At least nobody chased us off the property."

"Foo-what?" she asked.

"FUBAR," he told her with a smile. "It's an acronym for Fouled Up Beyond All Recognition, or words to that effect."

"I see." She almost smiled, then caught herself at it. "My rifle," she said. "It's still out there."

"Assuming it's found," Bolan said, "it might set off alarms, or maybe not. It wouldn't be the first time some out-of-season hunter got separated from his hardware, one way or another. Of course, if someone does find it and decides to trace the serial number—"

"No problem," she told him, finally permitting the smile. "I used a fake ID. Same with the rental car."

That could be good or bad, Bolan thought. There were ways of tracing fake IDs, the same as guns and motor vehicles. Some forgers did distinctive work, and some of *those* weren't above selling their clients out, if it would put a few more dollars in the bank. At the moment, though, he saw no reason to burden Chelsea Rawlings with any such long-shot concerns. His main problem would be finding a way to prevent her from taking another run at their mutual target, perhaps putting Phelan to flight and getting herself killed in the process.

"Looks like you thought of everything," he said, keeping it simple.

"So I thought," she answered. "At least, that is, until you showed up out of nowhere, and I really had to pull the trigger."

"I'm glad you didn't."

"I'm not," Rawlings said. "It's nothing personal, you understand, but now I guess I haven't got the stomach for it, like you said. No guts."

"Killing and courage aren't synonymous," Bolan replied. "I've seen cowards run up triple-digit body counts. Sometimes it takes more guts to realize that you're not suited for a job and pass it off to other hands."

"Like teamwork?" Her sudden hopeful tone set Bolan's nerves on edge.

"I work alone," he said. "That's nonnegotiable. We caught a break tonight, with Phelan either sleeping or away from home. He could have killed us both without half trying, while we scuffled in the yard."

"That doesn't have to be a problem."

"No," he said, "it doesn't."

Even understanding him, she forged ahead. "Because," she said, "now that I know somebody's on my side, there'd be no fighting. All I need is to be in on this. I won't get in your way."

"You would," he told her, "without meaning to. Just knowing there's a third person involved, I'm off my game before we start. I can't afford that loss of concentration when it's life or death."

"It's all a game to you," she said. "Some kind of academic exercise. This nameless, faceless friend you say my father had, he doesn't care enough to come himself, but sends you in his place—"

"He's not that kind of soldier," Bolan said. "I am."

"—and you give me this spiel about distracting you from God knows what, expecting me to go back home and make believe the whole thing's settled, when, for all I know, you might not do a goddamned thing."

"That's where the trust comes in," he said.

"The trust? Are you for real?" She couldn't stop the tears from spilling over now. Her cheeks were radiant with liquid pain. "I don't know you from John Doe on the street, and you want trust? I trusted my father, all right? I trusted him not to shoot total strangers, and then kill himself. I trusted the authorities to act, when he identified the men responsible. You pop in out of nowhere to protect the man who drove my father to his death, protect his ass from me, and now you want my trust? No, thanks."

"I guess you're out of luck, then," Bolan said, "because right now, I'm all you have."

"Here comes the stick, again," she said. "If I don't play along, I go directly to jail and don't collect my two hundred dollars."

"It could be worse," the Executioner replied.

"Oh, yeah? How's that?"

"I could pull out and leave you to it," Bolan said. "In which case, you'll need to reorganize, maybe hash it over with yourself and see if you can get your nerve back. That means wasted time, and when you go ahead with it—that's if you go ahead—Phelan will take you out like it was nothing. He won't even break a sweat."

"And if I play it your way...?"

"I confirm the target and proceed from there."

"I need to know it's done," she told him, leaning forward, almost coming off her chair. "It's not enough for you to promise."

"When it's done, you'll know."

She settled back, studying his face for close to a minute before she decided. "All right," she said at last, "since I don't seem to have much choice. I swear to God, though, if you let him get away, all bets are off. I'll have two scores to settle then. If I can't find the nerve myself, I'll hire someone to do it for me. Money talks. Remember that."

"We have a deal, then?" Bolan said.

"We have a deal...for now."

He let the ultimatum pass and rose to shake her hand. If Adam Phelan got away from him, it would make little difference to him what this young, determined woman said or did.

Because he would be dead.

CHAPTER FOUR

Peru

Peru is one of several nations that, though not strictly off-limits to American tourists, is branded with a State Department traveler's advisory suggesting that visitors go elsewhere in search of commerce or diversion. The traveler's advisory, in essence, is a legal disclaimer from Uncle Sam, divesting the government of any responsibility for protecting tourists who ignore the warning. If you wind up in such a place, by accident or otherwise, you might still find a U.S. Embassy, of course.

It just won't do you any good.

Peru owes its particular travel advisory to a matched set of distinct and separate problems. On one hand, the homeland of the once proud Inca produces sixty percent of the world's raw coca leaves, and the multibillion-dollar drug trade has produced no end of carnage, from tiny rural villages to the streets of Iquitos and Lima. On the other hand, political unrest has been a constant of Peruvian life since 1968, when the first of several military coups installed a brutal twelve-year junta as the nation's ruling power. Return to civilian rule in 1980 brought no cessation of violence, with terrorists from the left-wing Shining Path and Tupac Amaru guerrillas waging relentless, bloody war against the reigning government. Repressive measures followed automatically, evoking international criticism of Peru's disregard for human rights. The "good" news is that deaths from terrorism have been greatly reduced in Peru—to something like twelve hundred per year.

In short, the troubled nation was a happy hunting ground, from Adam Phelan's point of view.

He had done some private wet work in Peru, once upon a time, before he struck gold with the hunt club, and Phelan knew his way around the country well enough to keep himself alive. He also knew it well enough to understand that he shouldn't fly there directly with his client, from the States. Instead, they flew to Guayaquil, in friendly little Ecuador. From there, it was a short hop to Loja, on the right side of the Andes, and a shorter trip overland to the Peruvian frontier.

Phelan's million-dollar hunt club was a word-of-mouth operation, dependent on referrals for the most part, to keep him in business. A handful of hardcore clients came back for sloppy seconds or thirds, but most would never book a second hunt. They *did* talk to their friends, but discreetly, with Phelan's stern injunctions in mind. There had been no complaints or questions from the law so far, as if they could have made a case from one man's word against another, with Karl Shuker standing by to rubber-stamp whatever Phelan said. There were no records of the payments he received, no evidence to prove the hunts took place at all—on top of which, his clients each had a solid alibi that cut both ways, protecting Phelan equally.

Since he depended on those clients for his future business, though, Phelan took reasonable care to plan each trip with the abilities of his specific customer in mind. He wouldn't take a client with a heart condition under any circumstances—physicals were mandatory for all newbies—but he made allowances for other handicaps. If he was working with a porker, for example, he would look for someplace nice and flat to do their hunting, preferably with a moderate climate and no great potential for long-distance sprints.

The present client, Clifford Wix, seemed fit enough, in an early-middle-aged kind of way. He had love handles starting at his waist, hair thinning out on top, but he was sturdy and determined. There was no good reason why he couldn't pull his weight—in this case, forty pounds of camping gear and weaponry—while scrambling up and down the foothills of the Andes. With any luck at all, he might come out of the hunt a new man, in more ways than one, perhaps restored to the old fighting trim of his youth. The makeover would be a bonus gift, no extra charge.

They crossed the border sixty miles southeast of Loja, where the Cordillera del Condor mountain range straddled the line, providing a kind of natural boundary between Ecuador and Peru. There were no checkpoints or signs to mark their transit from one country to the other, passing from relative safety into a land fraught with peril, ravaged by drugs and political terror. Phelan knew where they were when they crossed because he had kept track of time and mileage, used his compass frequently and recognized landmarks along the way.

The Amazonas district had been a natural choice. Sprawled across three hundred miles of the Peruvian frontier with Ecuador, from Sullana to the Rio Pastaza, Amazonas provided free access in both directions, thereby earning favored status as a rebel sanctuary in the north. Guerrillas hiding there could always duck across the border if the heat got too intense, and then return at leisure to resume their raids. Whole villages in Amazonas were presumed guerrilla strongholds, and while several had been raided—razed would be more like it, the inhabitants packed off to prison camps or shot—such tactics were no longer favored in the light of UN scrutiny.

Phelan had managed to acquire the names of three such villages, along with their coordinates, and he had briefed his client—minus the specifics—on their plan of action. They would pick a rebel village, stake it out and see what opportunities arose for Wix to make his kill. If nothing happened for them in a day or to, they would move on and try again.

They had a week to get it done, before Wix was expected back at his brokerage house in San Francisco. If Phelan couldn't find a target for him in that length of time, he would almost be tempted to refund the fee.

Almost.

Wix understood, of course—and had agreed—that there were certain circumstances that absolved Phelan of his commitment to produce. The contract could be nullified by acts of God—earthquakes, typhoons, the usual—or by some unexpected act of man. Suppose, for instance, that the army found its balls and swept through Amazonas like a dose of salts, evacuating villages before they had a chance to score. In that case, Wix would be entitled to a second trip at cost—about $150,000—or he could elect to let it slide and eat the loss.

In either case, the million dollars paid up-front remained with Adam Phelan. It was history.

This time around, though, he felt good about their chances for a nice, clean kill. They had a favorable ten-day forecast on the weather, and the politicians in Lima were still more concerned with world opinion than with solving their guerrilla problem. They were now six miles from the village he had chosen and right on time.

All systems go.

CLIFFORD WIX HAD EXPECTED more heat, rain and insects, considering the fact that they were almost close enough to piss across the equator. He had expected something from a Tarzan movie, trees festooned with vines and serpents, dripping rain, with birds and monkeys shrieking in the canopy above him. He expected sluggish rivers occupied by crocodiles and quicksand that would swallow you in seconds if you left the trail.

What he got instead was a hike in the woods.

The altitude had something to do with it, Wix supposed. It was always cooler in the mountains than down on the flats. Hell, there was snow on Mount Kilimanjaro year-round, and that was in the heart of freaking Africa. As for the forest, it was nearly all deciduous up here—no evergreens, of course, but nothing in the way of classic jungle, either, with the massive ferns and creepers, moss and fungus swarming over everything in sight. Wix hadn't seen a snake of any size, much less the giant man-eaters that slithered through the average jungle flick. There were insects—he could hear them all around him, clicking, buzzing—but they seemed to have no interest in his flesh or blood. The streams they had encountered, so far, had been swift and narrow, foaming downhill in a rush, no stagnant eddies left behind to breed mosquitoes.

Wix could understand the rebels seeking high ground. It made perfect sense, the more he thought about it. They had found a better climate than the steaming jungle, down below, with cool, clear water, less risk of disease. There was probably game to be had in these woods if their rations ran low, and while the relatively open forest offered less concealment for an ambush than the jungle might have, any effort to surprise the rebels would be similarly handicapped. A raiding force would either have to climb up from the valley down below, or airlift in, with all the warning racket that entailed.

It struck him once again that he was several thousand miles away from home, on hostile turf, with only two men in the world who knew his present whereabouts. A man he'd never met was using Wix's name and credit cards in Oklahoma City at that very moment, nailing down the alibi that would also serve to render his disappearance an insoluble mystery if anything went wrong.

Wix thought about the rebels they were hunting, reminding himself once again that they were Communists, outlaws, thieves and killers pledged to the disruption of a lawful, progressive society. He only hoped that they weren't too skillful, too professional. He had no wish to die in Amazonas, at age forty-two, with some Commie's bullet in his heart or brain.

As for the thought of killing, Wix felt perfectly at ease. It wouldn't be his first time. That had been when he was just sixteen, a drunken joyride in a stolen car that turned into a hit-and-run, some homeless wino fished out of a roadside ditch days later. Once the adolescent nervousness subsided, Wix had cherished the event, replaying it in slow-motion daydreams, loving the sense of power it gave him. He had been tempted to try it again, but fear held him back. All the way through school and marriage, fathering two daughters, making money hand over fist, he had waited, wondered whether he would ever have another chance.

Now, here he was.

The Benelli M-1 Super 90 shotgun he carried had been Phelan's suggestion, after one trip to target range. Wix sucked with a rifle, and where handguns were concerned, he might as well have thrown them at his target as to aim and fire. The Benelli was different, though: an ass-kicking semiautomatic 12-gauge with an extended magazine that could crank out eight rounds—make it nine, if you started with one in the chamber—before your first empty shell hit the ground. As Phelan explained it, with double-aught buckshot loads, that would riddle a target with more than a hundred .33-caliber pellets in something like two seconds flat. Wix barely even had to aim with the Benelli, since the shotgun was designed for moving targets found in less than optimal conditions.

It was perfect.

Granted, Wix was only packing a hundred rounds of ammunition for the 12-gauge, slung across his chest in black elastic bandoliers, compared to Shuker and Phelan with their futuristic assault rifles, belt pouches filled with thick, curved magazines. Still, how much ammo could it take to kill one man? Wix didn't plan on facing down an army. If it took a hundred rounds for him to bag one freaking man, even in the middle of a foreign wilderness, it would be time for him to turn around and head for home.

Phelan and Shuker were his backup. They weren't supposed to fire at all if things went smoothly, but it helped to have them with him—even if the German sometimes smirked at him for no good reason, coming off with attitude like goddamned Eurotrash. The second time it happened, Wix had started thinking how sweet it would feel to cap the kraut. He wasn't about to try it, though, because he frankly didn't have the nerve. If he should go for broke and Shuker didn't kill him, Phelan surely would.

And that would definitely spoil his million-dollar hunting trip.

The lack of conversation as they traveled didn't grate on Wix's nerves. He was a man who kept his mouth shut when he had nothing to say, a trait that led his wife to bitch and moan from time to time about their failure to communicate. He knew that

Phelan or Shuker would let him know when they were closer to the target, ready to begin the final approach. Until then, he was satisfied just to be moving, enjoying the solid weight of the pack on his back, the shotgun in his hands.

Another chance, he thought. With no surprise, this time, no scabrous wino lurching out of the darkness and into his high beams. This time around, he would have a real chance to enjoy it, psyched from all the planning and anticipation, picking out his target. Making a deliberate choice.

No matter how he tried to dress it up, the first time had been a clumsy accident. There was even some doubt as to what he remembered, after more than a quarter-century of building it up in his mind. The hit-and-run itself had taken less than five seconds, images blurred by speed, whiskey and fear. The worst part—what had made him strike a deal with Phelan in the first place—was that he was losing it, the jerky, lavishly embellished memory of sudden death.

He needed more.

This time around, there would be no mistakes, no accident, no liquor to corrupt and fog his memories. The images of this kill would be with him till he died.

Wix only hoped that wouldn't be today.

KARL SHUKER SMELLED the rebel village from three-quarters of a mile away. Someone was cooking meat on an open fire, and they were downwind from the source of the mouth-watering aroma. They could follow it from here, as if they had been summoned by a homing beacon from afar.

But they would have to watch their step.

He glanced at Phelan, saw his boss had also picked up on the smell, one corner of his thin lips rising in an almost smile. The stockbroker was frowning, picking up on something, though he didn't seem to know exactly what it was.

The city life could do that to you, Shuker knew. With all the smog, carbon monoxide, piss and garbage in the streets, the sidewalk restaurants, construction sites, cologne splashed on too heavily, the reek of body odor as some homeless scarecrow shuffled past. It was a wonder city dwellers could smell anything at all.

"That's smoke," Wix said. And then he disappointed Shuker, when he asked, "Which way?"

"Southwest," Phelan stated, pointing. "Anywhere from this point on, they might have sentries posted. Take your time. Keep quiet. Watch your step."

Wix nodded, and the German gave him mental points for following instructions. Shuker didn't like Wix, any more than he liked Phelan's other clients. They were all somehow deficient in his eyes: some of them cowards, when it came down to the kill; some brash and boastful, jabbering endlessly about an easy shot that took the quarry down; a few of them psychotic, with the spark of madness in their eyes. The one called Wix, so far, had been better than most. He was simply a fat-cat poseur playing war in the woods, with two professionals on hand to save him if he made a critical mistake.

Another thirty minutes brought them to the village, unobserved. Shuker was curious about the lack of sentries, wondering if rebel forces this close to the border took safety for granted, confident in their ability to dodge pursuit. It hardly mattered in the last analysis, however. They had found the village, crept in close enough to watch the peasants go about their dreary lives, and still the enemy remained oblivious.

These peasants were "the enemy" in Shuker's mind, not only for their revolutionary politics and the support they gave to terrorists, but also for the simple reason that he had been paid to hunt them down. They would resist, of course, if given half a chance, and some of them were armed with modern military weapons. They would do their best to kill him, Shuker knew, if he gave them the opportunity. But before he let that happen, he would cheerfully slaughter every man, woman and child within range of his Steyr AUG.

They hunkered down and watched the villagers for close to forty minutes before Phelan signaled them back from the tree line, seeking out the shadows, gaining distance so that they could speak in whispers. Shuker kept watch while Phelan huddled with their client, eavesdropping while the two of them worked out a plan.

"They'll have to go for water sometime," Phelan said. "My guess would be the stream we crossed back there, a thousand yards or so." He jerked his head in the direction they had come from, and the broker nodded. "Most likely, even if they send their women for the water, they'll be covered. You can always drop the lookout."

So it was decided, without asking Shuker. If he had been asked, the German might have said that any water-bearing crew, especially if females hauled the buckets, would consist of several persons and would likely rate more than a single bodyguard. He kept the notion to himself, because he knew that Phelan would have worked it out himself. It was so obvious, in fact, that Shuker was a bit surprised their client didn't raise the point.

Instead of arguing the matter, though, Shuker dismissed it from his mind. The three of them were well armed, and an ambush gave them the advantage of surprise. If they were heavily outnumbered, Phelan would restrain Wix, make him wait for more propitious circumstances. On the other hand, unless the odds were too outrageous, they could have a merry time of it and bag their limit, give the man from San Francisco something to remember as his life wound down in tedium from that day on.

They moved back toward the stream, not holding any true formation, but keeping their eyes open, Wix swiveling his head from side to side as if he were some kind of robot, built with a surveillance camera in his melon. At least he kept his finger off the shotgun's trigger, Shuker noted, though he couldn't tell from his position whether Wix still had the safety catch engaged.

Distracted from the technical side, Shuker couldn't help wondering if they were headed in the wrong direction now. The stream they sought was swift and shallow—good enough for filling water buckets, he supposed, but no damned good at all for bathing, say, and it would barely do the trick for rinsing clothes. He had begun to wonder if there might not be another stream, perhaps a true river, somewhere beyond the rebel village, on the other side. They had no aerial reconnaissance to fill them in, and hadn't scouted out the land sufficiently to know what lay a mile farther on.

As he had smelled the village from a distance, so he heard the mountain stream before he saw it, the familiar burbling rush of water racing over stones. It sounded just the same, no matter where you were: scaling the Alps or plodding through an Asian jungle, tracking live game through a forest in Bavaria or sitting in the basement of a burned-out housing project, waiting for a rendezvous with someone you'd been hired to kill.

The sound of rushing water was the sound of life.

Unless, of course, you were already drowning.

Shuker smiled without knowing it, the slightest lift to one corner of his mouth, and lost the smile at once, unrecognized, as he came within sight of the stream.

It wasn't much of a patrol—five men, all young, some of them barely old enough to shave—but every man was armed, and three of those with automatic rifles. They had paused beside the stream, a couple of them kneeling, filling up canteens, but all five pairs of eyes were locked on Shuker in an instant, picking out the other men behind him.

Shuker froze, Wix almost bumping into him before he saw the danger and stopped dead in his tracks. Behind them, Phelan read the situation at a glance and drifted off to Shuker's right, away from Wix, to give himself some room. He was a cool one, Shuker knew from past experience, but he was still surprised when Phelan spoke.

"¿Qué pasa?" he inquired.

IT SEEMED A REASONABLE question in the circumstances, but Phelan wasn't really expecting an answer. He wanted to seize the initiative, throw his enemies off balance, buy himself an edge to offset the odds of nearly two to one against them. Make that nearly three to one, if Wix couldn't hold up his end.

There was no question in Phelan's mind that someone on the other team would open fire. They were guerrilla fighters, outlaws, facing long-term prison time or death if they were captured by the state. Three unfamiliar faces on their turf—three gringos, packing military hardware, dressed in camouflage fatigues—could only be the enemy, from where these soldiers stood. They wouldn't know exactly what to think, of course, and they would never come within a light-year of the truth. That moment of confusion, inescapable, was Adam Phelan's best hope of emerging from the next few moments with his life and limbs intact, the only hope he saw of bringing Wix and Shuker with him.

So, he asked again, *"¿Qué pasa, hombres?"*

They were gawking at him, the one on his far right half turning to speak with the next man in line, subtly shifting his grip on the AK-47 he was packing. Phelan saw his moment and shifted gears before the momentary spell was broken, trusting Shuker to follow along on his own, without verbal commands.

Phelan twisted, showing them his profile—smaller target—even as he raised the AUG to his shoulder, taking up the trigger slack. His target was the second man in line, not the distracted gunner, but his sidekick, facing Phelan squarely, his Kalashnikov slung muzzle down across one shoulder.

Phelan's burst ripped through the young man's chest and snuffed the light out of his eyes before the soldier had a chance to understand that he was dying. Away to his left, Phelan heard the rat-tat echo of Shuker's AUG and was vaguely aware of a second body tumbling to the ground, collapsing at the corner of his peripheral vision. No shotgun blast from Wix, but that might be all to the good. If the broker couldn't bring himself to find a mark and blaze away, make his kill here and now, the next best thing he could do was back off the firing line and keep his ass out of the way.

The three survivors on the far side of the stream were scrambling for cover now, the two lurching upright, discarding canteens and grabbing for the vintage M-1 carbines they carried. Their companion, armed with the last functional Kalashnikov, wasn't sure which way to turn, but he blew the indecision away with a long burst of automatic fire, tracking the muzzle from right to left, his perspective.

He thought Shuker might have been hit, but Phelan didn't spare a glance for his colleague, concentrating on the shooter, framing him in the AUG's optic sight from a distance of some sixty feet. It was more or less point-blank with the Steyr from that range, no correcting for windage or elevation as he stroked the smooth action, squeezing off five rounds.

His target staggered, reeling like a drunkard, one leg buckling under him, so that he wound up kneeling, like a would-be groom about to pop the question. Even then, even mortally wounded, the young man tried to swing around his AK, taking a last stab at payback.

Phelan's grin was fierce with admiration, and he whispered, *"Adios, amigo,"* as he slammed his kill shot through the soldier's forehead in a burst of gray and crimson.

Two gunners remained, one of them stretched prone and cutting loose with his carbine, somehow never bothering to aim. His friend was on the move, backpedaling toward cover at the tree line, firing from the hip without much care or thought behind it, seeking refuge in the noise.

Phelan was tracking the runner, when a sudden blast from the Benelli 12-gauge battered his eardrums, making him wince involuntarily. He bit off a curse and stuck with his target, pleased to find that the soldier was running directly away from him, no ducking and weaving or zigzag to make it a challenge. Phelan saw him turn to sprint the last few yards and shot him in the back, his 5.56 mm rounds slamming between the runner's shoulder blades, so that he was airborne, arms outflung like wings, when he collided head-on with the nearest of the trees.

And that left one.

Another shotgun blast rang out, the pellets splashing water short of Wix's target, as Phelan and Shuker both swung their sights toward the patrol's sole survivor. As if sensing Death at his elbow, the young man bolted to his feet, banging away at no one in particular with his World War II–vintage weapon. He might still have scored a hit—perhaps a kill—but panic had unhinged him, and it spelled his doom.

Converging streams of automatic fire ripped through the youthful warrior's face and torso, jerking him from side to side as if he were a marionette, with two crazed puppeteers fighting over his strings. He managed to empty the M-1's clip even so, but he never came close to a hit, his last half-dozen bullets wasted on the trees and sky. When he fell, after what seemed like minutes, he dropped in a loose, boneless sprawl.

Phelan scanned the field and made sure no one was moving before he turned to check on Wix. The broker had a strange expression on his face—a dazed and breathless look, yet not without some measure of excitement. He was breathing heavily, as if he had just finished a ten-mile run.

And he was bleeding from one arm.

It was a graze, Phelan determined at a glance, and not much of a graze at that. The bloody scratch wouldn't have qualified as a flesh wound in any MASH unit, but Wix had now noticed the blood, and it seemed to entrance him. He was smiling, as if in response to some personal achievement, the Benelli still clutched tightly in both hands.

"We'll clean that when we've put some ground between us and the village," Phelan said. "They must've heard this ruckus. They'll be on their way by now."

''This doesn't count,'' the broker told him, then thought better of his own pugnacious tone and added, ''does it?''

Shuker said, ''It damned well should. You had your chance—five chances—handed to you on a platter.''

''No one talked about this kind of thing,'' Wix said, still addressing Phelan, knowing where the power lay. ''I wasn't ready.''

Phelan thought about pulling the plug, ignoring the glare from Karl, and decided why not? If they could manage to avoid the hunting party from the village, why not give the dweeb another shot? They still had time.

''Well, if at first you don't succeed,'' he said to Wix, ''try, try again.''

CHAPTER FIVE

Bolan had left the surveillance to Hal Brognola and the Stony Man team. He had explained the glitch with Chelsea Rawlings, keeping his fingers crossed that she would honor their agreement, but he had no ready means of enforcing the deal, short of asking the big Fed to place her under house arrest. That notion didn't fly, considering the money and potential influence involved, and he was left to wait and see if Brognola could pin the tail on Phelan with a high-tech search.

In fact, as it turned out, the search hadn't been all that difficult. Within twenty-four hours, the big Fed had traced Phelan to the booking of a private charter flight from San Francisco International to Guayaquil, in Ecuador. The information came too late for Brognola to have the flight itself observed, the paying customer identified, but he confirmed three passengers were aboard when the charter took off, with a return trip scheduled six days later.

Bolan, for his part, had flown out of Baltimore, landing in Guayaquil some fourteen hours behind his quarry. Ready cash and a bit of subtle pressure from the U.S. Embassy combined to help him obtain the necessary information on Phelan and company—their flight to Loja, where a rented Jeep was waiting to carry them southward.

Toward Peru.

By the time he crossed the border—with a helpful pointer from the headman of a village his quarry had passed on their route of march—Bolan estimated that he had shaved their lead to ten hours, give or take, and he was counting on the civilian to slow them further, letting him make up more time. Phelan and his sidekick, Carl something, could doubtless keep up the pace, but unless their millionaire patron had done some serious training in preparation for the hunt, he was bound to hold them back. It was, after all, a pleasure trip of sorts, despite the setting and grim intentions. With a million dollars on the table, Bolan couldn't picture Phelan running his client into a state of exhaustion, double-timing him to the point of collapse.

The Executioner, for his part, was sparing no energy to close the gap, cutting into his enemy's lead. He ate and drank on the move, hiking at a steady ground-eating pace, pausing only when a call of nature demanded his urgent attention. Once he had found the trio's spoor, he never let it go. Indeed, they seemed to take no pains at all in covering their tracks, so intent on their goal that they gave no thought to the prospect of danger closing from behind.

Bolan had counted on a fair amount of arrogance in Phelan's nature, even though he knew the man would take precautions where it counted. There was no reason for Phelan to suspect he might be followed on a hunt, since it had never happened in the past. There had been no leak thus far of the fact that Quentin Rawlings had told all before he died, no alarm bells to make Phelan deviate from his normal routine. He had been far away from home, in fact, the night Bolan and Chelsea Rawlings dropped by.

As far as Adam Phelan knew, the only clouds on his horizon were the wisps of dainty white above the Cordillera del Condor. He had no reason to suspect that *he* was being hunted now, by one who knew the killing game at least as well as he did.

Even gaining ground, though, Bolan knew that it would take some time for him to overtake his prey. And in the meantime, there was nothing he could do to stop the trio from obtaining what they'd come for: one more human scalp for Phelan's grim collection, one more bloody memory for his paying client. How far afield would they range in their search for targets? How well prepared was Phelan, in terms of maps, reconnaissance, the rest of it?

For all he knew, they could have scored the kill already, but he doubted it. Adam Phelan was no idiot; he would intend to live and spend his money, rather than spill his blood in Peru for the sake of a total stranger. If anyone took a dive on this trip, Bolan guessed, it would be the anonymous client himself, and it wouldn't happen because Phelan was hasty or reckless.

So, he still had time. But how much?

The question was answered, hours later, by a distant rattle of gunfire from the east. It could have been anything, from target practice to a clash between Tupac Amaru guerrillas and government troops, but his gut told him otherwise. Distance was hard to judge with any great accuracy, but the sustained burst of gunfire—at least four different calibers of hardware, Bolan recognized—gave him a fix on the direction. Stepping up his pace to a trot, Bolan homed on the sounds until they were abruptly cut off, then used his compass to keep him on track. As he traveled, he picked out more traces of spoor from his quarry, confirming the hunch.

It was late afternoon before he reached the battlefield. By that time, there were locals on the scene, examining five bodies clad in olive drab and denim, picking over them and tromping all around the scene as if determined to obliterate whatever clues might have been left behind. Bolan hung back, using binoculars to watch them work, determining from glimpses of the dead and the apparent attitude of the survivors that the men killed here were friends of those who tramped around the scene. None of the dead were Anglos, none of them remotely similar in aspect to Adam Phelan or his faceless crony, Carl.

Bolan didn't read lips, nor would his basic Spanish have permitted him to translate much of what was said in any case. He gathered from the movement of the troops—two of them pointing off to the southwest, gesticulating angrily—that they had found some evidence to put them on the killers' tracks...or thought they had.

But should he assume the five dead men were killed by Phelan's team, or write them off as casualties in Peru's endless cycle of drug wars and political mayhem? Would the trophy hunters go out of their way to brace an armed five-man patrol? Or had the meeting been a grisly chance encounter, taking Phelan by surprise, forcing the hunters to defend themselves instead of picking off an isolated mark from ambush? Either way, could Bolan trust the rebels there in front of him to put him on the proper scent?

He watched and waited, conscious of the fact that if his prey *had* scored these kills, they would be making tracks with all deliberate speed, to head off a second clash with men as well armed as themselves. As far as where Phelan and company would go, he still had no idea.

The rebels made his mind up for him. Sending one man eastward, almost certainly a messenger, the others shouldered their rifles and set off in a straggling line to the southwest. With nothing but a hunch to guide him now, Bolan gave them a head start and fell in behind.

The hunters had definitely become the hunted.

Bolan wondered if they knew it yet.

CLIFFORD WIX HAD COME away from their engagement with the rebels terrified, embarrassed and exhilarated. The terror came from knowing that a hostile bullet had come close enough to crease his skin, draw blood, and yet had spared his life. Another inch or two, it could have torn his biceps, smashed the humerus and disabled his arm, or even clipped the brachial artery, letting him bleed to death.

But it hadn't.

The embarrassment came from his own reaction to the firefight—first freezing, then wasting two wild rounds that contributed nothing to the fight. He had seen the German's smirk of disdain, looked for something similar in Adam Phelan's face and found only questions there. Should they proceed? Was pressing on a waste of time? Had Wix already shown himself to be incompetent, or worse?

But they *were* pressing on. The hunt had been resumed.

That helped account for some of his elation, but the bulk of it was pure adrenaline, his second wind. The firefight had been thrilling, even as it scared him shitless. It had been a hundred times better than mowing down any number of winos in a stolen car. Wix could imagine how much better yet the thrill would be if he had made the kills himself.

And he meant to find out.

The had been marching for the best part of an hour, before Phelan called a rest stop. He had examined Wix's wound again, then left the broker to bandage it himself, while Phelan huddled with Shuker, presumably discussing strategy. When they were done, Phelan returned to Wix, his face inscrutable.

"We should be clear," he said, "but just in case, we ought to keep the pace up until nightfall. Can you handle that?"

"Damned right," Wix said, with more assurance than he felt. From the position of the sun, he guessed that nightfall was still several hours away, three or four at the least. And while he tried his best to keep in shape back home, Wix determined that he would, if necessary, run until his heart gave out and he collapsed. He wouldn't fail again, or give the German another cause to sneer.

"Okay," Phelan said. "There's supposed to be another rebel village roughly ten miles south. That way," he added, with a thumb cocked to identify their future line of march. "When it gets dark, we'll slow it down, but still keep moving. There'll be no fire when we camp tonight. If that suits you, we'll go ahead. If not, there'll never be a better time for us to turn around."

"We go," Wix told him, speaking through clenched teeth.

"We go," Phelan said to Shuker, eliciting a careless shrug.

And so, they went.

The jogging didn't hurt at first. It took the better part of half an hour before Wix started feeling winded, maybe half an hour more before the burning in his legs became a leaden weight that almost made him stumble, nearly brought him crashing down. He wouldn't let himself collapse, however, since it would have meant humiliation. Worse, it would have meant the termination of his hunt. He would have had to go back home without a kill, nothing to show for his million dollars except the pleasure of watching Phelan and Shuker shoot the targets.

No. That simply wasn't good enough.

Wix would run until his heart exploded in his chest, if need be, rather than disgrace himself again, deprive himself of what he knew could be his last chance to recapture the blood rush of killing. If his nerve or his body failed him now, he thought, that failure would be staring at him every time he faced a mirror.

He didn't know how many miles they covered or

exactly how much time elapsed before the sun went down. One blessing lay in the terrain, as it was downhill all the way. Of course, that meant they would be climbing when the trip was over and they turned around, but Wix ignored that prospect for the moment. He was busy trying to resist the pull of gravity, avoid a slip or stumble that would send him plunging headlong down the slope.

The hunt, so far, hadn't been as expected. Parts of it were better, and other parts were definitely worse. Wix had imagined scoring a trophy his first time at bat, no glitches, much less a nut-numbing freeze in the midst of an all-or-nothing firefight. Some of the problem he blamed on surprise. He hadn't, after all, come expecting to fight in a war. At the same time, a part of him thought that he should have been ready for anything, and that part mirrored the look of disdain he received from the German when the shooting was done.

He wondered now, not for the first time, if the whole damned trip had been one huge, tremendously expensive mistake. Perhaps his teenage reaction to killing the wino had owed as much to liquor as to raw enjoyment of the act. Perhaps the very fact that it had been an accident, so swift and sudden that he couldn't do a thing about it, had compelled him to imagine he enjoyed it, as a form of psychic self-defense against his breaking down or going right out of his mind.

No way.

Wix knew himself well enough to brush off the pipe dream. The problem, he decided, was that he had let so much time pass, had grown so staid and comfortable in his life that any edge he once possessed had been worn down to nothing by time and luxury. Over the past twenty-six years, his notion of a kill had been refined to economic terms—a killing in the market, maybe even at the racetrack. On the two or three occasions when he had gone hunting with a client, blasting quail or ducks out of the sky with too much firepower, Wix had the sense that something had been missing from the whole experience.

Now, here he was. He had been granted one more opportunity to prove himself, and it was costing him—he had screwed up in their first encounter with the enemy.

He would be ready next time, come what may, and he wouldn't hesitate, wouldn't miss. Wix was determined to go home with bloody hands, or he wouldn't, by God, go home at all.

THE WIND WASN'T with Shuker this time, and he had to trust his eyes instead to find the village. In a war zone, which described most of Peru, whether the signs were visible or not, guerrillas took precautions when they went to ground. They were more difficult to track in cities, he had found, because the crush of humankind concealed a multitude of sins. The city offered anonymity, a chance to blend and disappear. If a guerrilla was at all familiar with the tactics of disguise, he could remain at large for years within a city like Berlin, London or New York.

Out in the countryside, though, it was a different game. No matter where they tried to hide, subversive swine still had the basic human needs. They had to eat, drink, shit, piss, fuck. Well, Shuker thought, they didn't *have* to fuck, but it had been his personal experience that rebels—and particularly leftist rebels, when it came to that—depended more on sex to keep them going than your average human drone. In any case, whether the rebels built a rural base camp of their own or shacked up with a tribe of friendly villagers, they needed water, food, a place to answer calls of nature and escape routes, just in case. Suicide bombers were all the rage, in certain parts of the world, but Karl Shuker had never known a group of modern rebels who would fight to the death, like rats in a trap, if they were given any chance at all to run away.

He had surmised—and Phelan had agreed—that any village they encountered in this part of Amazonas would most likely shelter rebels. Maybe just a handful, here and there. But, after all, they needed only one.

One shot, one kill, and they could all go home.

He glanced back at their client in the settling dusk and wondered why he had ever teamed with Phelan in the first place. And the answer came to him immediately, as it always did.

The money.

Shuker earned a hundred grand per safari. Granted, it was only ten percent of what the client paid, but various expenses were deducted out of Phelan's cut, and Phelan had the headaches: greasing contacts in the different areas they hunted, setting up the clients' alibis, anticipating the potential shit storm that could bury both of them alive if Phelan's little operation was exposed.

Shuker could have found other work, to be sure. He could have handled wet work contracts until someone blew the whistle on him out of spite, or hired himself out as a mercenary in any one of a dozen minor wars. The hitch with either one of those scenarios was simply that he would have made less money while incurring vastly greater risk.

On balance, Shuker thought, he had no real complaints. And if their clients were predominantly snobs who walked around with noses in the air and thought their shit smelled like a rose garden, so what? The point was, they were wealthy snobs, and Shuker thought their *money* smelled just fine.

He spied the village when the rebels lit their evening fire. They had some kind of camouflage arrangement, nets strung up between the trees to hamper aerial surveillance, but there wasn't much that they could do about observers on the ground. The fire was built inside a pit, which helped, but there was no way to disguise the warm glow that reflected onto hungry faces in the night.

They stopped well back, perhaps a hundred yards from the firelight, and he watched the faces through binoculars, passing the glasses to Phelan, who in turn passed them to Wix. When Phelan spoke, his voice was lowered to a whisper.

"Feeding time."

Shuker retrieved the glasses, started counting heads, then gave it up. He didn't really care how many villagers there were, since they had no plan to attack. Phelan's safaris were the kindergarten version of search-and-destroy, tracking one man, two or three at the most. Once having found the village, they could only watch and wait.

But no rule said they had to watch and wait from so far back.

"I want a closer look," Phelan said. He turned to Wix and whispered to the client, "Any noise at all, from this point on, can get us killed. That isn't on my list of goals today."

Wix nodded, smart enough to keep his mouth shut, and he showed no signs of reticence when they moved out, this time with Phelan in the lead. Shuker was concentrating mostly on the fire ahead, and watching out for sentries in the darkness, but he still had time to check out the broker, right there in front of him. There seemed to be a new determination their client's attitude, a new determination not to fail that would have come in handy in their firefight earlier that afternoon.

It happened that way sometimes. Green recruits who choked their first time under hostile fire sometimes emerged as better men because of it—assuming they survived. Shuker wasn't prepared to call this one a soldier—far from it—but if his embarrassment from the first confrontation allowed him to make a quick, clean kill the second time around, so much the better. They could all pack up, in that case, and go home.

Shuker generally enjoyed their safaris, the clients aside, but this one had nearly gone sour already, and he wondered if there might be worse in store. It wasn't unheard-of for a client to miss his first shot and have to try again—he could remember half a dozen times when that had happened, in the past two years or so—but this continuing the hunt after a clash with hostile troops was something new. Shuker trusted Phelan's judgment in the matter, as much as he trusted anyone beside himself, yet he was still uneasy, troubled, as they crept in toward the village through the darkened woods.

It was extremely difficult, if not impossible, to travel silently through any forest in the world. True silence in the wild, in fact, was so unusual that it betrayed a threat of sudden death, some predator at large and waiting, poised to strike. The trick, in a successful hunt, was to avoid unusual or excessive noise. The hunter shouldn't thrash about in forest undergrowth as if he were a buffalo in rut. He should secure his gear, to ward off the metallic clanking sounds that have no place in nature. He should keep his mouth shut and control his breathing, so he didn't gasp and wheeze like the demented villain in a teenage slasher movie. He should never, under any circumstances, curse and slap the insects drawn to feed upon his blood.

A snapping twig or rustling leaf was nothing, in the forest's scheme of things. The trick was sounding natural and merging with the background noise that predated man's arrival on the scene by millions of years.

When Phelan raised his hand, the others stopped. They waited for his signal, beckoning them forward, to the vantage point behind a massive fallen tree he had selected for their watch. The village was some sixty yards to the south. Shuker sat and settled in to wait.

THE TRICK, Phelan decided, would be knowing what to do when daylight came. Before daylight, really, since they would have to make their next move in darkness, screened by the night from their adversaries—and potential targets—in the village. He would have to think it through, work out the best way in his mind for Wix to get his kill and still keep everyone who mattered safe and sound.

Phelan hadn't forgotten their encounter with the rebels earlier that afternoon, but he refused to let the killing prey upon his mind. They had survived the danger, and there was no evidence that they had been pursued. There was a risk of communication between villages, since even the poorest of rural guerrillas had access to cheap two-way radios, but if this village was forewarned, he would have counted on more visible security. Instead, they seemed to trust their camou nets to screen them from the air—a critical slip that would get them all killed the first time military gunships came along with infrared sensors installed—while mounting no sentries at all on the ground.

It was almost too easy, prompting him to question for a moment whether these were rebel villagers at all. The camou netting might be used by innocents, he reckoned, to prevent some trigger-happy pilot from attacking on a whim. There might be no guerrillas in the hamlet after all.

It came as something of a revelation, Phelan realizing in an instant that he didn't care.

What difference did it ultimately make to him? He hadn't been retained by Peruvian generals to track and kill rebels, though he would have earned his daily wage in that respect, as well. His client had signed on to track and kill a man in circumstances that, for all intents and purposes, precluded any future prosecution. Phelan's private rules forbade the deliberate killing of women and children, except when absolutely necessary for survival, but beyond that stricture, he couldn't have cared less about the chosen mark's identity. A peasant on a bladder break would serve as well as any member of the Shining Path. A coca farmer tending his illicit crop would die as readily as some guerrilla on the prowl.

He hoped that Clifford Wix agreed. If not, Phelan suspected he could help his client come to grips with the idea. One way or another.

"Stay here," he told Shuker and Wix, rising from his crouch. Both men watched him, but neither spoke as he left them, moved off through the darkness to circle the village, examine the layout and try to decide on the best course of action. Phelan kept his distance from the huts and firelight, listening to voices in the night, translating enough of what he heard to sense that there was no alarm in the village, no fear of impending attack.

They could rest easy on that score. The last thing Phelan wanted was to take on the whole damned village, rebels or not. This was a hunting party on the client's dime. He had no need to prove himself by facing killer odds for no good reason whatsoever. He would leave that to the grunts in green who drew their miserable paychecks from the treasury in Lima, and he only hoped that none of them would show their faces in the neighborhood until his threesome was long gone.

They needed distance from the village for their purpose, some way to draw one or two stragglers away from the herd. His mind went back to water, guessing they would have to draw some for a sit-down breakfast, maybe washing up, and Phelan knew the odds against encountering a village with a well in this terrain were damned near astronomical. They would rely upon some nearby pond or stream to slake their thirst. All Phelan had to do was find it, stake it out and wait. Simple.

It took the best part of an hour, but he found the water he was looking for. Unlike the stream where had met the enemy that afternoon, this was a waterfall of sorts gushing from a cleft in the hillside, spilling for some fifty feet along a wash paved with smooth, shiny stones, before it disappeared back underground. Phelan cupped a hand beneath the spill and found it clear, cold, utterly refreshing.

This, he judged, would be the place.

Scouting the area by moonlight, he was pleased to find a jumble of boulders away to the left, some twenty yards distant. That was pistol-shooting close, and should afford Wix a fair chance to score with the 12-gauge, once a target presented itself. The Benelli could kill well beyond that range, if handled properly, but Wix wasn't using rifled slugs, and Phelan didn't trust a newbie's marksmanship, even with a shotgun, at ranges where the shot pattern began to fade.

He prowled the rocks, confirmed that they could hide three shooters easily, with room to spare. There was even an angle of retreat around the curve of hillside, then up the slope and away. Not the best he had seen, and damned rugged in a sprint, but if Wix got his shot free and clear, there should be no need for a brisk retreat under enemy fire.

Phelan would keep his fingers crossed on that score, and hope for the best.

Returning to the others, he didn't retrace his steps, but rather finished skirting the village, making sure that he had seen it all before he rejoined Wix and Shuker. The broker twitched and spun to face him as Phelan approached, but he stopped short of raising the shotgun. Shuker, for his part, seemed fairly relaxed, lounging with his AUG braced across the fallen tree, its muzzle angled in the general direction of the village. Just in case.

"I found a spot that looks all right," Phelan told them without offering details. Wix kept his mouth shut, still obeying the injunction to silence, and Phelan was pleased. The man from Frisco would never be mistaken for a soldier, but he just might pass this test with breathing room to spare.

Or at the very least, still breathing.

"Come with me," he said, not waiting to see if the order was obeyed. Wix and Shuker would follow, and in half an hour, maybe less, they would be settled into their hide. Perhaps, he thought, there might even be time for a nap.

And tomorrow, he reckoned, not long past first light, they would have company. The weekend warrior who had paid a million dollars for a total stranger's scalp would have his last chance to collect.

Phelan was looking forward to it, and the trip back home.

CHAPTER SIX

Bolan trailed the rebel hunting party through darkness, keeping far enough back to avoid being seen if the last man in line should glance backward. The eleven-man party made noise enough on its passage through the woods that Bolan could have tracked them with his eyes closed.

Firelight in the distance, seen for the first time around 9:00 p.m., told him they were approaching another camp or village to the south. He dropped back farther, waiting for the guerrillas to meet outlying sentries, but there seemed to be no visible security in place. The trackers sent a scout ahead, double-timing toward the firelight and shouting in Spanish, presumably to keep himself from being shot. Ten minutes later, Bolan's party of unknowing guides were settled near the fire, while he observed them from the tree line, watching while they shared their news.

The villagers who had received them seemed to take it reasonably well. From what Bolan could see, his field glasses scanning the limits of firelight, none of those who occupied this hamlet were dressed in guerrilla chic, and the handful of weapons in evidence were vintage bolt-action rifles, instead of the Eastern Bloc automatics and war-surplus semiautos the rebels seemed to favor. He surmised from this that the village was, if not precisely neutral, at least something less than an armed rebel camp. At the same time, however, the camouflage netting strung overhead and the greeting they offered the trackers suggested an affinity for the rebel cause—or, perhaps, a simple recognition that to military raiding parties peasants in the Amazonas hill country all looked alike.

Bolan waited to see what would happen next, wondering if the rebels or their hosts would continue the search, but they seemed to be settling in for the night, accepting plates of food that they ate with their hands or from knife blades. Perhaps, after all, they were letting it go for the night.

And that made Bolan wonder briefly whether they had missed the trail somehow while trekking through the darkness. He had concentrated on the search party, trusting their woodcraft to keep him on course...but what if they had, in fact, led him astray? Where would he go from here, if Phelan and the others had made a clean getaway to parts unknown?

Retracing his steps was one option, trying to pick up the trail on his own, but he rankled at a further waste of time. If he couldn't prevent the hunters from killing and slipping away, then the best he could do was head back to the States, touch base with Brognola and try to do better the next time. Assuming the big Fed could find Phelan again and chart his next move.

It was enough to make him mutter curses underneath his breath, but Bolan had learned patience the hard way, lying still for hours or days at a time, insects nipping at his skin, while he waited for a certain special target to appear. He knew the game that Phelan played, albeit at a different level and for different motives. Patience was more than a virtue in hunting: it was an absolute essential element of a successful kill.

So, he would wait. But there was nothing that required him to do it sitting on his backside, watching the rebels feed their faces and later nod off by the fire. He could use the time to best advantage, study the lay of the land, and thus be better prepared for tomorrow, no matter what happened. If the trackers resumed their hunt, he would have an easier time keeping up. If they turned back, Bolan would have the option of trailing them back or remaining where he was, scouting the layout again in daylight, seeking any trace of his quarry.

He never came close to the circle of firelight, was never so much as suspected by those in the village. One more gliding shadow in the forest made no difference to the locals, even if they were alarmed by tales of raiders in the neighborhood. When guards were finally, belatedly assigned to the perimeter, he avoided them easily, giving no cause for alarm.

He found the waterfall around midnight, examined it briefly and went on his way. Tomorrow, in daylight, he thought he might stop there again.

THE SOLDIER CAME BY around midnight, as near as Wix could tell. He didn't want to check his watch, because there was a Velcro flap concealing and protecting the illuminated face. Besides, Phelan had heard or sensed the solitary figure coming, stretching out a hand that clamped hard on Wix's shoulder, shifting close enough that he could whisper in the broker's ear, barely breathing, "Do not make a move. Not a sound."

So they had watched the stranger as he walked by, paused near the gushing hillside, then finally moved on. Despite the moonlight, Wix couldn't have offered any meaningful description of the man, except that he was clearly armed and moved with stealth approximating Phelan's, or the German's. That troubled Wix, because it meant that he wasn't simply some coca farmer out to check his crops, some peasant sent to scout around the village for potential enemies.

Who was he? And what did he want?

Phelan lay still and silent for close to an hour after the stranger was gone, staring into the darkness where the man had disappeared. Wix didn't know if Phelan thought the man might double back, and he wasn't about to ask. By then, indeed, he had more pressing matters on his mind.

Wix didn't know exactly when his bladder had begun to ache, but it was aching now, the dull pain spreading to his kidneys. Thinking back, he guessed it had been something like eleven hours since he last relieved himself. One thing the broker knew, with perfect certainty: he couldn't wait eleven hours more—or even one—to find relief. It might disturb the others, but he couldn't help that. When you have to go...

He reached out to his left, tapped Phelan lightly on the shoulder, trying for the proper pained expression as the hunter turned his face toward Wix. The broker shifted closer to his guide, wincing at yet another cramp below, and leaned in close enough to whisper. Phelan didn't recoil from the move; neither did he meet Wix halfway.

"I need to go," Wix said.

"Go where?"

"To take a leak."

The frown on Phelan's face seemed contemplative rather than disgruntled. Glancing back into the darkness where the stranger had last been seen, he finally nodded. "Okay. Make it quick, and stay quiet."

Quick was no problem, but quiet posed strategic difficulties. City boy that he was, Wix had done his share of open-air pissing, and he wanted to avoid the telltale splashing sound, along with any splatter on his boots. His ultimate solution was to pick a good-sized tree and brace one hand against the trunk for balance, while he played his stream against the bark. No splash to speak of, and the muted trickling sound was barely audible to Wix himself. Feet splayed, he even managed to avoid the puddle he produced.

Returning to his place among the rocks, he caught a glare from Phelan, saw the guide's eyes flicking from his face to the Benelli shotgun, propped against a boulder where he'd left it, while he went off to relieve himself.

"You left your piece," Phelan said, in the same funereal whisper.

"Right," Wix said. "I thought—"

"Don't think," the hunter cut him off. "Out here, your weapon's your best friend. May be your only friend, but it won't do you any good if you can't reach it when the shit comes down."

Wix nodded, remembering Phelan's injunction to silence, and pulled the shotgun closer. At the moment, he didn't want to consider Phelan's words—"may be your *only* friend"—but he intended to be ready for the next barrage of shit, whatever form it took.

"You ought to try and get some sleep," Phelan suggested.

Wix responded with another nod, convinced that he could never sleep a wink under the present circumstances: fresh from one killing and primed for another, wedged into a stony crevice on hostile turf, with dozens of armed enemies just out of sight, a few hundred yards away. It would take a veteran soldier with nerves of steel to sleep in such conditions, even with the likes of Phelan and the German on guard to keep him safe. Besides, what if they fell asleep on watch? What would become of Wix if the professionals dozed off and let someone else—say, the dark man—creep into their makeshift camp?

It would be—

A NOT SO GENTLE PRODDING in the ribs woke Wix, eyes blinking in the first gray light of almost-dawn. He was about to swipe the grit from his eyelids, but caught himself in time to halt the move that could betray him to an unseen watcher, hiding somewhere in the woods.

He glanced at Phelan, would have said the hunter

hadn't moved a muscle since advising Wix to sleep—but, then again, for all he knew Phelan could just as easily have left their hide a dozen times without Wix knowing it.

"Look sharp," the hunter told him. "It should be almost time."

RAMON CADIZ WAS up before the sun, sipping bitter coffee from a metal cup that burned his lips, then checking the action of his old Kalashnikov as best he could by firelight. Females from the village had begun their breakfast preparations, extra food brought out to fill the growling stomachs of their uninvited guests. Cadiz could feel some of them watching him, and while he feigned indifference to their scrutiny, he was—as always—secretly delighted by the awe with which these simple peasants viewed a blooded member of the Shining Path.

Cadiz had once been a simple peasant himself, before he found his calling and went off to war against the greedy, fascist scum in Lima. Now, years later, while the war hadn't proceeded strictly in accordance with his plans, he was still alive, still fighting. He had scars to show for several near-miss confrontations with the enemy, but they would never break him, even if they took his life. He lived by fairly simple rules, and one of them was that an injury must be avenged.

Five of his soldiers had been killed the previous afternoon, and while Cadiz didn't know why, he guessed it had to have been what was called a "wrong" scenario: wrong place, wrong time. As for the killers, it was possible they could be soldiers or security police, but he suspected otherwise. When the official death squads found a rebel stronghold, they turned out in force, with everything from helicopter gunships to TV cameras, recording every moment of the raid. They swept through villages and slaughtered the inhabitants, or else destroyed their worldly goods before abducting them for "relocation" to a concentration camp, hundreds of miles from their ancestral homes.

A flying squad of executioners from Lima wouldn't kill five men within a half mile of their target, then reverse directions and evacuate on foot through hostile territory where their deeds were infamous and the majority of native-born inhabitants despised them. It was out of character, so strange, in fact, that Cadiz felt confident in dismissing the notion outright.

But if his men hadn't been killed by soldiers, then who?

Cadiz loved his homeland, but he was the first to admit that chaos ruled large portions of Peru. On one hand, there were feuding drug barons and their drug wars, killing one another for profit and meting out death to the peasants who served them as punishment for real or imagined infractions of their criminal code. On the other hand, the Shining Path wasn't the only outlawed paramilitary group active in Peru. The Tupac Amaru guerrillas were sometimes cooperative, sometimes hostile, and there were at least a half-dozen right-wing death squads, some clearly sponsored by the government itself, which hunted "criminals" and "Communists" at will. Throw in the government security patrols, and much of Amazonas—indeed, much of Peru—amounted to little more than a vast free-fire zone, where every living soul was a potential target, living on borrowed time.

He believed there would be time enough to find out why his men were murdered, once he found the killers and had time to question one or two of them. There was a chance, of course, that even when he found the men he sought, they might prefer to fight and die in lieu of being taken prisoner. They *would* die, certainly, whether they chose to fight or not, and while Cadiz would rather learn their names, their business in his district prior to killing them, he wasn't overly particular.

Sometimes, he knew, pure vengeance was enough to satisfy.

The village that had sheltered him the previous night, that was preparing breakfast for him now, wasn't a rebel stronghold, strictly speaking. Neither was it neutral, though, since every peasant in the province had at least some secondhand experience with the brutality employed by federal troops and state security police. The villagers were wise enough to string up camou netting as a hedge against a misdirected air strike, and they hadn't turned his men away once he explained their errand in the neighborhood.

A part of that was fear, Cadiz admitted to himself. There had been incidents, some recently, in which the peasants who assumed a die-hard neutral policy died hard, indeed. Mao taught that a guerrilla warrior was a fish, the larger population his aquatic sanctuary. There were certain times, however, when you had to prime the pump before the blessed water flowed in quantities sufficient for a rebel's needs.

Cadiz made no apology for anything his men, or others like themselves, had done to rally popular support from the oppressed majority. Someday, when victory was theirs, the peasants who regarded them with fear right now would recognize the grim necessity of discipline in wartime. They would praise the rebels and honor their long sacrifice, as a wayward child honored his parents on returning to the family.

And in the meantime, they would do as they were told.

Cadiz finished checking his AK, replaced the long banana magazine and cycled the action to chamber a round. He carefully engaged the safety switch and set the rifle down beside him, on the warm, hand-woven blanket that had covered him during the night. Methodically, he drew the Browning Model 35 Hi-Power pistol from the flap-top holster on his hip and started to double-check it, as he had done with the Kalashnikov.

If there was killing to be done this day, nothing would be left to chance if he could help it. While Cadiz might not be able to identify his enemies, or even guess their numbers, he could damned well see to his equipment, take precautions to insure that it wouldn't malfunction when he needed it the most.

From where he sat, Cadiz saw two young men collecting buckets, each balancing a six-foot pole across one shoulder, while other villagers slipped bucket handles over each end of the poles. He saw that notches had been carved into the wooden poles, roughly one foot apart, so that each could support six buckets, divided fore and aft. When the young men left the village, they took no guard along.

A notion struck him, and he started to call to his men by name, snapping until they rallied to him, weapons slung or ready in their hands. Cadiz didn't explain his notion, any more than he would bother justifying orders to a child. His men would do as they were told, and if they thought to question him, well, they were wise enough to keep the questions to themselves.

"Pablo, Raul, Jorge," he said, "stay here and watch the village. Be alert. Daylight does not mean safety." That left seven. More than ample, Cadiz thought, as he instructed them, "The rest of you, come with me."

PHELAN HEARD their quarry approaching the falls, and was worried at first, from the rattling, clanking sounds they made, that there might be too many. His doubt evaporated when he saw two young men coming through the trees, each one with a wooden pole over his shoulder, empty buckets swinging in front and behind.

The water brigade.

They weren't soldiers. That much was obvious, though one had an old revolver tucked inside the waistband of his baggy denim pants, while the other wore some kind of long knife on his hip, resembling the bastard offspring of a mating between a machete and a World War I bayonet. The young men seemed relaxed, no more cautious than normal for someone who lived in an off-and-on war zone. They were laughing at some comment one of them had made, eyes downcast to follow the path, and they paid no attention to the outcropping beyond the waterfall.

He glanced at Wix and found the broker staring at the water boys the way a snake might watch a mouse, his full attention concentrated on the targets. Wix was clutching the Benelli, but he hadn't raised it yet, waiting, perhaps, for Phelan's signal to proceed.

Not soldiers. Little more than boys, in fact. But they were male, and they were armed. After the firefight yesterday, he didn't feel that much like checking their ID or quibbling over age. He hadn't promised Wix a veteran soldier, after all. It came down to the client's choice.

"Your call," he whispered to the broker. "You can take them anytime. You want to wait for something else, that's okay, too. The downside being that we can't tell when you'll get another shot, or what may come along."

A little pressure there, to go ahead and get it over with, but Phelan didn't think Wix needed much in terms of nudging. The broker definitely didn't want to face down a guerrilla rifle squad, as he had proved the day before. There was at least a fifty-fifty chance he would have nerve enough to drop these two—or one of them, at least—but if he waited…

"I'll do these," Wix said.

"They're yours," Phelan replied.

He edged away from Wix to give the broker room, saw Shuker doing likewise on the other side. Phelan was ready with his AUG in case it went to hell. The see-through plastic magazine was fully loaded, but he double-checked it just in case, from force of habit. At the present range, he wouldn't need the built-in sight, but he was thankful for the Steyr's bullpup design, which reduced the weapon's overall length and made it simpler to maneuver in cramped quarters.

If he was forced to intervene and help Wix, the water boys would be both dead before they hit the ground.

Beside him, Wix was fidgeting, working his elbows and knees on the rock face as if it were loose dirt, something he could shift about to make himself more comfortable. He gave up in a moment and concentrated on the targets, closer now and well within the Benelli's striking range. At that distance, one buckshot round might conceivably drop both targets, but a wise shooter would spare one round for each, shifting the muzzle just a fraction, left or right, to do the job and do it properly.

Silently, Phelan urged the broker to hurry and take the shot.

And even though he knew the blast was coming, even braced for it, he winced a little when the 12-gauge roared three feet from his right ear.

BAM! BAM!

The shots came from the general direction of the waterfall, northwest of the village, and Bolan was moving before the echoes died away. He had already watched as eight of the guerrilla trackers left the village, headed in the same direction, but he hadn't followed them, since several of their number were left behind, the others clearly planning to return. He had no great desire to watch them bathe or deal with any other sanitary functions they might have in mind, so he had lingered in the woods outside the village, waiting.

Now it seemed to Bolan that he might have made the wrong choice, might have missed the kickoff, as it were.

He ran full speed, but it wasn't a blind rush through the trees toward an uncertain fate. He marked each tree and bush around him as he ran, alert to any sign of booby traps, an ambush, any other hazards that the human mind or Mother Nature could erect to block his path. A hidden root or rodent's hole could snap an ankle as effectively as any manmade trap with jaws of steel.

And *down* could well mean *dead,* in Bolan's present situation.

He was roughly halfway to the waterfall when more gunfire erupted from the same direction. Not a single gun, this time, but several weapons, firing all at once, their staccato reports overlapping. He recognized the stutter of Kalashnikovs—two or three, Bolan thought, maybe more—along with lighter weapons, smaller calibers. Some of the weapons, at least, were full-auto, while the first piece—a shotgun?—joined in seconds later.

The second firefight in two days, and this time Bolan hoped he wasn't too late for the party. As he closed the gap with loping strides, he double-checked the safety on his Colt Commando, making sure that it was in the off position, with the fire-selector switch set for 3-round bursts.

Unlike yesterday's firefight, the latest skirmish

wasn't resolved by a single exchange. Two minutes and counting, with Bolan on the move, and the guns were still hammering away, getting louder all the time. He wondered if Adam Phelan was one of the shooters or if, perhaps, he was about to join a battle wholly unrelated to his mission in Peru.

It was too late to second-guess the action, though. Bolan was nearly there, and closing fast. He slowed his pace a fraction, just enough to keep from running up an adversary's backside, and prepared himself for anything that might be happening around the waterfall.

Another moment...*there!*

He scoped the layout, found his bearings in a heartbeat and proceeded toward the killing ground.

CHAPTER SEVEN

Phelan was watching when the buckshot ripped through Wix's targets, one behind the other, dust exploding from their shabby clothes as if someone down there were beating dirty carpets with a baseball bat. The big Benelli's double blast had more or less the same impact, both water boys pitched backward, poles and empty buckets flying as they fell. By sheer coincidence, they wound up almost side by side, their arms outflung, so that it looked as if they went down holding hands.

It was the kind of thing *Life* magazine might feature as a cover shot, to prove that war was hell, but Phelan didn't plan to wait around for the photographers to show. Or the villagers, either, for that matter.

"Quick and clean," he said to Wix. "Not bad. Now, if we're done here, we should—"

That was when he heard the others shouting, coming through the trees. He didn't have to see them, didn't need to count heads or examine their hardware to know that some serious shit was about to hit the proverbial fan.

Too late to cut and run with any certainty of getting out unseen, he thought, and reached for Wix, yanking the broker down behind the nearest boulder when he tried to stand and find out where the howls were coming from. Karl Shuker, meanwhile, had his Steyr shouldered, finger on the trigger, ready to rip when the belated rescue party showed itself.

Phelan couldn't remember ever letting anything he wanted go without a knock-down-drag-out fight, and at the moment, what he wanted most of all was just to keep on living. Anyone who tried to tamper with that fairly simple plan should come prepared to rock and roll—most preferably in a suit of heavy-duty Kevlar underwear.

He saw the slow-response team coming through the trees now. It was difficult to get a head count, with them dodging back and forth through shadow as they were, but Phelan reckoned there were half a dozen, then adjusted that to nine or ten, for safety's sake. No one, in his experience, had ever died from overestimating an enemy's strength, though the reverse was often true.

The howling pack slowed at their first glimpse of bodies on the ground, and that was a mistake. Phelan picked out a target for himself and slammed a 3-round burst through the squat rebel's jacket, spinning him like a flamenco dancer before he went down. Shuker had found a mark by that time, cut the gunner's legs from under him and nailed him with a second short burst as he fell. Even Wix didn't freeze this time, with the smell of blood fresh in his nostrils, squeezing off a 12-gauge blast that went high, but encouraged the frightened survivors to beat a retreat toward the trees.

Those survivors were firing as they ran, though, and some of them weren't all that shaky, based on the flurry of incoming rounds that chipped stone and raised dust around Phelan, forcing him to duck for a heartbeat just when he was lined up on another moving target. Once they found the shelter of the tree line, his opponents settled in to pepper Phelan's team with more effective fire, pinning them down among the rocks.

Phelan knew what that meant. It was only a matter of time before some wise-ass tried to flank them or reinforcements arrived from the village, maybe both. Each moment wasted crouching in their makeshift fortress nudged the odds that much further in favor of their enemies. If they were cut off from behind, all three of them would be as good as dead.

Phelan didn't care squat about Wix, truth be told. He got along with Shuker well enough, but any half-way decent aide-de-camp could be replaced, if necessary. Bottom line, his primary concern lay where it always had and always would—with number one.

If Phelan could have rubbed a magic lamp and wished his ass back to the farmhouse in Virginia, he would happily have left the others to their fate and never missed a wink of sleep. Betrayal was a concept that he recognized, of course, but it required some vow of fealty on his part—to a military unit, for example; to a nation; to a friend. It rarely entered into business, where the profit motive ruled supreme, and dog-eat-dog produced more meals than diners any day.

The trick to getting out of this particular conundrum clearly lay in speed and raw audacity. It would be risky, granted, but the only visible alternative was certain death. Unleashing a short burst to keep the bastards occupied, he ducked back under cover, shifting so that Wix and Shuker both could hear him, without any need to shout.

"We're dead here if we fart around too long," he said. When no one challenged that assertion, he went on. "There's one way out, right now, and that's around the hillside behind us. Up and over, with the home team throwing everything they've got at us, the whole damned time. It won't be any picnic, but I like the odds a damned sight better than I like the thought of sitting here and waiting for the rest of their *muchachos* to drop by."

"I'm with you," Shuker said, not even taking time to think about it. He was grinning like a maniac, and Phelan wondered—not for the first time—if there was maybe one too many jokers in the German's deck.

"You know the drill if anything goes wrong?" he asked Shuker.

The German tapped an index finger on the handle of his sixteen-inch survival knife. "I know, all right," he said, and smiled again.

Wix missed it, which was just as well, but clenched his teeth and said, "I'm with you, too."

"Good man," Phelan said. "So, what say we blow this taco stand and head for home?"

RAMON CADIZ HAD LOST his taste for the battle when Jaime and Luis were cut down in the first fusillade, a second burst of automatic fire driving him and his surviving men back toward the cover of the trees. It wasn't much, at that, and each time bullets struck the tree that he had picked to hide behind, it made him flinch, a sign of weakness he didn't want any of his men to see. The good news, in regard to that, was that his men were busy ducking bullets at the moment, too, and they had no spare time for checking out their leader's reaction every time a shot was fired.

Cadiz had thought it would be simple. It was serendipitous, in fact, that those he hunted should not only choose this village as their target, but would also strike two water carriers a short distance off, while he and his soldiers were there. It had been a moment's whim to guard the two-man detail headed for the waterfall. On one hand, it would make Cadiz seem earnest to the other villagers; conversely, while he thought the hike would be a waste of time, there was at least an outside chance of finding spoor, some reason to believe his human prey was even in the neighborhood.

The sudden gunfire had erased all doubt. Unfortunately, it had also caught Cadiz with his guard down, simply going through the motions of scouting the trail. Instantly, though, from the echo of the loud reports that had made him bolt upright and whip his head around, Ramon was barking orders to his troops, driving them forward and into the fray.

It had been, he saw now, a critical mistake. In one short burst of automatic fire, the faceless enemy had already reduced his troop strength by some twenty percent, with three of the survivors stationed back in camp. He wondered, briefly, whether they would hear the gunfire and respond, then chided himself for being a fool. Everyone in the village would hear the deadly racket. As to how they responded, well, that remained to be seen.

Cadiz risked a glance around the bole of the tree that sheltered him, encouraged when a bullet didn't shear off half his face. He fired a short burst from his AK-47 toward the rocks, and knew it was a waste before his spent brass hit the ground. He saw his bullets ricochet from stone up there, the staggered rock formation providing excellent cover for his enemies.

Still, he thought, there had to be a way....

He knew a siege would cut them off and starve them out, but it would also be a waste of time and energy, on top of making him, Ramon Cadiz, look like a coward to the villagers. Based on the rock pile's size and the volume of incoming fire, he knew there were no more than three or four gunmen arrayed against him, pinned down in their makeshift fortress, unable to maneuver. If he kept his wits about him, he should still be able to—

Wait! Cadiz understood in a flash that he could be mistaken. The enemy still might elude him, slip out the back and away if he didn't move swiftly to block their retreat. There had to be some access to the fortress from behind, and that meant *he* could reach it, too. His men, if they were quick enough, could both eliminate the possibility of an escape and take their adversaries from behind, perhaps pick them off before the bastards knew what was happening.

It troubled Cadiz to split his force again, with two men already dead, but he had no better options. As it was, he had to risk his very life, lunging from the cover of the tree that sheltered him, across four yawning strides of open ground, to reach a fallen tree where three of his men were concealed. The other choice was to shout his instructions loudly enough to be heard over crackling gunfire—and by the very men he hoped to surprise.

Cadiz picked his moment, swallowed air and held it in his lungs before he made the desperate sprint. It wasn't really all that far, of course. He could have wrapped a note around a stone and tossed it underhand, if he had anything to write with—but it felt like a mile when the guns started hammering at him, bullets snapping at his heels. One actually struck his boot a glancing blow, or maybe it was just a stone dislodged by an incoming ricochet. Cadiz registered the stinging pain and kept on going, diving into cover behind the fallen tree, almost forcing one of his men out into the open with the impact of his arrival.

He took a moment to catch his breath, ridiculous to be winded after such a short run, heart slamming against his ribs as if he had just completed a marathon. His soldiers were watching him, keeping their heads down. Away behind him, two more peppered the rocks with random fire, wasting precious ammunition on invisible targets.

When he could breathe and speak again, Cadiz told them, "We must stop them from escaping. I need two of you to work your way around behind them. Pin them down, at least. With luck, you may have clear shots at them from behind."

"And if we don't?" The question came, predictably enough, from Arturo. Always questioning, never insubordinate enough to rate a beating or a bullet, he would be the obvious one to second-guess Ramon's plan.

"If you don't have a clear shot," Cadiz replied, "you can still prevent them from retreating. When the others get here, we encircle them and wipe them out."

Arturo frowned. "I meant," he said, "what happens if we don't go up the hill at all?"

A challenge. Now Cadiz could see that Arturo had merely been biding his time, waiting for the moment when true defiance would do the most harm. It was amazing, Cadiz thought, how the spreading chill of lethal anger helped to calm his fear.

"Well, now, Arturo," he replied, "that would be your decision."

Reaching for the Browning automatic as he spoke, Ramon drew, cocked and fired the pistol in one fluid motion. The first 9 mm bullet struck Arturo in the chest and drove the air out of his lungs. A second shot, at something close to skin-touch range, slammed his head back against the huge log and pinned it there, eyes locked open, blood dribbling from a tidy hole in his powder-scorched forehead.

"Mutiny," Ramon told the two survivors, "is punished by death. Any questions?"

"I wonder," young Guillermo said, "if we would save time going up or down the hill?"

"Your choice," Cadiz informed him. "Just be quick about it, and make sure you don't get lost. I'll know you're in position when I hear your guns."

THE SOUND of reinforcements coming through the woods struck fear into Wix's heart. He had been doing fairly well, he thought, until that moment, but the rising babble of voices unnerved him, reminding him that this could be the end. That he could die.

Of course, the notion had been with him since they crossed the border from Ecuador into Peru. For all Phelan's expertise, the reminders that he had never lost a client in the field, Wix understood the risks involved. His first real taste of danger had been the previous day, in their first clash with enemy troops. He had dropped the ball there, but he was doing better this time.

But he realized now that it might make no difference. Phelan's skill and the German's, much less his, could be irrelevant if they were heavily outnumbered, surrounded and cut off from all escape. Wix thought about the movies he had seen and stories he had read, describing treatment of white prisoners at the hands of Third World guerrillas, and steeled himself to die before surrendering. His tolerance for major pain was minimal, a weakness that he recognized, and for which he made no apology. He wouldn't submit to grueling torture at the hands of savages.

Then again, suppose they simply decided to hold him for ransom? He was wealthy, and his company was richer still. Wix could explain that to his captors, one way or another, if he should be taken prisoner. He could persuade them that he was more valuable to them alive and in one piece than staked out on an anthill or lashed to a stout post for burning.

The problem with that scenario, he realized, even as the thought took shape, was simply that he would be forced to explain his presence in Peru, should he return home safely from enemy hands. He was supposed to be in Oklahoma City at the moment, talking mythical business with nonexistent colleagues. How would he explain the lie to his partners and his family? What could he say to counter any statements from the rebels during ransom negotiations? There were bound to be charges against him, whether he was caged by Peruvian officials or ransomed by guerrillas. Either way, his link to Phelan and the hunt club would be publicized, his shame revealed.

A movement in the trees caught Wix's eye. He swung the Benelli around and squeezed off a blast, watching bark explode from two different tree trunks where his buckshot scored hits. It was impossible to say if he had found his mark—no scream of pain, no body flopping on the turf—and Wix recoiled as fire from an automatic rifle raked the boulders below him.

Throughout the brief exchange, his mind had been racing along other channels. Amazing, it was, how swiftly his brain had adapted to combat mode, allowing his personal fears to press forward, vying for attention with the men who meant to take his life.

Exposure of the hunt club meant a spotlight turned upon his private life, his background. If the press got hold of it, who knew what might turn up? It was entirely possible that he might be connected to the wino's death, so many years earlier. And as Wix knew well enough from watching cop shows on television, there was no statute of limitations for murder.

He thought it just might be better to die and get it over with, amazed despite himself at how icy calm he felt.

Beside him, Phelan fired a short burst toward the trees, then ducked back under cover of the rocks. ''We're running out of time,'' he said to no one in particular. ''If they've got one guy who can think out there, there should be someone circling around behind us now.''

''So, we should go,'' Shuker replied.

''Sounds like a plan.''

Phelan was shifting toward the rear of their position, when the reinforcements from the village finally arrived. Wix took a chance and risked a peek between two boulders, ducking back as bullets spattered off the rocks. There had been no time for a head count, but he knew the odds against them had increased dramatically. Some of the new arrivals he had glimpsed were armed with axes, hoes, machetes, but a number of them also carried firearms, old-model rifles and shotguns, already firing at will, despite the lack of visible targets.

It was time to go, Wix realized. If they delayed much longer, it would be too late.

Phelan had found himself a better vantage point. He was slipping another transparent magazine into his rifle when he said, ''Karl, you go first, then Wix. I'll cover you and follow right behind. Don't wait for me.''

Shuker didn't protest his orders, and neither did Wix. If Phelan could buy them some time, more power to him. He was a professional, with nothing to suggest a martyr complex. He clearly had faith in his own ability to escape, and Wix wasn't prepared to challenge him on that score. Not if it meant risking his own life in the process. Better to be out and away before the locals realized that they could overwhelm their enemies by sheer force of numbers.

The German made his break, slipping between two boulders that formed the rear wall of their fortress, crouching as he began the uphill jog. Wix followed, keeping his head down, uncertain as to whether any of the rebels behind him could see him from where they stood. Suppose they started climbing trees to find a better vantage point—had Phelan thought of that?

The next shots, when they came, were from in front of him, startling Wix to the point that he stumbled, nearly falling. As he slid to one knee, he glimpsed Shuker dodging to the left, back toward the rocks. Two other men were moving down the slope, as if to head him off, both firing automatic rifles as they came.

Wix reacted instinctively, firing from the hip. He was surprised to see one of the targets stagger, wounded, clutching at his abdomen before he fell. Wix felt an urge to crow with triumph, but he lost it as a bullet from his second adversary's weapon slammed into his chest. One moment, he was kneeling on the slope; a heartbeat later, he was crashing over backward, touching down with force enough to empty out his lungs.

Surprisingly, the pain was minimal. He imagined it had to feel this way to be struck by a speeding car: the crushing impact, followed instantly by numbness, as the body started shutting down. He couldn't feel his legs at all; the shotgun braced across his stomach was a deadweight, nothing more.

All things considered, the broker thought, it wasn't such a bad way to die.

KARL SHUKER SAW the client drop and cursed aloud, swinging his Steyr AUG toward the rebel whose shot had nailed Wix. He drilled the skinny bastard with a burst that sent him tumbling down the hillside like some drunken acrobat.

He scanned the slope, the trees, and saw no other gunmen waiting to surprise him. Glancing back at Wix, he could detect no signs of life. Disgusted, Shuker scuttled back to crouch beside the body, feeling for a pulse at Wix's throat. It was a waste of time, as he had known it would be, but he had to make the effort.

And he still had work to do.

It was the first time they had lost a client in the field, but Phelan had prepared for the event from day one, well before their first safari had become reality. The clients carried no ID, but it was still imperative that nothing should remain to let a corpse be processed and identified. Ideally, they would have cremated Wix and left his bones for scavengers, secure in the knowledge that forensic medicine wasn't a Peruvian specialty. In the present circumstances, though, Shuker knew he would have to cut corners.

A pocket of his camouflage fatigue pants yielded a large plastic bag, the zippered kind that was supposed to keep a sandwich fresh and tasty all day long. Shuker gripped the bag in his teeth and drew the foot-long fighting knife he carried on his belt. Leaning across Wix's body, he took the left hand first, clutching the dead fingers in his own left hand, while he hacked at the wrist with his knife. Four strokes cut through the bone, and he dropped the grisly relic beside him, moving on to the right.

When he had severed both hands—and the fingerprints they carried—Shuker stuffed them in the plastic bag and zipped it, sheathed his knife and reached for Wix's shotgun.

First the prints and now the dental work.

He loosed two blasts at close range, though one would probably have done the job. The dead man's wife or mother wouldn't know him now, much less a third-rate dentist out of Lima, if and when the regular authorities got around to examining the body.

Shuker left the shotgun, opened two buttons on his camou shirt and stuffed the bag inside. The hands were, despite their plastic sheath, warm against his skin, but that would swiftly change. He felt no queasiness about the relic he was carrying, any more than he did about hunting total strangers for money. Dead men had no need of hands, and he could ditch the severed parts next time they had a chance to stop and rest. It was enough, for now, that they weren't left with the body, hedging bets against that one-in-a-million chance that someone, somehow, would have the wherewithal to identify Clifford Wix.

He heard Phelan coming, boots scrabbling on

stone and gravel, a parting burst from his AUG for the rebels and peasants. Shuker rose and turned to face him, fastening one button of his bulging shirt as Phelan came into view.

"I told you not to—"

Phelan saw the mangled, faceless body of their client, stopping short. He didn't speak, though Shuker reckoned he could read his partner's mind. It would be *his* fault, somehow, that the prick had gotten killed, and the worst of it was that he couldn't contest the accusation. He had been the pointman, should have seen the bastards coming—or at least dealt with them before Wix got involved.

Tough shit.

Phelan saw that the necessary cleanup work had been done, casting a frosty glance at Shuker before he said, "They're right behind me. Let's shag out of here."

They turned up the slope, and Shuker heard the mob closing behind them, a few scattered shots ringing out as rebels stormed their rocky fortress overlooking the falls. A sharp command in Spanish, shouted loud enough for everyone to hear, and they were in pursuit. Shuker poured the speed on, hoping that he hadn't spent too long with Wix, that he wasn't about to die here in the company of peasants. Somehow, though he had always counted on dying in combat, it had never been like this.

It was tough going, slogging uphill for that first hundred yards, but Shuker was encouraged by the angry voices behind him, the gunfire that was picking up now that the enemy could glimpse their targets dodging through the woods. If someone didn't take the time to slow them, he realized, it might soon be too late.

Shuker lurched to a halt, swung around and brought the Steyr AUG to his shoulder. He used the built-in sight, but not for any special target. Picking out an enemy at random, he held down the rifle's trigger and let it rip in full-auto fire, unloading the plastic magazine at a cyclic rate of some 650 rounds per minute. When the bolt locked open on an empty chamber, he changed magazines swiftly, using the moment to dodge behind a nearby tree.

And almost made it.

The rifle slug that could have disemboweled him struck his belt buckle, instead. It was a fluke, but it still had the impact of a kick to the gut, and Shuker went down sprawling, nearly lost his weapon as he fell. He didn't lose it, though, and that made all the difference in the world.

Firing as he rose, still firing as he made it to his feet, he swept the skirmish line of rebels as they tried to close the gap, coming uphill. He saw the bullets strike some, take them down, while others broke and ran or dived for cover, dropping prone. The AUG was empty once again as Shuker turned and started slogging up the hillside after Phelan's dwindling silhouette.

The bastard didn't even stop, he thought. And then, he amended, Why should he? Shuker knew that *he* wouldn't have.

Behind him, his pursuers seemed disoriented, startled by the sheer ferocity of his counterattack. They had taken casualties, and some of those hit were still breathing, crying out for help, a relief from their pain. He hoped that it would slow the other bastards, give him a chance to catch up with Phelan and get the hell out of there.

Scattered shots still rang out behind him, but it seemed like a halfhearted effort, at best. The bullets sang past him, one or two striking trees, but none of them came close enough to matter.

Shuker caught his second wind, legs pumping furiously. He had cleared another hundred yards and was closing on Phelan when he realized that something was wrong. Reluctantly, he ducked behind another tree and clasped a hand to his belly, felt his shirt gaping where the buttons had come undone. It had to have happened when he fell, goddammit! There was no mistake.

The plastic bag with Clifford Wix's severed hands inside was gone.

THE CHOICE confronting Bolan when he reached the falls was relatively simple. He could wade into the middle of the fight and take fire from both sides, to no real benefit, or he could watch and wait. His main concern had been preventing Phelan's group from scoring a trophy, and since he was clearly too late in that respect, whatever happened next was more an academic exercise for Bolan, rather than a critical emergency.

Unless, of course, the hunters slipped away.

He was content to let the natives mete out punishment to Phelan and the rest, if they were capable of doing so. It mattered not to Bolan, in the end, who pulled the trigger, if their aim was true. Initially, when he was stateside, there had been some vague doubt in his mind about the hunt club, questions still remaining to be answered, but the former Army Ranger's presence here put those concerns to bed. The guy was guilty, and if someone other than the Executioner should drop the hammer on him, well, what difference did it make?

As to the hunter's paying customer, his fate was a matter of total indifference to Bolan. A stranger with money to burn had hired Phelan to help him commit murder, whitewashed as an "adventure," tricked out as "self-defense," no doubt, if they were caught in the act. The nameless, faceless guy had payback coming, and one delivery service was as good as another in Bolan's book.

The problem, simply stated, was that so far the locals seemed to be having no luck with the job. Two villagers and two rebels were down by the time Bolan reached the falls, hanging well back, on the far edge of the action, and it was impossible to say if the guerrillas had even glimpsed their enemy yet, much less scored any hits.

In other circumstances, given other players, Bolan would have waded in despite the odds, to give the Shining Path guerrillas an unwelcome surprise. As it was, though, he considered it a wash, content to hang back and observe until he satisfied himself that Phelan and associates had booked their last safari.

Even then, however, it occurred to Bolan that he could be missing something. There was no apparent access to the stony stronghold from where Bolan stood, which meant the great white hunters had to have come in from the other side—and could, presumably, go out again the same way. They could, in short, escape out the back door while their enemies were laying down a virtual firestorm in front.

Apparently, the same idea occurred to some of the guerrillas, for one of them huddled with three of his subordinates behind a massive fallen tree, surprising Bolan with a burst of pistol fire after one of them gave him some lip. It was stern discipline and seemed to do the trick. Moments later, the surviving rebels broke from cover, weaving through the trees as they jogged uphill and began to circle behind the outcrop, overlooking the falls.

Bolan was on his way to shadow them, when the rest of the village arrived. Well, not all of it, but from the numbers surging through the trees, he guessed that every able-bodied man and boy above the age of nine or ten years old was present, armed with everything from bolt-action rifles and vintage double-barreled shotguns to knives, hatchets and hammers. Some of them were bound to die the hard way, if they rushed the well-defended pile of boulders, but they didn't seem to care.

In retrospect, he told himself, it was the crowd of villagers that slowed him, forcing Bolan to make a wider circle through the trees, avoiding contact with civilians and rebels alike who were hyped up for hand-to-hand combat with any unfamiliar face. No doubt, he would have made better time if not for the reinforcements, but excuses hardly mattered in the end.

The bottom line was that he was too late.

It took perhaps ten minutes for Bolan to slog his way up hill, then parallel to the action, and finally start downhill again. In the meantime, he could hear the firing pick up from below, more weapons joining the fray. Mixed in with the general snap-pop-crackle was another burst of fire that seemed off center somehow, as if emanating from a somewhat different source. He chalked it up to echoes at the time, and only recognized his error when he saw the bodies scattered on the slope, some distance westward—or *behind*—the rocky fortress.

Two of them were rebels Bolan recognized, the same men who had been dispatched to outflank Phelan's team. The third was unfamiliar and unrecognizable, his whole face blown away by close-range fire, blood draining from the stumpy wrists where hands were once attached. The corpse's camou clothing didn't match that worn by any of the villagers or rebels. Likewise, it was obvious the dead guerrillas never had a chance to use their knives on Mr. X, since they had died some thirty yards from where he lay.

Which left the pressing questions who and why?

The answers came to him at once, and left him cold.

There were more bodies scattered farther down the slope, where reinforcements had attempted to pursue the fleeing hunters but were driven back by plunging automatic fire. Apparently, the villagers and handful of guerrillas had decided it was best to cut their losses and retreat, with all deliberate speed. This night, around the campfire, they could dress it up and make themselves the heroes, but for now, the home team had its hands full, hauling ass.

Bolan spent a moment with the faceless corpse, rifling pockets in search of clues that he knew he wouldn't find. That done, he started following the hunters who had left one of their own behind. He had proceeded fifty yards uphill, perhaps a little more, before he found the hands in a plastic bag, sealed tight and bulging with its contents that resembled two pink spiders, grown to an outlandish size.

He made the mental match, scooped up the bag and took it with him as he kept on going. Something for Brognola to analyze, assuming that he got the fleshy remnants back to Stony Man intact.

And why not? Bolan thought. They had to have ice somewhere in Ecuador.

CHAPTER EIGHT

"Some gift you sent me," Hal Brognola said. There was a bone-deep weariness about his voice. For once, Bolan was almost glad he couldn't see his old friend's face. It helped sometimes to have the miles of wire between them when they spoke. "Where'd you come up with dry ice and the sealed container for a thing like that?"

"I found a hospital in Cuenca," Bolan said. "Money talks, just like at home. The shipping was the tricky part."

"Well, it came through all right," the big Fed said. "A little gamy, but the lab boys have seen worse, I guarantee."

"So, any word on the ID?" It was a lot to hope for, Bolan realized. Despite the paranoia voiced by certain groups and individuals about Big Brother tracking citizens of the United States with everything from microchips to tattooed bar codes, there were tens of millions of Americans whose fingerprints weren't on file with any local, state or federal agency. If they hadn't been arrested, never joined the military or applied for government employment, if they lived in states where thumbprints weren't required for driver's licenses, they might pass from cradle to grave without leaving a fingerprint record behind. As for DNA matches or any peculiar medical condition, forget it. Bolan would have to start out with a suspect, including tissue samples and full medical records, to match a pair of disembodied hands to anyone on earth.

He was surprised, therefore—and pleasantly, for once—when Brognola replied, "Indeed, there is. We've got your man, or, rather, we know who he was."

"I'm listening."

"The mitts belong to Clifford Richard Wix, age forty-two and holding for eternity. We made him off the thumbprint taken for a California driver's license, scheduled for renewal on his next birthday. He is, or *was,* a stockbroker in San Francisco, partner in a well-respected firm out there. He leaves a wife, two children and a sizable estate. He also leaves a paper trail in Oklahoma City, credit cards and such, that runs a full day past the time you found his last remains."

"The cover," Bolan said.

"Bingo. The other Wix apparently received a call at his hotel about the time you shipped your parcel back from Ecuador. Call came from Dallas-Fort Worth International Airport, one of umpteen-hundred public telephones they've got there. Smart money says Phelan or one of his cronies dropped a dime and told the ringer to skedaddle, as soon as they got back to the States."

"No way to trace the ringer, I suppose," Bolan said.

"There's a clerk at the hotel who thinks he could ID the guy, but that means finding him, of course. A hotel room's got prints up the wazoo, and there's a question of priorities. The most we've got to charge the ringer on would be defrauding the hotel, maybe grand larceny. OCPD's not interested, and I frankly don't see much percentage in chasing the small fry."

"Which brings us back to Phelan," Bolan said. Somebody had to state the obvious. He simply beat Brognola to the punch.

"About that end of things. We hit another snag. I started by assuming that the call from Dallas-Fort Worth might suggest a transit point, and went from there."

"Makes sense," the Executioner replied.

"I thought so," Brognola continued, "but it didn't scan. First thing we found out was that Phelan and his traveling companion didn't use the same air charter service coming home. In fact, I couldn't tell you if they took a charter flight or flew commercial. We've got Anglo types and Europeans flying in and out of Guayaquil like there was no tomorrow, and we can't rule out a flight from Quito, either. As to where they went from Ecuador, the first leg of their trip back to the States, it could be anywhere from Bogotá to Miami or Los Angeles. It's gonna take us weeks to run the U.S. passports down, forget about the foreigners."

"The call from Dallas-Fort Worth?" Bolan prodded him.

"It's still the only lead we've got, but what the hell. It could've been a relay, or they might have had some gofer make the call, to lay another phony trail. How much could it cost?"

Nothing much, Bolan thought. And he said, "So, that's it?"

"What we know is that Phelan's not home, meaning, back in Virginia. Of course, that doesn't really tell us anything. He could have half a dozen homes-away-from-home, in half a dozen names. Give me some time, and I probably can track them down."

"But time's the problem," Bolan said.

"It could be, yeah," the big Fed agreed. "We don't know how our boy reacts to failure, after all. He's covered well enough, as far as any link to Clifford Wix, and I'm assuming that he never caught a glimpse of you."

Brognola didn't phrase the observation as a question, but Bolan answered him, anyway. "He didn't." Both men knew that if Phelan had been close enough to get a look at Bolan, he would be dead.

"So now we're trying to outguess him," the big Fed went on. "I don't know if he'll cut and run, maybe decide it's time to suddenly retire, or else stay in business."

"I don't see him retiring," Bolan said. "Why should he, after all? I mean, win some, lose some. The client pays the tab and takes the lumps, whatever happens, right? It's not like Phelan advertises when he drops the ball. Who'd even know?"

"Makes sense," Brognola replied. "And if he goes ahead with business as usual..."

"There has to be a trail," Bolan finished for him. "All we have to do it find it."

"Great. You wouldn't have a phone number for Sherlock Holmes, by any chance?"

"I'm talking to him," Bolan answered. "I'll get back to you when you've had time to huddle with the Baker Street Irregulars."

"And in the meantime?"

"I'll be working on some angles of my own."

He severed the connection, frowning as he stepped out of the phone booth into glaring Texas sunlight. His first task, though he gladly would have passed it off to someone else, involved delivering bad news. And he didn't expect the lady to receive it well.

Louisiana

KARL SHUKER SIPPED sipped his Lowenbräu beer and waited for the other shoe to drop. He had been waiting since they climbed aboard the flight from Guayaquil to Ciudad Juarez, since he had broken the bad news to Phelan about the client's missing hands. Still nothing from the boss, so far, and Shuker didn't know if that was good or bad.

The situation was unique, so there was no established precedent to guide him. They had never previously lost a client, and Shuker himself had never once flubbed an assignment. The task itself had been simple: sever Wix's lifeless hands and transport them to some unspecified point where they could be disposed of safely and efficiently. It galled and embarrassed him that he had failed, but there was nothing he could do about it now.

Except to wait to see what Phelan had in mind.

The bastard was taking his time, making Shuker sweat. When he had first learned of the problem, Phelan made no comment at all, simply cocking one eyebrow at Shuker, as if to ask him how could he possibly be so stupid? They had barely spoken on the flight to Ciudad Juarez, and only briefly on the drive across the border, chauffeured by one of Phelan's contacts from El Paso. It had been arranged, in little more than terse monosyllables, for Shuker to fly from El Paso to Dallas-Fort Worth, where he had telephoned their ringer in Oklahoma City and advised him to bail out. Two days of silence had followed that order, until he got the call to meet Phelan in New Orleans.

And now, here he was, sipping imported beer and waiting for the boss to speak his mind. The silence didn't trouble him so much, since Phelan had never been loquacious, but he would have liked to hear whatever judgment was in store. At least that way Shuker would know if it was time for him to seek another job.

He had no fear of Phelan making an attempt upon his life. The man was clearly capable of killing, but he wouldn't have delayed the move this long. If Phelan wanted Shuker dead, he would have made his move in Ecuador, perhaps in Mexico, where such things were more easily ignored. The two of them wouldn't be in New Orleans, drinking beer in a hotel room where their fingerprints could readily be found, should the police become involved. That knowledge helped Karl Shuker to relax a bit, convinced that if he ever had to test his skill against Adam Phelan's, at least it wouldn't be this day.

That helped, although he told himself once more that he wasn't afraid of Phelan. He could handle the American if it was required. Shuker simply hoped that there was no such test in store for him anytime soon. The challenge, if and when it came, should be on Shuker's terms, his choice of time and place. Why yield a critical advantage if there was no pressing need?

They had dispensed with small talk early on, almost before the hotel's air-conditioning had chilled Shuker, drying up the perspiration that had soaked his shirt on the cab ride from the airport. It seemed hotter to him in New Orleans—well, more humid, at the very least—than it had been in Amazonas, while the two of them were running for their lives and leaving Clifford Wix for buzzard bait.

"No comebacks yet, I take it," Shuker said when he was halfway through his beer and nearly out of patience. "No alarm bells going off, or such?"

"We had some luck," Phelan replied.

"I think you mean to say we made some luck," Shuker said. "I've heard you tell the clients often enough that a man makes his own and must take responsibility."

"That's still the way I feel, Karl...good or bad."

The subtle shift in tone didn't escape the German's notice. The hotel, he told himself again. A public place. And still, he shifted in his chair and took a firm grip on his beer bottle. Just in case.

"You'd say Wix made his own luck, I suppose," Phelan remarked.

"I'd say his luck ran out. Christ, he was an amateur. They're all of them amateurs, babes in the woods."

"Which is why they hire guides, Karl. To bring them back out of the woods, safe and sound. We've never lost a man before."

"The flankers jumped us, and he froze," Shuker replied. "He lost himself."

"He didn't lose the hands," Phelan said quietly.

"So, we've come back to that again," Shuker stated, putting on an irritated tone. "I've told you what happened. There's no more to say. You think those peasants have the hands? So what? If anything, they'll make a stew of them to feed their brats. It's not as if they can report what happened to the army or security police."

"I thought of that, as well," Phelan replied.

"So, what's the problem, then?"

"Karl, a program like the one we operate demands precision in all things, from the initial paperwork and cover, through extraction. I insist on that. More to the point, I keep my focus where it needs to be—on number one."

"And have I ever let you down?" Shuker asked. "Besides this business with the hands, I mean?"

"Once is enough," Phelan replied. "Once is too much."

Shuker could feel the angry color rising in his face. "Well, if you feel that way about it—"

"Karl." The tone of Phelan's voice was all it took to silence him. "I see this as a lesson to the both of us. Imagine that you've left a piece of valuable luggage at the airport by mistake, and you don't notice it until you're half an hour down the road. Your heart stops for an instant, and your guts twist into knots. You race back to the lost-and-found department, knowing that you're screwed...and there it is! No harm, no foul. But it's a warning, Karl. You watch your bags a bit more closely after that."

"I understand."

"Good. I value your participation in these field excursions, Karl. I'd hate to lose you."

"I'm not going anywhere," the German said. Relief was worming through his veins, relaxing him, as if the beer he held had been his third or fourth, and not the first. A smile tugged at the corners of his mouth, but Shuker kept it to himself.

"Just one more thing, about the business in Peru," Phelan said.

"One more thing?" Relief began to duck and cover, like a cockroach when the kitchen lights come on.

"I would assume our client's people must have checked with the hotel in Oklahoma City by this time."

"Is that a problem?" Shuker asked.

"It shouldn't be. The odds against them tracking down the ringer are—what would you say? A million and something to one?" The frown on Phelan's face spoke volumes. Shuker didn't need a psychic friend to know what the boss man was thinking.

"The odds would be even better," Shuker volunteered, "if there was no one to find."

"Perhaps we should take care of that," Phelan said. "Just this once, to make things absolutely safe."

This time, Shuker made no effort to suppress his smile. "I'll see to it myself," he said.

Texas

IT WAS another sunny day in Houston, hot enough to fry eggs on the sidewalk, if you didn't mind the taste of city filth for breakfast. Houston wasn't bad, as cities went—in terms of urban rot, it couldn't hold a candle to New York, Chicago or the nation's capital—but it was still impossible to roam the streets for any length of time without encountering gang signs and vandalism, homeless people, spaced-out runaways and hookers wearing just enough to dodge arrest on charges of indecent exposure. The air was cleaner than L.A.'s, but it was getting worse each year. Texas exterminated killers at a rate exceeding that of any other U.S. state—or several states combined—but there were seldom any vacancies along Death Row.

Suburban Bellaire—like most bedroom communities bearing that name—was cleaner, quieter, and noticeably lighter skinned. Racial discrimination in housing was illegal, of course, but Bolan knew there were a thousand different ways to wriggle through the loopholes in such legislation. Overpricing was the simplest and among the most reliable techniques, bearing the added benefit of ego strokes for those who managed to afford a home in an exclusive neighborhood.

Bellaire wasn't for Houston's superrich, but it was close enough, and Chelsea Rawlings hadn't yet shifted from her house there to her father's lately vacant mansion. Perhaps she never would, conflicted as she seemed to be about the dead man's money and some of the uses he had found for it, but she had ample time to work that out. The family fortune wasn't going anywhere. In fact, each time another sweaty driver pulled up to the gas pumps, it increased.

Some life, Bolan thought, then remembered Chelsea's father and amended it to add, some death.

They weren't meeting at the lady's home, though she had first suggested it. Bolan had a whole laundry list of reasons for demurring, but he kept them to himself when he suggested that she choose a semipublic place for their meeting instead. The compromise site was a stylish steak house on Chimney Rock Road, the layout providing extra privacy for preferred patrons, in the form of smaller rooms separated from the main dining area by floor-to-ceiling partitions.

"The manager's a friend of mine," Rawlings told him as they were seated. "Well, more a friend of my father's. I sort of inherited him."

"It's a nice place," Bolan allowed, leaning toward innocuous small talk until the young waitress had taken their order and left them in peace.

"So," Rawlings said, leaning forward with her elbows on the table, "what happened? Did you get him?"

In the interest of restraining the woman, Bolan had sketched his recent mission for her in advance, and in the vaguest possible terms, telling her that he was onto something that might bring Adam Phelan to book, leaving the details elusive. Now, he had the unenviable task of letting her down without sparking a tantrum, still without providing any solid details of the hunting party in Peru.

"Let's say I managed to confirm a portion of your father's statement," he began. "By which I mean, the so-called hunt club is real enough." He saw the flash of eagerness in Rawlings's eyes, and quickly brought her down. "Unfortunately, I've uncovered nothing that would pass a test as evidence in court. Assuming there were charges filed, the worst an American prosecutor could claim is solicitation to commit murder, and that would be filed against Phelan's clients. They approach him, after all. It's not the other way around."

"Conspiracy," she said. "I've done some reading up on that. If two or more agree to violate the law—"

"To prove conspiracy, you need some eyes and ears inside. The clients have nothing to gain and everything to lose if they cooperate. As far as taps and bugs, I think we can assume he takes precautions."

"But my father's tape—"

"Is true in all respects, as far as I can tell," he interrupted her. "As far as evidentiary value, it's a washout. We've been over this."

"You also told me bringing cases into court wasn't your job. You led me to believe—"

The waitress cut her off this time, appearing with their food. Rawlings restrained herself and forced a smile, assuring the waitress that they required nothing more.

"You led me to believe," she said again, "that this could all be settled out of court. I thought—"

"I'm not responsible for what you thought, inferred, suspected or surmised," he said. "I've broken every rule there is just meeting you to have this conversation. I'm not on your payroll, and we have no arrangement to 'settle' anything."

"You said we had a deal."

"For you to step aside and let me do my job. It's not done yet."

"Oh, right. I'm just supposed to trust you, come what may."

He sat in silence for a moment, holding her gaze. Bolan didn't believe that she was wired, had no fear of prosecution, much less blackmail, even if she was. He knew that sharing information with the lady was a gamble, but he also knew that he was balanced on a razor's edge, leaning toward action that could get her killed, while putting Adam Phelan in the wind.

He gambled. "Since we talked," he said, "there's been another hunt. I can't go into detail, but they hit a snag. The client didn't make it back."

"Too bad." Her voice was frosty. "What's that mean to me?"

"He's been identified," said Bolan, "which is one step closer to a proved link with Phelan."

"One step. Terrific."

"If you want to speed things up," he told her, "you can always hire a couple of crack monsters to do the job for peanuts. If they live long enough to pull it off, you'll be jailed as a conspirator and put away. Catch yourself a sympathetic judge, with any luck at all, you should be out in six or seven years."

"It might be worth it."

Bolan knew she meant it, and he also knew that there were limits beyond which Chelsea Rawlings wouldn't be pushed. A further effort to intimidate her could have the exact reverse of his intended effect, propelling her into self-destructive action.

Softening his tone, he said, "I don't think you'll regret it if you wait a bit."

"Define 'a bit,'" she challenged him.

"Can't help you there. Right now, the ball's in Phelan's court."

"From what I've seen," she said, "it never left. His ball, his game, his rules. And I'm supposed to take that as a sign he's nearly on the ropes?"

"Your options aren't the most attractive in the world," he said.

"I guess that all depends on where you're coming from." As Rawlings spoke, she reached into her purse, produced a wad of bills and dropped three twenties on the table, near her plate. "My treat," she said, already on her feet and turning toward the exit. "If you have another bulletin to share sometime, you've got my number. I won't hold my breath."

Instead of going after her, attracting more attention from the other diners, Bolan gave her a head start, with ample time to clear the parking lot. The waitress had returned by then, apparently concerned that something Bolan may have done to piss off the lady would somehow jeopardize her tip. The sixty dollars seemed to put her mind at ease, and she was smiling again—this time with a suggestion of sympathy—as Bolan left the restaurant.

Another snag, he thought, and wondered if he should alert Brognola to the possibility that Rawlings might cause trouble. He finally decided against it, judging that what little the big Fed could do, within the law, would only make things worse.

Bolan had done his bit, such as it was, in trying to calm down Rawlings. He hoped that she still had enough common sense to avoid doing anything rash. Anything fatal.

In the meantime, he had other things to do. Like tracking down Adam Phelan before another hunt was organized and under way. Like ending it, before the butcher's bill got any worse.

But first, he had to find his mark.

And that could take some time.

ADAM PHELAN never second-guessed himself. He wasted no time whatsoever wondering if he had been too harsh—much less too easy—on Karl Shuker for the blunder in Peru. He could have executed Shuker for his screwup with the hands, but what would be the point? In truth, he knew the odds against the severed members being found and identified were huge, perhaps astronomical.

Unless…

Unless nothing, he told himself. Forget about it.

The mechanics of it were fantastic. No, make that unthinkable. It would require Clifford Wix's severed hands to be discovered and preserved, then shipped off to a crime lab, God knew where, that could not only lift his rotting fingerprints but match them to a lifelong resident of California. The FBI lab in Washington might have a shot, with its vast fingerprint index, but shipping the hands from Peru to the States raised a whole different set of obstacles.

Again, he told himself to forget it.

At the moment, Phelan had more pressing—and more pleasant—business on his mind. Specifically, he had an all-time record waiting list of seven wealthy clients, ready to front a million dollars and follow him to parts unknown on one week's notice. Sitting in his makeshift office with the files spread out in front of him, he wondered which of the fat cats he should boost to the head of the list.

There was, of course, no question of canceling. Losing Clifford Wix had disturbed Phelan, in the same way that mechanical problems disturb a professional race-car driver, but he knew the loss wasn't his fault. Responsibility for Wix's death lay first with Wix himself, and secondarily with Shuker—though, in truth, he doubted whether Karl Shuker could have done much more to prevent their client's demise. The hunt had been dogged by problems from their first encounter with guerrillas, and the end result, while not predictable, was hardly out of character with the events that had preceded it.

In fact, Phelan thought, he and Shuker were lucky to have made it out alive. Luckier still that Wix—identified or otherwise—couldn't be traced to them in any way. Once Shuker had disposed of the Okie City ringer, they would be entirely in the clear, untouchable.

And since he had no doubt that Shuker would polish off that job with all deliberate speed, Phelan felt confident in looking forward to the next hunt...and the next.

The good news was there was still no shortage of hot zones to visit, no dearth of corrupt authorities in those or adjoining nations, who would rubber-stamp travel documents and keep their eyes shut for a price. No shortage of peasants, guerrillas, poorly trained soldiers and half-assed militiamen, blundering around the region, virtually begging to be shot or blown apart by someone.

In the past five years, he had led safaris on five continents, excluding only Antarctica and Australia. Two of the trips—into Vietnam and Laos, respectively—had been semiofficial, with monetary incentive from the CIA heaped on top of the fee from his clients, the cloak-and-dagger types asking only that Phelan keep his eyes peeled for any trace of Anglo-type "missing persons" in the area. He had informed his clients of the extra duty, and they had been thrilled, participating in a patriotic search for MIAs to mask whatever subconscious guilt still surrounded their venture with Phelan.

He had never found an MIA in Asia, but he'd kept the CIA's down payment, all the same. That part was understood, up-front, and there had been no beef from Langley, where the cash flowed like champagne at a Hollywood wrap party.

His one rule on geography was hard and fast: no hunts in the United States. "You don't shit where you eat," his daddy used to say, and it was one of the sorry old drunk's few philosophical gems. From time to time, a well-heeled redneck type would ask about the possibility of setting up a "coon hunt," waving money under Phelan's nose, but he had always turned them down and always would.

You don't shit where you eat.

Stateside was Phelan's sanctuary, even though the bulk of all his money went offshore. He also had an island refuge, screened by artful paperwork from any prying federal eyes, but that one was held in reserve. It was the last resort.

Meanwhile, he walked the line at home, paid taxes on the arms trade—after a fashion—and had weathered two IRS audits with flying colors. The second time, Uncle Sam wound up owing *him* money, and Phelan had laughed all the way to the bank.

He turned his mind back to the list of clients in waiting, ticking them off from memory. He had a movie star on tap, best known for action flicks that cleaned up at the box office, even as they were clobbered by critics. These days, it seemed, the "star" was tired of having others do his stunts, watching the bad guys he riddled with make-believe bullets on set get up and go for coffee when the director yelled, "Cut!"

He had a department-store magnate and classic sportsman, who had been everywhere and shot everything on four legs. The guy was in his fifties now, and running out of trophies—not to mention countries that would let him roam and slaughter wildlife as he pleased. A little something different might be just the ticket to revive the guy's interest in life...and in death.

Phelan rolled on through the list. He had the CEO of a global publishing empire, a closet sadist primed to graduate from domestic violence to murder—as long as it carried no penalties, of course. He had another oilman waiting, this one from Louisiana, convinced that his vast bank account placed him above the law. There was a best-selling romance author, anxious for a look at the dark side of life. A renowned televangelist, apparently convinced that Jay-sus would forgive him for breaking that commandment, just this once....

So many would-be murderers, so little time.

It was good, Phelan thought, to be in on the ground floor of a dynamic growth industry. If a miracle ever transpired, and people stopped killing each other for fun or profit, he would have enough hard cash on hand to live in luxury for the rest of his days, wherever he chose to settle down.

In the meantime, however, it was still a mad, mad world, and there was killing to be done. He lined the files up, left to right across his desk, and tapped them with his index finger, one by one, as he recited, "Eeny, meeny, miney, moe..."

CHAPTER NINE

Chelsea Rawlings had given Mike Belasko, or whatever the hell his name really was, her full attention while he made his pitch. In fact, she had been looking for a reason to believe him, hoping she could dredge up trust enough in someone else, just once, to let the whole thing go, absolve herself of the responsibility to see justice done.

It wasn't working, though.

Belasko seemed sincere enough, had maybe saved her life and all, but when you got down to the all-important bottom line, she didn't know him any better than a total stranger on the street. His hints about some government connection could be total crap, for all she knew, and there was no way she could check it out. As far as trusting him to punish Adam Phelan went, she simply wasn't buying it.

Belasko's story of another hunt conducted since her father's death had saddened her, but it had come as no surprise. Why should the bastards give up earning money when they knew damned well nobody cared enough to try to stop them? She hadn't asked if this had been the only hunting party since her father's suicide, and didn't want to know. The other deaths were bad enough, but they had no impact on her life, except to reaffirm her personal conviction that the sons of bitches had to pay.

When Rawlings punished them, it would be for her father's death, and not for any faceless strangers in Rangoon, Brazil or Africa. And anyway, the punishment she had in mind would wipe the slate, one penalty for all of their accumulated sins.

She had failed once, but she wasn't about to let that hold her back. Besides, she told herself, her failure on the first attempt was more Belasko's fault than hers. Confronted by a stranger in the darkness, Rawlings knew she should have fired her rifle, but there had been light enough to see the stranger wasn't Phelan, and her hesitation had betrayed her.

Chelsea Rawlings wouldn't hesitate a second time.

She had been working out, after a fashion, while she waited for Belasko to report his "progress" on the case. She had a copy of her father's tape made before she started making the official rounds and she had watched it by the hour since her first attempt on Phelan. Like an actress in rehearsal for a remake of a classic film, she memorized her father's every word, cough, gesture, until she could give his parting speech from memory. And she had done just that the night before her latest meeting with Belasko, sitting naked in a straight-backed chair in front of the mirror of her vanity.

She wondered if that meant she was insane, but didn't care.

A little psycho action just might come in handy for her next attempt on the elusive Adam Phelan.

This time, she would watch her step, let no one take her by surprise. And if somebody tried to stop her, she would do whatever was required to finish the job.

She had acquired another rifle at a gun show in Houston, thus avoiding the five-day waiting period and registration hassles. This time, she had opted for a Plainfield Model M-1 carbine, resembling one of the guns she had seen in a hundred old movies about World War II. The rifle used detachable clips, and the dealer had sold her four that held thirty shots each, assuring her with a wink that the clips were "pre-ban," whatever that meant.

All the woman cared about was that the carbine functioned properly, and she had tested that for herself on a Sunday-morning drive into the desert. She'd found that after half a dozen misses, once she tweaked the sights a little, she could topple soda cans and shatter bottles with sufficient regularity to put her mind at ease. The carbine lacked the shoulder-slamming kick of her lost Winchester, but it made up for that with rapid fire and six times the lever-action's magazine capacity. Besides, if Uncle Sam had issued M-1 carbines to Marines for storming jungle islands in the face of hostile fire, they had to be deadly, right?

If one shot didn't drop her target in his tracks, well, she would simply shoot him ten or fifteen times, and thus erase all prospects of the bastard ever getting up again.

Besides the carbine, she had also bought a special knife to keep her company the next time she went prowling after dark. The blade was seven inches long, jet-black and double-edged, honed to a razor's sharpness on both sides. The handle, forged from tarnished-looking brass, had finger loops with stubby little spikes, and a wedge-shaped pommel seemingly designed for cracking coconuts—or skulls. The salesman had described it as a trench knife, but she reckoned it would serve her just as well on Phelan's patio, or in his living room, as in some muddy ditch somewhere.

The carbine was her first choice, but if all else failed…

The trick now would be finding her target, and Chelsea Rawlings only knew of one place to begin the search. She had been sidetracked on her last attempt, never reaching the house, and while she still had no idea if Phelan had discovered any traces of her visit, there was only one way to find out. If he had fled the property, she might still find a clue to point her in the right direction, tell her where he could be found. And if the rural spot was still his residence, well, then, so much the better.

She would make it Adam Phelan's final resting place.

And God help anyone who tried to interfere.

Arkansas

THE STAND-IN they had used for Clifford Wix in Oklahoma City actually lived in Fort Smith, Arkansas. It would have been too risky to use someone who resided in the city where they ran the scam, since he walked the streets each day and might encounter witnesses from the hotel at any time. Fort

Smith, by contrast, was at least 150 miles away, and Phelan's ringer—a marginal character named Bobby Dukes—had been warned to stay out of Oklahoma City for six months minimum after completing the job. Just in case.

It should have been an easy promise to keep, since Bobby Dukes had no business or social connections to Oklahoma City—no real business or social connections much of anywhere, in fact. He was an ex-soldier and full-time fringe dweller, convinced in his heart that global society was on the verge of collapse. He kept to himself for the most part, stockpiled supplies for the Apocalypse and did odd jobs to make ends meet.

If there had been no problems in Peru, if Wix had come home safe and sound, Karl Shuker knew that Phelan would have left Dukes to his fantasies of Armageddon in the Ozarks. They had never rubbed out a ringer before, but this time it was critical that no trace of the Wix safari should remain, connecting either one of them to the late broker from San Francisco. And if killing Bobby Dukes was what it took to burn that bridge once and for all, Shuker had zero difficulty pulling off that little chore.

His commuter flight arrived at Fort Smith Municipal Airport on time, at an improbably precise 3:17 p.m. A rental car was waiting for him in the Budget lot, and Shuker wasted no time picking up an extra set of license plates from a minivan parked outside a bar. Once he had switched the plates to give himself a little extra camouflage, he picked up Interstate 540, and followed the northbound flow of traffic toward the Arkansas River.

It was standard procedure for Phelan and Shuker to run extensive background checks on one-time-only employees, the same way they did on their clients. How else could a cautious businessman avoid the hazards of entrapment by police or federal officers, betrayal by unstable individuals, the odd attempted shakedown by some would-be extortionist? Aside from checking out a player's past and present, they would also know exactly where and how to reach him—or his loved ones—if a sudden need arose.

The fact that Bobby Dukes had no apparent loved ones didn't concern Karl Shuker. He had no intention of coercing Dukes in any way, to guarantee his silence. Shuker simply meant to kill him.

After all, it was the only iron-clad guarantee.

Dukes lived across the river from Fort Smith, although his mail went to a post office box in the city. For this special delivery, however, Shuker needed to see the man in person. Nothing less would do.

He took the first off-ramp after the bridge, picking up State Highway 59 and its southward course for several miles, until he found the turnoff. Coming up on the vicinity of Bobby Dukes's hideaway, he took it slow and easy, found a place to stash the car and took his suitcase from the trunk.

A moment later, he had changed from running shoes to hiking boots. The denim shirt and jeans he wore were adequate for tramping through the countryside, but Shuker slipped on a camou Army jacket to help him pass unnoticed through the trees. The final item in his bag, unnoticed by airport security since he had checked the luggage through, was an

Italian Spectre submachine gun. Phelan preferred the slightly smaller MP-5 K, from Heckler & Koch, but the Spectre had a higher cyclic rate of fire—850 rounds per minute, versus the H&K's 800 rpm—and it featured a unique four-column 50-round magazine, nearly doubling the H&K's maximum firepower, while taking up less room than a 30-round mag of conventional double-column design. Equally important from Shuker's point of view, the Spectre was a double-action gun and fired from a closed bolt, allowing him to carry it cocked, a live round in the chamber, without fear of accidentally shooting himself.

It was a brisk ten-minute walk from where he left the car to Bobby Dukes's cabin-bunker in the woods. Shuker had known enough so-called survivalists to understand where they were coming from, in terms of paranoia, but he always wondered why so many of them felt the need to live in houses that resembled something from a low-budget Hollywood Western. Perhaps it was part of the "ethic," a return to values and a life-style from the so-called good old days, but Shuker failed to see the attraction.

And so, apparently, did Bobby Dukes—at least insofar as the six-foot-wide satellite dish in his yard was concerned.

The harsh noise of a revving chain saw led Shuker around the north end of the cabin, skirting the tree line and watching for any sign of movement at the small, dark windows he could see. The cabin sat atop a mound of earth that would be Duke's bunker, the repository of his weapons, ammunition, food and bottled water for the imminent apocalypse. Shuker considered taking the man down below, when he was done, but then dismissed the notion. All he needed was a simple kill; there was no need to make the target disappear.

Dukes had his back to Shuker when the German first saw him, and was using a Stihl chain saw to cut foot-long chunks of firewood from a tree trunk braced across two sawhorses and secured by rusty-looking chains. A last glance at the cabin gave Shuker no reason to think Dukes had company on this of all days, and he stepped out of cover, moving closer to his target, the sound of his footsteps on dry leaves amply covered by the chain saw.

He could have shot Dukes in the back, but decided why rush it? Instead, he closed the gap to roughly fifteen feet, remaining well outside the reach of the chain saw. Shuker saw a Ruger Mini-14 rifle propped against the cabin wall, some thirty feet from where Dukes stood, and knew his man would never have a chance to reach it.

Perfect.

Moments later, Dukes switched off the chain saw and drew a flannel sleeve across his sweaty face, below the plastic safety goggles that he wore. Shuker decided there was no time like the present to announce himself.

"Wood-burning stove?" he asked.

Dukes jumped and spun to face him, color draining from his face, replaced a heartbeat later by a pink flush of embarrassment. He recognized the German in a flash, almost relaxed...until he saw the SMG in Shuker's hands.

"Wha-what brings you all the way out here?" he asked.

"Unfinished business," Shuker said.

"Hey, man, we're cool. I did exactly like you told me to." A quick glance toward the rifle told him it was hopelessly beyond his reach. "We got no beef that I'm aware of."

"Nothing personal," Shuker said, as he brought up the Spectre and slammed a short burst into Dukes's chest. The man toppled backward, with the chain saw clutched against his groin, as if to shield his genitals. In fact, he was already well past caring, eyes glazing over as they tried to focus on some point beyond the sun.

Shuker stood over him and squeezed off one more burst, another six or seven rounds. It was a waste of ammunition, but he had come this far to shoot the man, so why not see that it was well and truly done?

Back at the rental car, he took a moment switching plates again, repacked his bag and headed back into Fort Smith. Along the way, he threw the stolen license plates into a roadside ditch, first one and then the other, half a mile apart.

His job was done.

California

THE LONG FLIGHT into San Francisco International left Bolan feeling stiff and vaguely out of sorts, a feeling he experienced from time to time when flying coach. He could have pulled some strings with Hal Brognola to catch a military flight, but there had seemed to be no point. The only urgency about his mission would arise if and when Brognola got another fix on Adam Phelan. In the meantime, Bolan's mission to the city by the bay required more tact than haste.

He had decided on a visit to the family of Clifford Wix. It could turn out to be a waste of time, but Bolan wouldn't know for sure until he tried. If nothing else, he thought the broker's family deserved to know that Wix wouldn't be coming home.

Brognola had initially opposed the move, suggesting that an FBI agent or U.S. marshal break the news. Instead of caving in, though, Bolan had insisted, hoping that the dead man's widow might possess some knowledge, possibly a written record she was unaware of at the moment, that would bring him closer to the man behind the lethal hunting club. If nothing else, the Executioner hoped to achieve a better feel for Wix himself, the kind of white-bread businessman who spent a million dollars for the opportunity to kill another human being.

Wix had lived on Nob Hill in a house that was less than a mansion but still plenty stylish despite its appearance of age. He parked on the street, front wheels turned to the curb as required by city ordinance, in case his parking brake failed and the rental went hurtling downhill on its own. The neighborhood was quiet at what Bolan took to be the dinner hour. Streetlamps cast pools of light that offered an illusion of security without a hint of warmth. The city's famous fog wasn't in evidence, and he wondered idly if it ever reached this high.

He climbed a flight of flagstone steps and rang the doorbell, waited for a minute and a half until a shadow blocked the pencil beam of light that shone out through a peephole in the center of the heavy door around eye level. Bolan showed a profile to the peephole, turned to face the porch light when it blazed and had the bogus FBI credentials ready when the door was opened to the limit of a stout brass chain.

"Good evening. Mrs. Wix?"

One eye, framed by a spill of auburn hair, regarded him suspiciously. "I don't know you," the woman said.

He flashed the federal ID card and said, "I'm Agent Blanski, with the FBI. I'm here about your husband, Mrs. Wix."

The eye blinked twice, and then the door closed in his face. He heard a rattling as the chain was disengaged, and then the door swung wide. Before him stood a woman in her mid-to-late thirties, well preserved, but obviously under stress. She wore a long-sleeved turtleneck that almost matched the color of her hair, with black designer jeans and hand-stitched moccasins.

"Where is he?" she demanded. "Is he safe?"

"May I come in?"

His question seemed to take the wind out of her sails. She backed away to let him pass and closed the door behind him, ignoring the dead bolt and chain. Bolan noticed that her lower lip was trembling when she said, "What's happened? Is he...?"

"Perhaps we should sit down."

"Will you just tell me, dammit!" Flushed with angry color, she recoiled from Bolan as if he had cursed at her, and not the other way around. "I'm sorry. I just...please...just tell me."

"It's bad news," he said. "The worst, in fact. I'm sorry, Mrs. Wix."

Tears spilled from underneath her lashes, but she kept her poise. "I knew it. When they said he had checked out of the hotel in Oklahoma City, I just knew it."

"Mrs. Wix—"

"Was it a mugging? Cliff carries—carried—lots of plastic, but he wasn't much for cash."

"It wasn't robbery," Bolan said. "And your husband wasn't killed in Oklahoma City, Mrs. Wix."

She blinked at him again, both eyes this time. "What do you mean?" she asked.

"Your husband wasn't killed in the United States."

"There must be some mistake." For just a moment, Bolan thought the lady saw a ray of hope. "He had a business meeting in Oklahoma City. I've confirmed all this with the hotel. Arrival and departure dates, the credit card..."

"We don't believe your husband ever went to Oklahoma City, Mrs. Wix."

"I'm sorry, I don't understand."

"Would he have any business that your know of in Peru?"

"Peru, Indiana? Vermont? Illinois?"

"No, ma'am," Bolan said. "I was thinking Peru, South America."

"What? Now I know you're mistaken. My husband would no more fly off to Peru than he'd, well, than he'd go to...I mean."

"It's confirmed, I'm afraid," Bolan told her.

"Confirmed? Confirmed, how?"

"You should really sit down, Mrs. Wix."

"Confirmed how?" she repeated, insistent.

"From fingerprints," Bolan replied.

"You... I don't understand."

"I'm sorry, Mrs. Wix. Partial remains were found."

"Oh, God!" She staggered, Bolan catching her before she fell. He helped her through an archway to the living room, and got her settled on the sofa. When he felt convinced that she wasn't about to faint, he sat on the far end of the couch, with several feet of empty space between them.

"Partial remains?" she said at last. Her voice was small and faraway.

"The details aren't important," Bolan told her.

"Yes, they are," she said. "To me."

It would defeat his purpose to reveal too much, but there was nothing to be gained from an elaborate lie. "We have—by 'we,' I mean the FBI—your husband's hands."

"Oh, God!"

Committed now, he forged ahead. "They were discovered under circumstances still not clear, delivered to the U.S. Embassy in Ecuador."

"You said Peru."

"That's right. According to the man who found them—"

"Who was that?" she interrupted him.

"A missionary," Bolan said. "He's not a suspect in your husband's death."

"Don't be so sure." She wore a bitter smile.

"I've known some preachers who would kill you in a New York minute if they thought there was a nickel in it for themselves."

"The man checks out," Bolan replied, and let it go at that. "He found the...evidence in Amazonas. That's the northern district of Peru, next door to Ecuador. Since he was headed for Iquitos anyway, he stopped in at the embassy."

"And left my husband's hands on someone's desk," she said. "A Good Samaritan. So, what about the rest of him?"

There was a sharp edge to her voice now, as she found a measure of control. The lady had a tough streak, Bolan realized, and she would need it in the days ahead.

"I'm sorry, I don't know," he said. "The Amazonas district is a hotbed of bandit and guerrilla activity. In fact, the State Department has maintained a traveler's advisory on Peru for a decade or more. I need to ask if you have any notion why your husband would have gone there, after telling you that he was on his way to Oklahoma City."

"I still say there's been some mistake," she said. "I've spoken to the hotel manager, confirmed his stay and the departure time. He paid by credit card. I just don't see—"

"There's no mistake. We believe a ringer—someone chosen to impersonate your husband—used his card and left a paper trail in Oklahoma City to cover his trip down south."

"This sounds like a movie from Oliver Stone. My husband, in Peru, for heaven's sake? With bandits and guerrillas? It's ridiculous."

"I take it, then, that you don't know of anyone who would have joined him on a trip like that?"

"If you're referring to another woman, Mr.... What's your name again?"

"Blanski," he said. "And I was thinking more of men. Someone your husband might have mentioned recently? A new acquaintance?"

"No one comes to mind," she said after a moment's thought. "I'm sure he didn't mention anything about new friends from South America."

"Well," Bolan said, "it was a long shot. Mrs. Wix, I'm sorry that you had to hear the news this way."

"Is there a better way to hear it, Mr. Blanski?"

"Not that I'm aware of, ma'am."

"Then you're absolved. One thing, before you go...about my husband's... Well, you understand. I need to make arrangements, and—"

Her voice failed as he palmed a business card and gave it to her. It bore Hal Brognola's name and office number, with the Justice seal. "The paperwork should be no problem, ma'am. The number there is in Washington, D.C."

"I can afford the call," she told him with a crooked smile. "My husband was extremely well insured. Double indemnity for accidental death or dismemberment. It would appear I'm set for life."

WHEN ADAM PHELAN THOUGHT of going home, these days, the farmhouse in Virginia came most readily to mind. He wasn't born in Stafford, had no deep roots in Virginia soil—no family ties at all, in fact—but he enjoyed the place as much as any he had occupied since leaving military service.

Anyplace except the island, that would be. And for the moment, he wasn't inclined to disappear entirely. He had business to conduct, safaris to arrange. Clients to satisfy.

The island would be waiting for him when he caught another break, when he felt more inclined toward rest. Another hunt or two was what he needed at the moment. Get back on the horse that threw him and restore his confidence, before defeatist thinking sank its claws too deep.

Phelan didn't believe that he was being tracked or followed, but he took no chances. From El Paso, he flew up from Denver, where he picked up a connecting flight to Baltimore. He would retrieve his Chevy Blazer from the long-term parking lot at the Baltimore-Washington International Airport, and spend the night at a small hotel in the city, where room service included prime rib and prime women. The next morning, rested and refreshed, he would complete the last leg of his journey overland, bypassing D.C. on Highway 301 south, through Anne Arundel and Prince Georges Counties. Cross the Potomac by toll bridge above Morgantown, and another hour, hour and a half should see him safely home.

He would allow himself a day or two of rest, then start to think about which client he should tap for the next excursion, where they should go to try their luck.

Not South America, this time. The whole Western Hemisphere needed time to cool off, in Phelan's estimation. It had been a year or so since he had taken anyone to Southeast Asia. Sipping whiskey in the Denver departure lounge, he considered possibilities and made a mental list.

There was trouble in Indonesia, as always, with economic ills, student riots and violence against the ethnic Chinese minority. Skirmishing continued in Sri Lanka, where rebel forces had been fighting for years to overthrow the ruling government. Military roundups of civilian insurgents continued in Myanmar, formerly Burma, with no end in sight. Guerrilla warfare in the Philippines dragged on interminably, with Western visitors caught in the cross fire from time to time. Malaysia and Singapore were on the verge of border warfare once again, while Chinese government troops in Nepal were locked in combat with insurgents.

Turning his thoughts to sub-Saharan Africa, Phelan ticked off another list of killing grounds. Liberia and neighboring Sierra Leone were both torn by domestic dissent verging on civil warfare, while each country blamed the other for a series of cross-border guerrilla raids and skirmishes. UNITA rebels in Angola continued their efforts to topple the military junta that ruled, however tenuously, from Luanda. Ethiopia and Eritrea continued their long tradition of border raids and artillery duels, with hapless civilians caught in the middle. The Congo had become a bloody free-for-all, with troops from Chad, Rwanda and Uganda on hand to assist various domestic factions. Sudan remained under U.S. sanctions, with local warlords raising hell, skirmishing across the Eritrean border. Tribesmen in Namibia's

Caprivi Strip were in revolt, demanding independence from the distant government in Windhoek.

It was, in short, a crazy world of mayhem, where mercenaries were never out of work, and a circumspect hunter could have his pick of white, black, brown or yellow targets. All he had to do was pay the tab, and Phelan's rich clients would take care of that.

They were calling his flight as he finished his drink, left a tip on the bar and moved off toward the departure gate. There was no rush about deciding on the next hunt's location, but he didn't want to stall unnecessarily, either. Perhaps it would be better if he chose a client from his waiting list, and let the customer decide where they should go—within reason, of course. Phelan retained the veto power over any choice that offered too much risk or bumped the cost too high.

He was the master of the hunt, and there would be no change in that, at any price.

CHAPTER TEN

Virginia

Chelsea Rawlings flew to Richmond this time, breaking patterns. She used the same fake driver's license, but a different rental agency than last time. A wig and shades helped with the disguise, in case the clerk had anything beyond an average memory. This time, she told herself, she'd do it right.

The problem with a daytime flight was that it left her hours to kill before she could begin the hunt itself. The drive to Stafford took an hour, give or take, depending on the traffic, and since Rawlings didn't want to wind up in a small town with so much extra time, she stayed in Richmond through the afternoon and early evening. She went window shopping at a mall and sat through a demented movie, wherein teenagers were being killed for no apparent reason by a hulking brute who wore a jumpsuit and a Richard Nixon mask, announcing his presence in every scene with an asthmatic wheeze like Darth Vader's. At one point, midway through the film, Rawlings caught herself laughing aloud at its absurdity, drawing reproachful glares from members of the audience who seemed to take it seriously.

Well, she thought, to each his own.

It was well after dark when she left the theater, disoriented for a moment in the strange surroundings, looking for an unfamiliar vehicle. She got her bearings quickly, though, and found the rental car where she had left it, with her suitcase in the trunk, her weapons and night-prowling gear in the bag.

Driving north on Interstate 95, she took her time, obeyed the speed limits and watched for highway patrol cars. Rawlings was familiar with the sense of paranoia that had dogged her on the first attempt to murder Adam Phelan. She knew how to handle it now, keep the feeling under control, so that she wasn't jumping at shadows. Of course, considering the way her first attempt had gone FUBAR, in Mike Belasko's words, perhaps she should be paranoid.

Relax, she told herself. Most anything that could go wrong already had. Except for meeting Adam Phelan. Except for killing him, or getting killed herself.

Then again, perhaps he wouldn't even be at home. Perhaps this was another wasted trip. It shamed her to find herself secretly hoping the trip was a washout, her money wasted on another failed attempt.

This night, he died.

She left her rental car the same place she had parked the first one, and to hell with breaking patterns. She remembered Belasko's trick with the dome light, but couldn't find a way to reach the bulb without inflicting damage on the car that would be questioned later, so she let it go. Better to hurry when she stepped out of the car and shut the door behind her, locking it.

Rawlings opened the trunk, then her suitcase, taking one last glance around the darkened woods before she kicked her shoes off. She stripped down to her underwear, feeling the night air cool against her skin before she pulled on the black jeans and wriggled into the snug turtleneck. She saved the itchy ski mask for last, seeing first to her weapons.

The trench knife felt heavy on her hip, suspended from her narrow belt in a black leather sheath, but she liked it, drawing comfort from the weight that slapped against her thigh when she walked. Having the nerve to use it on a man—even Phelan—would be something of a challenge, but she hoped it wouldn't come to that. The trench knife was insurance, brought along in case the carbine failed her and the fight went hand-to-hand.

The Plainfield carbine had a folding stock of wire and a pistol grip. The salesman at the gun show had described it as a paratrooper model, and she had selected it deliberately, because the folding stock would let it fit inside her suitcase. Rawlings drew the stock to full extension and tested it against her shoulder one more time. It still felt wobbly, but she reckoned it would do. The carbine's clips filled canvas pouches on her belt, and she took one out to load it, working the bolt to put a live round in the chamber. She was careful with the safety, flicked it on and off again, for practice, finally leaving it engaged.

At last, wishing she had some of the war paint Belasko had used on his face and hands, she pulled on the ski mask, adjusting it until she could both see and breathe. There was a trick to ignoring the itch, she remembered from last time. When she was nervous or frightened enough, the lesser irritant faded from her mind and was, at least for the moment, forgotten.

She knew her way through the trees, more or less, to the farmhouse. Unfortunately, she couldn't be sure of the exact path she had followed last time, coming back with Belasko, and she couldn't check to see if anyone had found the Winchester. Too bad. It would have given her a clue, perhaps, as to whether her first intrusion had been recognized, whether a trap was waiting for her in the dark. Then again, as Belasko had explained, a missing rifle might not prove anything. If hunters lost guns in the woods from time to time, she assumed they had to also find some.

Rawlings seemed to find the house in no time, as if coming home. There were lights on this time—well, one light, around toward the rear—but still no vehicles in evidence. She wasn't sure quite what to make of that, but she proceeded with caution, keeping to the darker shadows at the tree line, circling clockwise around the house.

At last, some ten or fifteen minutes later, she could see the lighted windows, disappointed to find that the curtains were drawn. So much for peeping or sniping from a distance. She would have to get up close and personal, to learn if Phelan was at home.

And if she saw him through the window, what then? Could she bring herself to use the carbine?

Yes. Damned right.

Would she be able to aim through a hairline crack in the drapes?

First things first.

She approached the house, unconsciously moving on tiptoe, clutching the carbine in a white-knuckled grip. If she could only see between or through the curtains, find her target, she was confident that she could make the shot. A few more paces, almost there. Reaching the window, she craned her neck to find a gap between the drapes.

The movement left her throat exposed, a cold blade barely kissing it as someone told her, "One move and you're dead."

PHELAN WAS JUST ABOUT to leave the one-time barn that served as his garage when he discovered he wasn't alone. The prowler wasn't particularly skilled, but he gave the man credit for coming this far. Indeed, he gave the bastard credit for finding him at all.

There was no question of any mistake in Phelan's mind, no possibility that this could be a simple burglary in progress. Granted, Stafford had its share of thefts and other crimes, but while burglars might well dress in black, even down to the ski mask, he had never heard of one who carried a rifle to facilitate breaking and entering.

From where he stood, watching the prowler through a darkened window of the barn-garage, Phelan couldn't identify the weapon more specifically than some kind of carbine or submachine gun. These days, it could be damned near anything, and he was more concerned with the shooter's caliber than that of his weapon. If the guy was a pro, hard-core, then Phelan could well be in trouble.

It was pure dumb luck, apparently, that he had killed the lights inside the barn before the gunman closed in. Likewise, if he had left the barn short moments earlier instead of lingering in darkness to appreciate the rural silence, he might well have walked into the shooter's sights, unconscious of the danger that he faced.

That was the good news.

On the flip side, he had left most of his weapons in the house. Even his Glock was out of reach, resting beside the easy chair he occupied while watching television, in what passed for Phelan's recreation room. He had the knife, of course—a cold steel Tanto with an eight-inch blade, stashed underneath the front seat of his Chevy Blazer in a special sheath, attached with Velcro tabs.

When all else failed…

Reluctantly, he backtracked to the car, opened the driver's door and found the knife by touch. He eased the door shut, stopped it short of latching to avoid the telltale sound, and moved back to the exit, where the door was cracked an inch or two. There was a heartbeat of uncertainty, when Phelan was afraid he might have lost the prowler, but he found his man again, emerging from a pool of shadow at the southwest corner of the house and gliding toward the rec-room windows.

He was following the light, trying to learn if there was anybody home. The drapes were drawn, of course—Phelan had killed too many unsuspecting men to ever walk around in front of open windows if he had a choice—but they weren't blackout curtains, and the spill of light that he could see from where he stood told him the shooter would have at least a partial view of the rec room.

It was a tiny lapse, produced by years of living in comparative security, and it could even work to Phelan's advantage this time, distracting his enemy from danger at his back.

Phelan wasted no time attempting to guess who the shooter was or who might have sent him. There would be time enough for questions later if he managed to take the man alive. And if he couldn't, well, there was still an outside chance of finding some ID, perhaps some other lead that would help him understand the attempt on his life.

This was nothing less, Phelan knew, than a flat-out assassination attempt. As far as whether the shooter hated him personally or was employed by someone else, he could have flipped a coin. It made no difference at the moment. His first order of business was disarming and disabling the prowler, preferably without inflicting any mortal wounds. If he succeeded there, he could ask questions to his heart's content, use any means at his disposal to produce the answers he desired.

There were far too many prospects for a list of enemies who would delight in Phelan's death. Some were the relatives, associates or friends of others he had killed. Some held a grudge because their side had come out second best in one of the conflicts where Phelan had served as a soldier for hire. Others might even be enemies of this or that client whom

Phelan had supplied with military hardware through the years.

The one aspect of Phelan's life that never even crossed his mind, in that regard, was the millionaire hunt club. Most of his clients were well satisfied, a few of them repeat customers, and the few who regretted their association with Phelan were spineless cowards, repulsed by violence to the point of folding when the chips were down. Clifford Wix might have been a candidate for revenge, but Wix was dead, and none of his surviving relatives or business partners had any way of learning Phelan's name, much less tracking him to his very doorstep.

Phelan put the problem out of mind as he slipped through the doorway, thankful for his own foresight in keeping the hinges well oiled. He was behind the shooter, in his blind spot, but that could change at any moment. Silence was essential, coming up behind the other man. Phelan could throw a knife with fair accuracy, but it was never a reliable means of killing, despite how it looked in the movies. Even if he scored a decent, disabling hit, the gunner could still go down shooting, and it only took one round to do the job.

He tried for a mixture of stealth and speed, coming up behind the shooter as his adversary stretched to peer in the window. A small man, that was something, though Phelan was skilled enough in unarmed combat to know that size really didn't matter all that much, if your opponent had the necessary skills.

A few more yards...

He made it, sliding in behind the shooter, and brought the knife up against his throat, the blade dimpling the skin, as he cautioned, "One move and you're dead."

Of course, some guys didn't give a shit.

Phelan was startled when, instead of freezing, his opponent kicked out toward the wall, beneath his rec-room window, and propelled himself backward with a snarl. There was something about the guy's voice, something odd, but Phelan had no time to dwell on it as the hooded skull cracked him under his chin, momentum driving him backward, off balance, stumbling just to stay upright. He nearly slashed the gunner's throat then and there, but something made him hesitate, lashing downward with the knife instead, scoring a gash across one of the enemy's forearms, rewarded with a cry of pain and the clatter of the weapon hitting the ground.

Incredibly, the smaller man slipped out of Phelan's grasp, losing blood in the process, but drawing a knife of his own. It was a wicked-looking tool, but Phelan wasn't intimidated. He had a longer reach than his opponent and, he strongly suspected, a superior skill with edged weapons. In fact, from the way the prowler held his knife, Phelan questioned whether he had ever done any serious cutting at all.

The hunter moved in, ducking and feinting, keeping his adversary on the move, driving him backward toward the barn. It took some time, but he was gaining, moving closer, into the position for a strike. When it was time, he feinted to his left, then lunged with the knife in his right hand, low and fast, slicing flesh and fabric on the prowler's left side. Another gasp of pained surprise, and his opponent made the unpardonable error of glancing down to check his wound, taking his eyes off Phelan's face and blade.

Phelan seized the time without hesitation, stepped in close and struck his adversary with an open palm, square in the face. If he had used more force, it could have been a killing blow, but Phelan managed to restrain himself, striking just hard enough to put the prowler down and out.

When he had caught his breath and claimed the trench knife for himself, Phelan bent and hooked his fingers underneath the ski mask, peeling it away. He blinked twice at the blood-smeared face, then cracked his first smile of the day.

"Well, well," he said. "What have we here?"

COLD STEEL...

The flat side of the blade was lightly tapping Rawlings's face. First one cheek, and then the other, back and forth, with just enough insistent force to make the pain inside her skull flare up again.

She didn't want to see the man who held the knife, didn't want to see anything at all, in fact. Her head was throbbing viciously. It felt as if she had been kicked in the forehead, perhaps more than once. If she opened her eyes and there was a reflective surface in the room, she was afraid that she might find her skull caved in, her face irreparably scarred.

No, that was wrong. She would be bleeding, in that case, but she sensed that she wasn't. There was no sticky wetness on her face, no wet warmth soaking through her turtleneck or jeans. She had been struck with something—had it been an open hand?—but she was still alive and capable of coherent thought.

The blade withdrew, came back and found her left cheek. Tap-tap-tap. She knew it was a knife because she felt the cutting edge, just barely, on her skin. Phelan could slit her throat, could cut her head off if he wanted to, but all he seemed to want, so far, was her attention.

She groaned, a sound not altogether feigned, and shifted sluggishly, attempting to project the image of a person still unconscious, coming back by slow degrees. It gave her time to test her hands, bound tight behind her back with something that felt like thin strips of plastic, and her legs, secured at the ankles to the front legs of a heavy chair, keeping her knees a foot or so apart. She guessed the chair was made of wood, a straight-back, maybe one of those designed for looks instead of comfort. It was smooth against her back, no slats or carvings there.

The blade withdrew again, and she was ready for the tap-tap on her right cheek, but it never came. Instead, the needle tip pricked her underneath her chin, exerting pressure, forcing her to lift her head or risk a bone-deep wound.

"What do you want?" she asked, embarrassed at the dry croak of her voice.

"That's better," Adam Phelan said. "I knew you were awake. The question isn't what I want, though. After all, you came to me."

It was her first glimpse of the man behind her father's death. She had expected something more—or maybe less—than what she saw. A gangster type, perhaps, or something like a jungle mercenary from an Arnold Schwarzenegger movie. That was foolish, she realized. The only men who wore their camouflage fatigues around the house were playing soldier. Playing with themselves.

This man was serious.

His shirt was charcoal-gray, short-sleeved, displaying powerful arms with minimal hair and no sign of tattoos. A pale scar looped halfway around his right forearm, above the hand that held a long and wicked-looking knife. His matching slacks were tailored, loose enough for modesty's sake, still hinting at powerful thighs and calves underneath. Black shoes, some new athletic style, with Velcro flaps instead of ordinary laces.

Mr. Cool at home.

"I don't know what you mean," she said.

The knife rushed in and flicked the tip of Rawlings's nose. She yelped and jerked her head back, unable to tell if she was cut, surprised and frightened by the raw intensity of pain from such a minor contact.

"*Chinatown,*" he said. "You ever see that movie? Where Polanski takes Jack Nicholson and slits his nostril open?"

"Please," she said.

"Please what?"

"Please tell me what you want."

"That's simple, babe." His smile seemed genuine, as if he were enjoying this. "I want to know what brings you out to my place in the middle of the night, dressed like a K mart ninja, with an M-1 carbine and a trench knife, peeping in my rec-room window. That's for starters. If I like your answer, maybe you'll live long enough for us to talk about some other things.''

Rawlings considered her limited options. The ski mask and weapons ruled out any innocent excuse, and Phelan was too smart, too experienced, to fall for some lame mistaken-identity dodge. Instead, she decided on a variation of the truth.

''I came out looking for the man who lives here,'' she replied.

''You found him, babe. The question on my mind is, why?''

''It's what I do,'' she said.

''It's 'what you do'? That makes you, what, some kind of hit woman?''

''That's right.'' She tried to put defiance in her tone, but didn't think she made it.

''You should think about another line of work,'' Phelan said. ''Something in the field of agriculture, maybe. I was thinking plant food.''

Rawlings kept her chin up, glaring at him, resolute. Her nose still burned, making her want to sneeze. She bit her tongue to counter the sensation, and made no reply.

''So, tell me, Hit Babe,'' Phelan said, ''who was it sent you here to punch my ticket?''

She didn't know how to respond. If she made up a name, picked one out of thin air, the odds were fifty-fifty that Phelan would laugh in her face. If he didn't laugh, though, she could well be dooming someone she had never met to death at Phelan's hands. Another downside, if he bought the made-up name, was that there would be no incentive left for keeping her alive.

"You never heard of confidentiality?" she challenged him.

"That's doctors, priests and lawyers," he replied. "Besides, in case you hadn't noticed, babe, we're not in court. That's not a witness stand you're sitting on, and I'm the only judge you'll ever have. If I find you in contempt, you'll be one sorry bitch."

He moved to her right. His rubber soles produced a rustling sound that puzzled her, until she glanced at the floor and saw the broad, blue plastic tarpaulin spread out beneath her chair.

To catch the blood, she thought, and felt her stomach twist into a painful knot.

Phelan was at her side, slightly behind her now. "If somebody hired you, he should get his money back. I don't believe it for a minute, understand, but it's a place to start."

The fingers of his left hand brushed her hair aside and tugged at the collar of her turtleneck. She stiffened as the long blade of his knife slid in between the clingy fabric and her skin. "It's getting warm in here," he said. "You're overdressed."

There was a whisper as the knife sliced through her collar, Rawlings holding deathly still. She felt the flat edge of the blade slide past her clavicle, almost caressing her, parting the fabric as it went. It grazed her chest and slipped into the valley of her cleavage, nicking her stomach as it sheared through the front of her sports bra, moving down toward her lap. In seconds, the turtleneck hung loose and open, split down the front from collar to hem.

Phelan used his blade to flick away the ruined shirt and bra, first one side, then the other. Rawlings tried to squirm away from him, but there was nowhere to go. He examined her coldly, almost clinically, his dead eyes doing more to frighten her than any leer or lecherous remark.

"Okay, babe, let's start over, shall we?" he prompted, scraping lightly at one nipple with the knife blade. "Once more, from the top."

Maryland

KARL SHUKER WAS DOZING in his Baltimore apartment when the telephone woke him from a dream of death. He had fallen asleep in front of the television, midway through his sixth or seventh beer, and it pissed him off to see that he had missed the last half hour of *Commando.* It was no big deal, of course, since he had seen the film at least a dozen times already, but he liked the climax, where the studly hero massacred at least a hundred enemies, while suffering no more than superficial scratches in the process.

His dream had been more realistic than the movie, incorporating snatches from real life, but for all its violence, it hadn't been a nightmare. Not even vaguely unpleasant, in fact. Shuker enjoyed the dreams of blood. They were his favorite kind. And now the telephone had ruined it for him, delicious images of slaughter lost beyond recall.

Shuker's number was unpublished, but he still got six or seven calls a week from telephone solicitors. He had complained to his local billing office, and was told that some solicitors employed a random-dialing apparatus that could reach him, even though his number was unlisted. That explained why some of those who called didn't appear to know his name. They simply called him ''sir'' and launched into their spiel. Buy this, buy that. In such a case, Shuker would cradle the receiver, check his Caller ID box, and phone back to the solicitor, screaming curses in German and cackling like a madman until the shaken stranger finally hung up.

This late at night, whenever someone called, he always checked the Caller ID in advance. Shuker didn't believe in answering machines, despised the thought of having messages recorded in his absence, or encouraging strangers to think he might actually return their mindless calls. He had no friends, as such, and would not have returned their calls, either, nine times out of ten.

This time, when he glanced at the plastic ID box beside his plain black telephone, Shuker recognized the caller's number. Adam Phelan called when there was business to be done, but their next meeting was already scheduled for the middle of next week, to discuss the location of their next hunt. It was uncommon—nearly unheard-of, in fact—for Phelan to call at odd hours this way.

The phone was on its fifth ring when he lifted the receiver. ''Yes,'' Shuker said. No cheery hello, made to sound like a question, as if he expected some pleasant surprise.

''We have a problem,'' Phelan said without preliminaries.

''What?''

''Not on the phone. How soon can you be here?''

Shuker could have asked where ''here'' was, but

he didn't like playing foolish games. The number on the box had told him Phelan was at home, in Stafford. Call it sixty miles by air, and add another twenty for the highways circumventing Washington and Arlington.

"Maybe two hours," Shuker told him, "if I leave right now."

"I'll see you then."

Phelan hung up without another word, the dial tone humming in Shuker's ear until he replaced the handset in its cradle. He was curious about the problem, verging on concerned, but that was the extent of his response. Karl Shuker didn't worry; it was just that simple. He knew well enough that fretting over the unknown was a colossal waste of time and energy. If Phelan said there was a problem, they would deal with it. And if worse came to worst, Shuker could always leave the Yank to face the music on his own.

Another thought kicked in and made him frown. Suppose, for some unknown reason, that Phelan had decided to dissolve their partnership. Perhaps he wanted to retire, after the trouble in Peru, or maybe he had thought some more about Shuker's mistake with the hands, deciding he was better off without this particular colleague.

There was no question of severance pay, naturally. Shuker had been paid his share of the proceeds from each hunt, agreed on in advance, and personal finances were his own responsibility. If and when the end came, he expected no more from Phelan than a parting handshake...but suppose there was more to the story?

Paranoia started to gnaw at him, making Shuker scowl as he moved toward his bedroom for a quick change of clothes. When he had changed his shirt, he slipped the Galco shoulder holster on and double-checked the SIG-Sauer P-226 semiauto pistol, loaded with the same Olin 9 mm Parabellum subsonic rounds favored by the FBI. The 147-grain bullets provided lethal stopping power without the overpenetration common to lighter, fully jacketed military loads. The Olins gave his P-226 the stopping power of a .45 automatic, but with more than double the ammunition capacity. Two spare clips, suspended in leather pouches below his right armpit, gave Shuker a total of forty-six rounds.

Not enough, he decided, and went to the closet, retrieving the Spectre SMG. He slipped it into a gym bag, with half a dozen spare magazines and a Sionics suppressor tailored to fit the stuttergun's threaded muzzle.

Shuker had no reason to suspect Phelan of treachery, but warriors stayed alive by anticipating the unexpected, making allowances for every feasible event. If Phelan meant to kill him at the Stafford house, he would most likely wear a Kevlar vest, but that still left his head, groin, arms, legs—every spot a lethal target if you placed your bullets properly.

Phelan would want him close enough to press the muzzle of his favorite Glock against Shuker's skull before he squeezed the trigger, but Karl would be ready for him, if and when. If Phelan had a surprise in store for his partner, it just might rebound and bite him on the ass.

And if the German's preparations were in vain,

so much the better. He would rather be prepared and wrong than unprepared and dead.

Shuker was whistling as he hefted the gym bag, locked up and walked out to his car.

CHAPTER ELEVEN

The flight from San Francisco International to Byrd Field, outside Richmond, wound up taking seven hours, with a stopover and change of planes in Dallas. Bolan understood that modern airline flights were scheduled for convenience of the companies involved, and not the paying passengers. Half a dozen hub airports attracted travelers from all across the country, even if it took them in the opposite direction from their destination, but Bolan sometimes wondered how long it would be before the whole system bogged down.

Not this night, he thought as he stood in line at the car-rental counter, his suitcase heavy with hardware.

Trust and privacy were still the glaring flaws in America's public-security system. Whereas certain European and Middle Eastern nations had learned the hard way with terrorists, driven to extremes where all check-through luggage was X-rayed for weapons and explosives, American "security" consisted of two or three questions at the ticket counter, the answers accepted on blind faith. "Did you pack that bag yourself, sir? Has it been out of your personal control since it was packed? Enjoy your flight."

Apparently, the concept that a terrorist or other criminal might lie hadn't occurred to anyone associated with the FAA or any major airline. It was still a crapshoot every time a bag was checked on board an aircraft leaving any airport in the U.S.A. A few airports used dogs, but they were mostly trained to sniff for drugs, and most of them were utilized to check incoming bags of foreign origin.

This night, the lax security had worked to Bolan's advantage, allowing him to skip the military flight Brognola could have managed on an hour's notice, while taking some rudimentary hardware along for the ride. It was nothing fancy, granted: the Beretta 93-R, plus the Desert Eagle and an MP-5 K submachine gun with suppressor, with spare magazines all around. With leather and ammo, the weapons added some fifteen pounds to his bag, but it was still well within the airline's standard weight limit, no questions asked.

And he would be grateful for all of it, Bolan thought, if Adam Phelan was waiting for him at home.

He hadn't called ahead to check, although he had the man's unlisted number memorized. Assuming Phelan *was* at home, any suspicious calls might spook him, put him more on edge. The odds were good that Phelan kept his guard up, as it was. Bolan had no desire to rattle him, perhaps even put him to flight, if he had any chance of catching the hunter at home.

This time, he thought, he'd finish it.

It was a slightly longer drive to Stafford, north from Richmond on Interstate 95, than it had been rolling south from Washington. The extra ten or fifteen miles gave Bolan time to think about his target and his angle of attack. At last, though, he could think of nothing that would change about his first approach—except, that is, for leaving Chelsea Rawlings out of it.

He parked and left his car in more or less the same place, changed into his blacksuit, donned his combat gear and went in through the trees. So far, so good. He stayed alert for sensors, anything at all, but it appeared that nothing had been added to the landscape since his previous visit. It was only when he reached the house itself that Bolan noted anything at all to set his teeth on edge.

His first time there, the house had been blacked out, as if abandoned. This time, there were two lights burning, on the porch and in what he took to be the living room. There was no oddity in that, per se, but Bolan's stomach tightened when he saw the piece of paper thumbtacked to the door.

He tried field glasses, but the paper had been folded over once, and he couldn't make out the two words written on the side that was exposed. Alarms were going off in Bolan's mind as he began to circle wide around the house and barn, looking for traps. Leaving a note to advertise his absence struck him as the last thing on earth Adam Phelan would do...unless, of course, he was expecting company.

It happened in the daily world of social intercourse, the landscape strewed with sticky notes and scraps of paper left on windshields, slipped through mail slots, wedged into the cracks of doors. The messages were typically mundane: "Love you. I'll be back soon. The party's out in back."

But Bolan couldn't find the party this time—couldn't find a single sign of life around the place, in fact. Night-vision goggles let him penetrate the windows on three sides, where curtains had been thoughtfully flung wide on darkened rooms.

Nobody home.

Which left him with two options: he could leave, or he could read the note.

The porch light left him critically exposed, but Bolan had already satisfied himself that there was no one in the barn. As for the woods around the house, well, he would simply have to take his chances on a sniper creeping up to pick him off. He reached the porch without incident, felt himself go cold and dead inside as he read the external address on the note.

Mike Belasko.

Bolan pried out the thumbtack and flicked it away, ignoring the microscopic risk of contact toxins on the tack or paper. That wouldn't be Phelan's style, assuming he possessed the requisite technology. Bolan unfolded the single sheet of paper, reading silently: "*Mi casa es su casa.* Make yourself at home."

The next step would be entry, if he followed through. There was an element of danger, Bolan realized. Phelan could have the house wired up to blow a dozen different ways. He could have trap guns rigged inside, to strafe the door with automatic fire or punch a charge of buckshot through the first intruder's chest. He could have run electric wires between the doorknob and the nearest wall socket. Or Phelan could be waiting in the house himself, hidden from any outside view, prepared to blaze away at any home invaders, confident that local law would rubber-stamp his plea of self-defense.

All possible, but somehow none of it rang true.

He tried the knob and wasn't surprised to feel it turn. No one was waiting for him in the living room. Despite its ample furniture, the house felt vacant, almost dead, as if the structure somehow knew its human had departed for the last time.

The second note was smaller, but he saw it on his second sweep of the room. It was a yellow sticky note, affixed by its adhesive to a videocassette cartridge, resting on the glass-topped coffee table.

It read: "Play me."

Bolan found the television with its built-in VCR and ran the tape. It opened with a shot of Chelsea Rawlings, bound securely to a straight-backed chair, her turtleneck and bra slit open and pulled back to bare her breasts. Several small cuts had been inflicted on her upper body, bright red blood a striking contrast to her tan.

"I'm sorry, Mike," she said, fighting the tears. "It's all my fault, I know. He says that if you do exactly as you're told, he'll let me live. I don't believe it, though."

The tape appeared to jerk, a clumsy cut, and when he next saw Rawlings, she was bleeding from a split and swollen lip, the livid imprint of a fist clearly visible on her face. She spoke with difficulty now, as if she had a wad of cotton in her mouth.

"No editorials, he says." She tried a smile, but didn't have it in her. "You're supposed to join us at a special place he has. I don't know where it is, exactly. He says you should fly to Santa Rosalia—that's in Baja California somewhere—and check into the hotel. There's only one in town, I guess. Someone will watch for you and get in touch with your instructions for the rest of it."

She hesitated, seemed about to try another warning, but thought better of it. When she spoke again, it was to say, "He says for you to bring this tape along, and don't make any copies. If you show it to the cops or anybody else, he says I'll die. 'Die screaming,' are the words he used. He'll see them coming, and you'll never find him till *he* comes for *you.* I'm sorry, Mike. I screwed up really bad."

He stopped the tape, ejected it and took it with him as he finished checking out the house. Phelan was well and truly gone, the bedroom closet empty, dresser drawers cleaned out. He tried to picture Phelan packing, Rawlings bound and bleeding in the other room, and couldn't make the image gel. He wondered, finally, if there had been a great deal there to pack, or if his target lived a rootless kind of life, accustomed to way stations on the road.

It made no difference, either way. He had a choice to make, and while no time limit was specified—Phelan couldn't have known when, or even definitely *if* Bolan would see the tape—but simple logic told him it was not an open-ended deal. Call it a few days, at the most, and every hour Chelsea Rawlings spent in Phelan's company increased the odds that she would die.

Die screaming.

Bolan left the front door standing open as he put the place behind him and retraced his path through darkness, toward the waiting rental car.

PHELAN HAD KNOWN that he was gambling when he made the tape and left it at his house. He placed the odds of his enemy paying a visit—a second visit, at that—around sixty-forty against, and while it was better than nothing, it left Phelan dissatisfied, haunted by a feeling that his life had started to unravel.

Quentin Rawlings, for Christ's sake!

Phelan remembered the man as a weakling of sorts, who had picked off one target from ambush, then froze when the second began to return fire. There was nothing remarkable in that, of course. The majority of his clients went looking for a clean, uncomplicated kill. Only a hale and hardy handful wanted to engage an enemy who was capable of defending himself, and most of those few lacked the discipline to pull it off.

So, Rawlings had been nothing special, pro or con. The suicide surprised Phelan, though. He had missed the media coverage, if there was any, but the act seemed out of character. A man who paid a million dollars for the chance to kill another human being was, generally speaking, devoid of traditional conscience. It had occurred to Phelan that one of his clients might rat him out someday, if cornered on some other charge and anxious for a deal, but he had never seriously considered the prospect of a spontaneous—much less posthumous—confession to murder.

Well, he thought, a person lived and learned.

Once he'd identified the woman, found out who her father was—correction, had been—Phelan felt he had begun to get a better handle on the situation. There were still critical gaps in his information, of course, the first and foremost dealing with this Mike Belasko character. His true name held less interest for Phelan than the question of his government affiliation. The Rawlings woman had been clear in her belief that Belasko—"a big, dark, good-looking man," the best she could describe him—had some link to Washington, perhaps to Justice and the FBI. For his part, Phelan was inclined to doubt it, since the SOP in such a case would have his property aswarm with uniforms and warrants, but he couldn't absolutely rule it out.

And that was where the gambling part kicked in.

He had been careful with the videocassette, from start to finish. He hadn't appeared on tape, made sure the woman didn't speak his name, arranged a neutral background for the shoot, and wiped the cartridge down for fingerprints before he left it on the coffee table. On the downside, if Belasko turned it in, the very fact that it had been recovered from his house would serve to link him with the taping.

Still, what would it prove?

To prosecute a murder charge, or even kidnapping, the law would need a victim, some small part of Chelsea Rawlings to convince a jury she was dead and gone. Without a body or a witness, all the government could really prove was that the woman had been bound and videotaped by *someone*. Her apparent injuries could be explained away as makeup, simplistic special effects of the sort advertised for sale to amateur filmmakers in a hundred different magazines. Her spiel about the trip to Baja was a simple piece of acting. Let the state prove otherwise.

But it would never come to that, Phelan was reasonably sure. This Belasko sounded like a one-man show, to hear the woman tell it. He was here and there and everywhere, with no apparent clock to punch. His first apparent visit to the Stafford house, where he met Chelsea Rawlings to begin with, sounded like a classic black op hunting party, search and destroy. Phelan hadn't been home, of course, but he still felt almost as if he owed the woman something for diverting the stalker's attention, taking him down a blind alley.

She was something, this one. Full of piss and vinegar, as Phelan's old man used to say of the rare people he admired. Two solo trips to kill him, even knowing what she might be up against if he was home. He wondered if her Winchester was still out in the woods, where she had dropped it on her first attempt. If so, and it was found, it would rebound against the Feds in any effort to construct a case against him. Rawlings's credibility on tape was suspect from the get-go, since she clearly blamed him for her father's death and had attempted—twice, no less—to take him out by extralegal means.

The rest of it was bullshit, anyway. The Feds would never find a way to prosecute him for the hunting parties he had organized. The only client who had blown the whistle on him, so far, was deceased, a mentally unbalanced suicide. The Feds would never get another name from Phelan's lips, no matter how they piled the pressure on. The other option was to splash his face and name across the headlines, pleading with his various unknown accomplices to sacrifice themselves, their families and fortunes, in the interest of justice.

Right, he thought. And anyone who held his breath on that one was a dead man.

Hell would freeze over before one of Adam Phelan's clients put his own head on the chopping block. An offer of immunity would mean no more to any of those men than breath mints to a vampire. Phelan's fat-cat clients feared embarrassment far more than prosecution. Any one of them who joined the Quentin Rawlings one-man whistle-blowing team could take immunity and shove it up his ass. The real punishment, for men of their stature, lay in public humiliation, loss of social status and employment, the prospect of a multimillion-dollar divorce, restricted visitation rights with their children. In short, a whole life down the crapper—and for what?

To help Uncle Sam nail Adam Phelan on a third-rate felony or Class A misdemeanor that would probably put him back on the street inside of six months. His clients had to know there was no evidence remaining of their hunts that would support a murder charge in any foreign jurisdiction. They also had to know that Phelan, once released with a slap on the wrist, would move heaven and earth to punish those who had betrayed him. And their loved ones. Their friends and acquaintances. Their pets.

It was a lose-lose situation for the men who had employed him as a hunting guide and travel agent. Most of them would probably prefer the Quentin Rawlings exit method—sans confession tape—in lieu of watching their deepest, darkest secrets become tabloid fodder.

That left only Mike Belasko to be dealt with, Phelan gambling that his faceless enemy would return to the Stafford house, find the videotape of Chelsea Rawlings and do something about it himself without calling in the cavalry. It was a heavy-duty risk, but that was Adam Phelan's stock-in-trade. Assuming that Belasko took the bait, it would mean a final farewell to his favorite hideout, but that was a small price to pay for survival.

And in the meantime, he was working on a scheme to turn the problem around, make it yet another opportunity for profit. One last hunt, to let him go out with a bang—and a few extra million to cushion his retirement.

Whoever said crime doesn't pay had been a total idiot.

CHELSEA RAWLINGS KNEW in her heart that she was doomed. She had pegged her last hope on the flight to Baja California, trusting that a trip to any airport, much less on board a plane, would present her with an opportunity to save herself, sometime between departure from Virginia and arrival on Mexican soil. Even if it cost her life, she could still score a victory of sorts by forcing Adam Phelan to kill her in a public place, with witnesses, where he could be identified, perhaps even captured at the scene.

Of course, she had reckoned without a private plane.

Rawlings had no way of knowing whether the Piper Cheyenne IIXL belonged to Phelan, but he clearly had access and knew how to fly, while his sidekick—the same Karl her father had referred to in his suicide tape—kept a watchful eye on her. A private plane meant no examination of their luggage for weapons or other contraband, no security checkpoint in the terminal—no entry to the terminal at all, in fact. Phelan's plane was parked five hundred yards or so from the Byrd Field terminal proper, near a string of hangars rented out to private charter services. Their flight plan was already filed when they got there, and Phelan kept her company on board the Piper while the scowling German went to drop his Blazer in the long-term parking lot. When he returned, some twenty minutes later, they were ready to fly, all systems go.

Rawlings gave up hope as the airplane lifted off. She had done her best, and piss poor it had been. Instead of avenging her father, she had dropped the ball twice, with disastrous results. Besides her own impending death, she had allowed Phelan to bait a trap for Belasko that could lead him to his death. She should have forced Phelan to kill her at the Stafford house, and never mind the pain, instead of helping to destroy the only person who had tried to help her since her father's suicide.

Of course, the "good" news was that Belasko might not find the tape. She had no reason to believe he would be visiting the Stafford house again, though Phelan somehow seemed convinced of it.

Assuming that he *did* stop by and find the bait, however, there was still no guarantee that he would follow them across the country, on to Santa Rosalia. It was suicide to do so. Surely he would recognize that fact and stay away.

The bad news was that Rawlings didn't think so. If Belasko made another trip to Stafford and he found the tape, she thought the odds were excellent that he would try to set her free, regardless of the danger to himself. He struck her as that kind of man, the hero type, and that would make his dying in a lost cause all the more pathetic. All the more her fault.

Rawlings felt a blush warming her cheeks as she thought of Belasko watching the videotape, seeing her half-naked, bound to a chair. Would the image excite him somehow, or would he simply find her pitiful? He didn't seem the kind of man to relish someone else's pain—but, then again, neither was Adam Phelan.

When Phelan hurt her, when he cut her clothes away and started poking at her with his knife, she had known the work was strictly business. He required whatever information she possessed, and would do anything to wring it from her. Anything. He didn't have the sadist's smile or glassy stare, but he would press her to the limits of endurance, to the last breath of her life, if necessary. She had seen that in his eyes, and it had broken her before the torture had progressed beyond the kind of superficial damage that was treatable with adhesive bandages.

He had broken Rawlings with the same ease that he might have broken down a child, and she was shamed by that. In the moment that she spoke Belasko's name, began to spill the details of their meeting, she had willed the knife blade closer, wished she had the nerve to throw herself upon it and deny the bastard what he needed to survive. If Phelan lived through this, if Belasko died, it would he her fault, no one else's.

Once again, the "good" news was that she wouldn't live long enough to truly suffer from her guilt. It was entirely possible that Phelan would kill her as soon as they reached their Mexican destination. Indeed, it wouldn't have surprised her if he had ordered Karl to open the Piper's door and pitch her out while they were airborne over Dixie, maybe crossing the arid Southwest. At times, while her mind gnawed on itself, the plunge would have been a relief.

She was wearing one of Phelan's T-shirts, with a light windbreaker over it, to replace the clothing he had slashed as a prelude to interrogation. The garments were too large, but she still felt trapped inside them, hating the feel of the fabric against her skin. It was an irrational response, Rawlings knew, but she couldn't help feeling violated. Every time she moved, the small, insistent tug of bandages on her breasts reminded her of how little pain it had taken to break her will, destroy her resolve.

They stopped to refuel at an airport near Roswell, New Mexico, but she had no chance to make a bid for freedom in the town where aliens from outer space had once supposedly crash-landed decades before she was born. Karl remained with her inside the aircraft, while Phelan took care of the refueling bill, and then the men took turns visiting a public rest room, no offer of a similar courtesy to their captive. Rawlings could have used the toilet, true enough, but it was no emergency. More than anything else, she wanted out of the airplane, wanted to feel the wind on her face, in her hair. She wanted a chance to run for it, even if it cost her her life.

It was midafternoon when they took off again, chasing the sun toward the Pacific Ocean. She had a window seat, for what it was worth, and she studied the desert below them, watching the occasional small town pass by in their flickering shadow. She prayed for an engine to fail, begged gravity to exert itself and pull them down, but all in vain. The twin turboprop engines ran smoothly, bearing them on toward the spot that would be her graveyard.

Rawlings had no idea when they crossed into Mexican airspace, but she recognized the Gulf of California, with Baja dead ahead, mainland Mexico fading behind them. They spent the last three-quarters of an hour flying over water, headed nearly due south, until she reckoned they had to soon run out of gulf and hit the ocean proper.

Phelan had allowed her to keep her wristwatch, and it was nearly five o'clock when she felt the aircraft begin its descent. Glancing out her window, she still saw nothing but water below them, hoping for an instant that her prayers for destruction had finally been answered. Too late, she realized that they were homing on an island, situated ten or twelve miles offshore.

Phelan made one pass, then banked and brought the Piper back to line up on a narrow airstrip, dirt and dried grass, by the look of it. One final chance to crash, but Phelan brought them in safe and sound, with just enough bouncing to remind Rawlings that she really *did* need that toilet now.

A fair judge of distance, she guessed that the island was roughly two miles long and shaped like a teardrop, perhaps a mile wide at its broad southern end. Except for the landing field and a narrow strip of beach, it was heavily wooded, with a rocky spine running down the north-south axis. She had glimpsed no sign of human habitation, but she knew much could be hidden by the trees.

A grave, for instance.

Rawlings knew her corpse wouldn't take up much room at all.

"I CAN'T BELIEVE you're falling for a trap like this," Brognola said. He didn't sound disgusted quite so much as sad.

"I see the trap," Bolan said, understanding his old friend's concern. "I've seen them before. It doesn't change anything."

"Doesn't change—" The big Fed seemed to catch himself, pulling back from the edge of anger, knowing it would get him nowhere with the Executioner. "Look, Striker, this woman did it to herself."

"What difference does that make?" Bolan asked.

"I mean to say, it's not your fault."

"I know that. But it *is* my *job.*"

"Uh-uh. No way," the man from Justice countered. "Your job was to get the goods on Adam

Phelan and wrap up the hunt club, assuming it existed."

"It does," Bolan replied. "We know that now. He's killing people, and he'll keep on killing until something stops him cold."

"So, stop him," Brognola suggested.

"That's the plan."

"But on your own terms, guy, not his. He wants you down in Baja, for Christ's sake! Check into some hotel and wait for him to get in touch with you. He'll get in touch, all right. A rocket through the window at siesta time. I wouldn't be surprised."

"You put your finger on it, Hal—surprise. He knows I'll be on guard when I arrive. He might try something right away, but I don't think so. If he tries and blows it, then he's lost his only chance. He has to figure I'll pack up and split."

"Too bad he's wrong," Brognola groused.

"My thinking is, the stop in Santa Rosalia's just phase one. He's talked to Chelsea, so he's thinking I'm some kind of Fed. He wants me somewhere well away from U.S. soil, where I won't have the cavalry on tap."

"Now, that's a thought," Brognola said. "I'll ring up Able Team. They're down in Costa Rica, but the job can wait another day or two, and—"

"No, Hal," Bolan said, cutting him off. "I'm handling this myself."

"Goddammit! Well, I had to try. Go on, then. Let me hear the rest of it."

"He'll come for me at the hotel, all right—or, more than likely, send a gofer—but it won't be a straightforward hit. More like an escort. Take me somewhere else, where he can work without an audience. Remember, Hal, he's thinking I'm official, more or less."

"You are," Brognola answered, "more or less."

Times changes, Bolan thought, flashing briefly to the days when Brognola had hunted him with all the force at his disposal, placing Bolan's name at the top of the FBI's most-wanted list. And he stopped himself before the flashback turned into a time-wasting detour down memory lane.

"He'll want to find out who I work for, how high up it goes, and whether he can even go back home again. If he just whacks me, he won't learn anything."

"Suppose he's just pissed off by now, and doesn't give a shit?" Brognola asked.

"It doesn't scan," Bolan replied. "This one's a thinker, not some wind-up thug. You don't just point him at a target and let go. Phelan selects his target, time and place. He thinks it through. Self-interest put him where he is. It's all that's keeping him alive."

"You need to follow his example," Brognola suggested.

"I'm not suicidal," Bolan told him. "If I thought this was a kamikaze mission—"

"You'd go anyway," Brognola interrupted him. "We both know that. Show you a damsel in distress, you're off like Don Quixote. What you've got here is a rich, spoiled brat who blew her first attempt on Phelan—"

"Thanks to me."

Brognola forged ahead, refusing to be sidetracked.

"Blew her first attempt on Phelan," he repeated, "and then promised you she wouldn't try again. Which was a lie, in case you haven't noticed it. So, then, she blows the second try and winds up in the bag. Phelan applies a little pressure and she rats you out, on top of which she now expects a white knight to come riding in and save her ass."

"Her personality's irrelevant," Bolan replied.

"Okay. Two things to think about, in that case. Number one, she might be dead already. Maybe never left Virginia, come to that. If Phelan's thinking, like you say, he's also got to figure that the more excess baggage he carries around, the worse off he is. Why not kill her and dump her as soon as he finished the tape?"

"I want him, anyway," Bolan replied. "I need to know. What's number two?"

"The lady might not be on your side, after all. The whole damned thing could be a suck."

"How's that?" Bolan asked, through a frown.

"Well, now, we know she's Chelsea Rawlings. That part checks out, five by five," Brognola said. "But think about it—daddy dearest left his little girl chin deep in money, stocks and real estate when he checked out. It wouldn't be the first time someone helped a family member shuffle off this mortal coil, to speed up an inheritance."

"You think she faked the tapes somehow, then made the old man shoot himself?"

"Not necessarily. Maybe, though, she heard opportunity knocking and decided to open the door."

"I'm not following you," Bolan said.

"Quentin Rawlings left the suicide tape with his

lawyer, right?'' Brognola said. ''It was supposed to kick off an investigation of the hunt club.''

''But it obviously didn't,'' Bolan said, ''until we got involved.''

''Correct. Now, maybe darling daughter starts to think about what happens if the hunt club is exposed, and daddy dearest is the only client publicly identified. Suppose the victims—hell, the other countries—start to feel litigious. Say they run through Phelan's cash, assuming they can find it, and they start to look around for someone else to blame. Who's left? A confessed accomplice who's already dead, but whose estate has deep, deep pockets.''

''So, she draws me into it...exactly why, again?''

''To bury Phelan's operation, if you can. You tried it in Peru, and came back telling her—against my best advice, you might recall—that it would take more time. Suppose that spooked her, and she cut a deal with Phelan. Bury you, instead of him, and put the lid back on, before the thing goes public.''

''You've been watching *JFK* again,'' Bolan said, smiling now. ''But even if you had it right, I'd still want Phelan. And I'd want the woman, too. You've given me no reason yet to stay away from Santa Rosalia.''

''How about survival?'' Brognola suggested. ''I would truly hate to see you killed.''

''I'm not too thrilled about that notion, either,'' Bolan told his friend. ''Of course, the flip side is that I refuse to live in fear with a job unfinished from a lack of trying.''

''That's the side you always play,'' Brognola

chided him. "How about another tune to make me happy, just this once?"

"I'm going, Hal," he said.

"Uh-huh. Well, watch your back. Give a call, if you can think of anything you need. Able Team—"

"I'll see you, Hal."

"I hope so, Mack." The line went dead.

The Executioner hoped so, too.

CHAPTER TWELVE

Baja, California

Santa Rosalia is one of three major ports on Baja's east coast, serving the Gulf of California. All three—the other two being Loreto, roughly one hundred miles to the south, and Pichilingue, perhaps ninety miles farther on—have airports, while Loreto and Santa Rosalia also offer regular ferry service to the Mexican mainland, some eighty or ninety miles distant. Despite their status as centers of commerce in eastern Baja California, however, the port towns go begging, for the most part, when it comes to Yankee tourism. Why go to dusty Baja, after all, when for a few more dollars and an extra thirty minutes on the airplane, you can be in Acapulco or Cancun?

Baja, through no real fault of its own, has become stigmatized in most American minds as a kind of death-wish destination. A long list of movies, TV shows and torture-test commercials for off-road vehicles have portrayed Baja California as a godforsaken wasteland, where only the toughest men and vehicles survive amid sun-scorched boulders, scorpions and rattlesnakes. Border dwellers and generations of military servicemen are familiar with the free-wheeling, anything-goes atmosphere in Tijuana and Mexicali, but anything south of Ensenada is widely regarded as the exclusive province of drug lords and bandits, outlaw bikers and Gila monsters. Anyone unwise enough to follow Highway 1 southbound beyond Ensenada takes his life in his own shaky hands.

In fact, while sparsely settled in parts, Baja California is no more remote, uncivilized or dangerous than many other parts of Mexico. If drug gangs traffic there, the same can easily be said about Nogales, Ciudad Juarez and Matamoros. If the Baja desert shows no mercy to unwary transients, neither do the arid wastelands of Sonora, Chihuahua or Coahuila. If the cops in Tijuana have their hands out, so do their compatriots in Monterrey, Tampico and Mexico City.

Politically, Baja California was divided into two states, north and south. The capital of Baja South, Lapaz was some two hundred miles below Bolan's destination at Santa Rosalia, but it hardly mattered, since he gave no thought to seeking any aid and comfort from the locals. In the present circumstance, he was as much an outlaw as was Adam Phelan, and he would conduct himself accordingly—within certain limits.

Because Mexico was a prime source of illegal narcotics and other contraband flowing into the United States, her customs agents had no interest whatsoever in incoming luggage. Like most Mexican officials, they couldn't care less what gringos brought with them to Mexico, as long as they left some money behind when they returned home. Bolan thus had no trouble transporting a small arsenal in his luggage on the flight to Santa Rosalia, though he knew that he would have to dump the guns before he left.

Assuming he went home at all.

He had considered options—flying into Loreto, for instance, and driving north to Santa Rosalia, in case Phelan's people were watching the airport—but finally decided any dodge would be a waste of time and energy. He wanted Phelan to find him, and there was no reason to believe that any airport watchers would have orders to waste him on the spot. It would have been too public, for one thing, and a quick kill would eliminate any hope Phelan had of interrogating Bolan, finding out who he worked for and what he was after.

Phelan would want some time, Bolan surmised, if nothing else, to make an example of the soldier, reassure himself that he was still in charge, officially untouchable. He had to be sweating, though, maybe just a little bit, at the thought of trackers hunting him for a change, turning around the whole game.

Bolan bypassed the line of beat-up taxis and rented a two-year-old, four-door sedan at the airport, detouring past a men's room where he armed himself, before proceeding to the car and stowing his bags in the trunk. There was, in fact, only one hotel of any size in town, and while Bolan considered signing the register with yet another alias, he finally saw no reason to make things more difficult on Phelan or the gofers he might send to do his dirty work. Bolan had come this far to find his enemy, after all, not to hide in his room while the game went on without him.

At the hotel, he checked in, took a shower—keeping the Beretta 93-R handy, just in case—and changed into jeans and a long-sleeved shirt, Doc Marten boots and a loose denim vest to hide the shoulder rig. It was warm out, even at the tag end of the day, but Bolan chose long sleeves in the knowledge that he could always roll them up for comfort, roll them down again if he had any pressing need to cover up—as in a headlong dash through thorny desert brush, for instance.

He had finished dressing and was checking out the dog-eared room-service menu when the old-fashioned rotary telephone beside his bed gave a halfhearted jangle. Bolan waited for a second ring, to make sure it was not some switchboard glitch, and picked up on the third.

"Belasko."

"It is good you've come," a male voice, vaguely foreign—German?—told him.

"How could I resist the invitation?"

"Come downstairs," the caller said. "We take a ride."

"What, no siesta?" Bolan prodded him.

"You want to play? The woman's tasty, don't you think?"

"How will I know you?"

"You'll have escorts. They should be outside your door by now."

"I'm on my way," Bolan said, hanging up the telephone before the caller had another chance to speak. He didn't fancy going for a ride Chicago-style, and reckoned this would be as good a time as any to assert himself, start throwing the opposition off balance. While reluctant to jeopardize Chelsea Rawlings any further, he knew there was still something to be said for selective resistance. With any luck at all, he might turn the tables on Phelan and company, gain the upper hand with his opening move.

Two Mexicans were waiting for him in the hallway when Bolan opened his door. They both wore baggy linen shirts, the tails outside their pants. One made a move in the direction of his waistband when Bolan flashed him a grin, but he was unprepared for the elbow smash that flattened his nose, dropping him senseless to the floor.

By the time number one hit the deck, Bolan had rounded on his partner with a left-handed jab to the throat, cutting off the tough guy's wind. Bolan then slammed the steel-capped toe of his boot into the guy's crotch and put him down. In parting, he relieved both men of side arms: an Iver Johnson X-300 Pony autoloader from Broken Nose, and a Colt Diamondback revolver from No Nuts. Bolan bypassed the elevator, pausing long enough to drop the captured weapons into a wheezing ice machine, and started down the service stairs.

KARL SHUKER WAITED in the car while two of the local peons entered the hotel and made their way upstairs. It had been simple, obtaining the target's room number from a scrawny porter, the German slipping him the equivalent of five U.S. dollars and cautioning him to forget the transaction. From the young man's spaced-out expression, Shuker suspected that forgetting would be no problem at all.

He called Belasko on the mobile phone he carried, no concern about eavesdropping police in this Mexican backwater town, where even the roaches and scorpions took their siesta time seriously. It amused Shuker to think what would happen if he entered the hotel himself, dragged this Belasko from his room and down the stairs, out to the waiting vehicle. Would anyone bother to call the police? Would the lawmen respond to a call?

Instead of risking it, however, Shuker counted on the man to do as he was told. Why else would he have come to Baja in the first place, if he wasn't concerned about the woman? It would make no sense for him to cause a problem now, when he had come this far. Unless…

Shuker glanced at his watch and muttered a curse in German. What was taking so long? The lazy bastards should have returned with Belasko by now. He had considered giving one of them a walkie-talkie when they went inside, but had decided they were probably too simpleminded to operate the two-way radio. Now, he cursed his own failure to take the precaution, regardless of its prospects for success.

Another minute passed. Shuker shifted in his seat and reached into the gym bag resting on the floorboards. The feel of his Spectre SMG reassured him, but only to a point. While he felt capable of going into the hotel and taking out their man, Phelan had ordered him to avoid deadly force. Without this Mike Belasko character alive and talking, Phelan said, they would have no idea of who was stalking them or how much trouble they were facing in the States.

Phelan's demand explained the other item in the gym bag, a Crossman air pistol loaded with a fresh CO_2 cartridge and a needle-tipped tranquilizer dart. Shuker had been forced to guess at the dosage, working from their prisoner's description of the target as a man over six feet tall and about two hundred pounds. Few soporific drugs are instantaneous in their effect, however, and the best Shuker could do was to calculate a marginal overdose—enough dope, say, for a man six feet two and 225 pounds. Anything beyond that dosage ran the risk of an accidental fatality, and while Shuker wouldn't mind killing this pest, Phelan would be furious if he did so.

So what? Shuker thought to himself, then blinked it away in a heartbeat. This wasn't the time or place for a rebellion against his employer. If such a move was necessary at some future time, Shuker would plan his actions well ahead and execute them flawlessly.

Right now he had a different problem. There was still no sign of his two gofers or the man they were sent to lift. He tried the room again, with his cellular phone, and waited through five rings before disconnecting.

What now?

Should he send his last two men inside to find the first two and their human cargo? Maybe leave the driver with the vehicle and join the second local, to give it the personal touch? Or should he simply wait a little longer for the lazy pigs Phelan had hired to do their job?

Broken communications aside, Shuker had another problem at the moment. Even if he entered the hotel himself, he wouldn't recognize this Belasko without the escorts he had sent to fetch the stranger back. He had a vague description from the woman—"dark, good-looking"—but he didn't know the bitch's standards when it came to physical attraction. Christ! He could be looking for anyone from Pierce Brosnan to Mr. Bean. The bastard could walk right past him, without the two locals, and Shuker would never know it.

Another minute gone, and he was down to plotting alternative strategies, sending one man around to cover the back while he went in to ask the clerk how many white men were registered today, getting the information out of him one way or another, when a man stepped through the front door, alone, glancing left and right before his eyes met Shuker's and locked on target.

The woman had been close. He was a little over six feet tall, about two hundred pounds, with dark hair and a dark complexion. If Shuker had been a woman, he might have called the stranger handsome, but his mind didn't work that way, and he dismissed the notion out of hand. Was this, in fact, their man?

He recognized the possibility of error, however small, without the locals to confirm which room this particular man had come from. Where were they, goddammit? They should have had him flanked and covered, coming out of the hotel. Instead, Shuker was looking at a man who met his gaze and gave him the bare suggestion of a smile, before he turned and started walking eastward, toward the waterfront.

Getting away, Shuker thought, although he had no clear idea of where the stranger thought he could hide or why he would make the attempt. He had a split second to decide, no time to hesitate. Make the move? Sit and wait?

"*¿Qué pasa?*" asked the driver, smart enough despite the dull expression on his face to know that something had gone wrong.

"Emilio!" Shuker snapped at the Mexican in the shotgun seat. "Go in and see what's keeping your friends. *Pronto!*"

"*Sí, señor.*"

The Mexican bailed out and shut the door behind him, moving swiftly toward the double doors of the hotel. Shuker leaned forward, clamped his left hand on the driver's shoulder as he spoke again. "Luis," he said, "I want us on that gringo's ass, no matter where he goes. Understand?"

"*Sí, jefe.*"

A heartbeat later, they were rolling, following the tall, dark stranger as he moved along the sidewalk, still eastbound. He seemed to take his time, glancing back only once, as if to make sure the car was following him before he continued on his way. No hurry, pacing off the sidewalk, glancing at shop windows now and then, but never really slowing down enough to window-shop. Assuming this was Belasko—and the German hoped it was, with all his heart—their progress eastward was ironic, for a man attempting to escape. The waterfront had been their destination all along, of course. A launch was waiting for them there, gassed up and ready for a quick run to the island, out and back.

The other guests would be arriving in the next twelve hours or so. And none of them would be amused if Shuker let the man who called himself Belasko slip away.

They still had four or five blocks left before they reached the docks, and Shuker thought it was as good a time as any to make his move. There were no witnesses in sight; it should be relatively easy. Take the Crossman from his gym bag, roll the starboard window down and—

He was thinking through the shot, rehearsing it, when his intended target veered into an alley, bolted and was gone.

"YOU SHOULDN'T HAVE to wait much longer," Adam Phelan said. The woman didn't answer him, but he could feel her glaring at his back as he stood gazing through the window, toward the forest pressing close around the house.

"Reunions are a funny thing sometimes," he said, turning to face her. "You'd be surprised how quickly people change. Or maybe not. Your father changed, I take it, after he and I did business."

"Business." She tried the word on for size, testing its limits, still watching Phelan, her contempt tinged with fear. "Is that what you call it?"

"What would you suggest?" he asked her.

"Murder," Chelsea Rawlings said, her tone and affect curiously flat. "They call it murder where I come from."

"Right. Deep in the heart of Texas, that would

be. Where the men are men, and the women are glad of it.''

''Depends on the man,'' she said, and her eyes shifted away from his. She was handcuffed to the bed, and while the bed itself wasn't bolted down, neither would it fit through the door in one piece, much less through the window. She couldn't dismantle the bed without tools, which the hunter had failed to provide. She couldn't use the toilet, next door to her room, without Phelan's permission and help.

''This Belasko measures up, I take it,'' Phelan said.

''I wouldn't know,'' Rawlings replied. ''I only met him twice. We talked, he made some promises, he went away. What can I tell you?''

''So he's not much of a hero, then. That's disappointing, Chelsea. You don't mind if I call you by your given name? I feel as if we know each other...intimately.''

''Go to hell!'' she snapped, the color rising in her cheeks.

''I'm not a great believer in the afterlife,'' Phelan said.

''I hope you get a rude surprise.''

''Unfortunately, you won't be around to see it,'' Phelan told her, moving closer as he spoke, enjoying how she edged away from him, her getaway restricted by the cuffs. He sat down on the bed beside her, kissing close. ''Your friend is in the bag by now, I would imagine. He can't help you anymore. I, on the other hand, can grant your fondest wish.''

''Which is?''

"Survival," Phelan said.

"Wrong answer," she replied. "You want to grant my wish? It's simple. All you have to do is kill yourself and let me watch."

His smile felt carved in stone. "You've got some nerve," he said. "I hope your would-be savior measures up. It will be disappointing otherwise."

"What do you mean?"

Instead of answering, he rose to leave. "Last chance," he said from the doorway. "If you need anything, want anything, before I go...?"

"Nothing."

"Your call. Someone will be around to feed you later on."

He closed the door behind him, blotting out the image of her face, her burning eyes. Whatever thoughts he'd had of keeping her around a while, for personal amusement, were dismissed. The bitch would slit his throat first chance she got. He would be better off when she was dead.

But not just yet.

Phelan had determined that it made little difference whether Belasko spilled his guts or not. He would be questioned, certainly, but any serious interrogation would defeat Phelan's greater purpose, if it left Belasko seriously weakened.

Call it a revelation or a whim, but Phelan had decided there was little more the Feds back home could do to him once Chelsea Rawlings and Belasko were eliminated. Killing them on U.S. soil would have complicated matters, perhaps even giving the government grounds for a long-shot indictment, but if the duo simply disappeared—outside the States, at that—the investigation would disintegrate, unraveling into a hopeless pile of loose ends. The FBI or whoever could make what they liked of the Quentin Rawlings videotape, assorted statements from his missing daughter and whatever field reports "Belasko" might have filed. It all came down to hearsay in the end. Without a witness who could testify in court, the case was going nowhere fast.

Despite his confidence, Phelan believed that he would take a long vacation when his business here was done, beginning in a day or two. The money he received from the four men already on their way to join him, coupled with his stash in offshore banks, would tide him over nicely in his semiretirement. In truth, Phelan could live out the rest of his life in fair style on the cash he had now, but that wasn't his plan.

A soldier needed action, after all, to keep both his mind and body in tune. Like the songwriter said, it was better to burn out than to rust. Give it a year or so, for things to cool down, and Phelan would be back in business, if not at the same old stand, then from some other new, improved headquarters. He was already thinking of Europe, or perhaps Bangkok.

It was a small world after all, he thought, grinning on his way to the kitchen for another cup of coffee. Between satellite communications and the Internet, supersonic airliners and other marvels, any fat cat with a taste for blood could make connections with a tour guide in a matter of hours, see the details of his safari finalized within days. Payment up-front was achieved in the wink of an eye, as rapidly as funds could be transferred from one numbered account to another.

It was, to Phelan's way of thinking, the perfect racket. Unlike lesser crimes—gambling, prostitution, what have you—his clients were basically barred from cutting deals to rat him out. *They* were the killers, after all. *They* approached *him* with a desire to murder total strangers. Phelan simply followed their lead for a price, serving the fat cats as a combination travel agent, tour guide and bodyguard. Any time he pulled a trigger on their behalf, he had done so in self-defense—and on foreign soil. No American court could charge him with murder, and what foreign prosecutor would ignore the triggerman and sponsor of the manhunting trip in order to nail a relatively minor functionary?

Phelan's clients would keep their mouths shut because they had more to lose than he did, and because, for most of them, their brief outing with Phelan had been the experience of a lifetime, surpassing any thrill of conquest achieved in the bedroom or the boardroom.

The one and only witness left who could damage Phelan, with all said and done, was Karl Shuker. Himself a killer many times over, the German could still cut a deal for relative leniency, if he was so inclined. There was a precedent for such bargains, in federal court. And while Shuker hardly seemed like an informer, circumstances changed from day to day. Lepke Buchalter had trusted Abe Reles, before he rolled over in 1940. Four decades later, John Gotti had trusted Sammy the Bull.

Those who failed to learn from the mistakes of

history were doomed to repeat them, but Adam Phelan had learned his lesson well. He had a certain bonus hunt in mind for the weekend, with a special reward for whoever scored the kill.

It promised to be a rewarding event, all around.

BOLAN HADN'T PLANNED much beyond the act of turning tables on his enemies. They were expecting him to play the game by their rules, start to finish, cowed by fears of what might happen to the woman if he missed his cue. Unfortunately for the home team, there had been no opportunity for them to study Bolan's background, analyze his mind-set, as they went into the game. They couldn't know that he had killed more men than all of them combined, that he had lost more colleagues, friends and loved ones in the long years of his private war than they could even contemplate.

For all that, Bolan's choice to break the rules wasn't a rash, impulsive act. He wasn't writing off Chelsea Rawlings as lost, although he knew the odds of her survival to the present moment were fifty-fifty, at best. Phelan could have killed her at any time since the videotape was recorded, counting it a smart move on his part. And so it might have been—unless he reckoned on the fury of the Executioner.

Bolan didn't intend to duck his enemies entirely. Dodging them to the extent that they lost track of him wasn't the plan. Instead, he had set out to test them, maybe thin the herd a little, and he had achieved that goal. If he could shake them up enough to make them cut and run back to their boss, so much the better.

But to pull that off, he had to stay alive.

As he emerged from the hotel, Bolan had glimpsed a man he took to be the leader of the pickup team, watching from a sedan, parked at the curb. Not Phelan, he saw, remembering the military ID photos Hal Brognola had managed to retrieve. Someone else, then. Perhaps the mysterious Carl that Quentin Rawlings had mentioned in his suicide tape. An expendable target, if push came to shove.

Bolan turned right, or east, and headed toward the waterfront. He had no special destination in mind, but knew he would run out of town a mile or so in the other direction, with nothing but desert beyond. The gulf offered no hiding place, per se, but long experience had taught him that a waterfront meant piers and warehouses, taverns and shops, streets and alleys. He would take his chances near the water, as opposed to running headlong toward an arid wasteland to the west.

Bolan could smell the waterfront ahead of him—a tart, distinctive aroma combining the tang of salt water with the reek of rotting fish and kelp—when he was still some blocks away. The sedan had trailed him this far, after disgorging one of its passengers outside the hotel, two men remaining in the car as it crept along behind him. Bolan guessed the bail-out would be checking on his friends in the hotel, perhaps attempting to revive them, but he knew that neither of the Mexicans he had encountered in the hall outside his room would feel like double-timing to another fight.

Not yet, at least.

He saw an alley coming up, a half block farther

on his right, and picked up the pace just enough to make the trailing driver edgy. Even then, he didn't telegraph his move, but waited until he was halfway past the alley's mouth, then pivoted and broke into a run, rewarded by the squeal of brakes behind him, then an engine racing as the four-door tried to follow him.

The alley wasn't wide enough, although the driver crunched a fender finding out for himself. Bolan was near the far end of the alley by the time the car backed out again, its passenger leaping clear before the car continued eastward to circle the block.

Bolan thought he could finish a part of it here, turn and face the man who was pursuing him on foot. They would be under orders not to kill him outright, he surmised; otherwise they would have rushed his room in force, or perhaps pulled a drive-by once he had cleared the hotel. He could make a stand here, drop his pursuer with a silenced round or two from the Beretta 93-R and be on his way before the driver made his way around the block.

A moment later, Bolan reached the alley's southern mouth. It would be now or never, if he meant to do his killing in the shadows, with no risk of involving passersby. A running battle in the street meant witnesses, perhaps civilian casualties.

But there had been no battle yet. His enemies had yet to fire a shot, although the man pursuing him on foot did have some kind of weapon in his hand. The odd shape made him think it might be some kind of exotic target pistol, or perhaps a simple autoloader with a homemade silencer attached. In any case, the shooter wasn't using it, which validated Bolan's notion that his adversaries wanted him alive.

There was more to the trap, so it seemed, than simply luring Mike Belasko into killing range. And that, in turn, gave Bolan added hope—however slim and ill defined—that Chelsea Rawlings might still be alive.

He left his pistol in its holster, under his left arm, and stepped into the street. No longer running now, he walked "with purpose," as his old drill sergeant used to say in boot camp a lifetime ago. Bolan heard the footsteps of his pedestrian adversary, hastening along the alleyway behind him, closing up the gap.

Bolan left the sidewalk, stepped into the street, jaywalking in the absence of any significant vehicular traffic. The street was lined with seedy-looking shops on either side: a pharmacy of sorts, a tattoo parlor, a couple of pawnshops, some hole-in-the-wall restaurants. All were apparently closed for siesta, giving Bolan the street to himself.

Until a familiar sedan took the corner at speed, its driver hunched forward at the wheel, aiming the vehicle directly at Bolan. Caught in the middle of the street, he could go either way, but a glimpse of movement at the alley's mouth made his decision for him. He was breaking for the south side of the street when something stung his thigh, an inch or two below his buttocks. Glancing down, he saw the dart protruding from his leg and understood the funny-looking pistol that his tracker carried.

Understood too late.

He managed three more steps before the sidewalk rose to meet him in a rush and smacked into his face.

CHAPTER THIRTEEN

Phelan declined the glass of bourbon Shuker offered him, but lingered near the bar until his paying guests were served and satisfied. The latest of them had arrived ten minutes earlier, which meant the rest already had a head start on the liquor. Phelan wondered if they drank for courage or from simple camaraderie, deciding it was probably a bit of both.

They weren't friends, of course—had never met before today, in fact—but they were gathered in a common purpose, curious to find that there were others like themselves. They knew that, going in, but knowing it was worlds away from meeting flesh-and-blood examples.

The oldest of the four, and latest to arrive, was Arthur Estcott, a department-store magnate and classic old-fashioned sportsman who collected rare trophies, a pursuit that was increasingly difficult in a world circumscribed by political correctness and endangered-species legislation. If it walked and breathed, Estcott liked to say, he had shot it—including two young members of UNITA he had picked off on a visit to Angola some eighteen months earlier.

Wayne Melbourne was the next in line, chronologically. A Louisiana native, he was the last of the successful wildcat oilmen, a self-made billionaire who honestly believed that might—financial or otherwise—made right. It was his privilege to do as he wished, Melbourne frequently said, since he paid "more damned taxes last year than the rest of the state's population combined." The fact that he had also dodged more taxes only made it sweeter, a more enticing game. Much like their hunt in Chechnya had been.

Gregory Fiske, at forty-something, was the CEO of a global media empire that stretched from New York to New Zealand, encompassing newspapers, magazines, books, TV and radio stations, plus a fat slice of the Internet. He was also, as Phelan had reason to know, a closet sadist who had graduated from domestic violence to murder nine months earlier on an excursion to Colombia.

The youngest and most recognizable of the lot was Vernon Blake, thirty-six-year-old star of a dozen box-office hits in the action-adventure genre. His flicks were long on pyrotechnics, short on logic, and while it was doubtful Blake would ever win an acting award for his slash-and-burn extravaganzas, he was rolling in the dough. He also craved a taste of the real thing, perhaps to see if he could handle it. He had done well enough on their trip to Rwanda the previous year, and had immediately placed his name on the waiting list for a replay.

"Good evening, gentlemen." The hunter didn't have to raise his voice. His visitors were speaking quietly among themselves, with none of the hilarity that was heard when old friends got together for a social gathering. They each had business here, and Phelan was the man. Each guest kept one eye on his host, no matter how engrossed he was in conversation with another of his kind.

"I'm glad that all of you were able to make it on such short notice," Phelan said. "As I mentioned briefly on the telephone, I have something extra-special planned. A competition, in fact, between four of my most favored clients."

"What kind of competition?" Estcott asked.

"A hunt," Phelan replied. "Restricted to this island, but with very special prey...and an added bonus for the winner."

"What makes the target special?" Fiske inquired.

"Long story short, he chose to meddle in my business," Phelan said. He noted flickers of concern behind four pairs of eyes. "The details aren't important," he went on. "Suffice to say that an investigation of our little hunt club has been scuttled as we speak. The agent seems professional enough, perhaps a soldier in his day. He's been disarmed, demobilized for now, but he'll be ready for you in the morning."

"So, what's the bonus," Melbourne wondered aloud, "helping you take out the trash?"

"The bonus is in two parts," Phelan told the room at large. "First up, the man who makes the kill will be refunded one-third of his entry fee—$330,000, give or take. Aside from that, the target has a young female associate who also needs to disappear. You'll meet her in the morning. She belongs to the victor, with my compliments."

"To do with as we like?" The question came, predictably, from Fiske.

"That is affirmative," Phelan said, listening to thoughtful murmurs from his guests. "Now, since the hunt won't begin until tomorrow after breakfast, feel free to relax. Enjoy yourselves. The bar is open, but I will remind you that you have an early day tomorrow. Breakfast will be served at 0600 hours, with the hunt commencing at 0730. There is no allowance or refund for hangovers."

That brought chuckles from the clientele, but Phelan saw that two of them, Blake and Estcott, casually set their whiskey glasses aside. Fiske drained his double shot almost defiantly, and made a beeline for the bar to get a refill. Melbourne stood apart and sipped his drink, watching the others, like a man accustomed to judging friends—and enemies—by first impressions.

And what would he make of this bunch? Phelan wondered. What did he make of himself, when he looked in the mirror?

Phelan frankly didn't give a damn. As far as he could tell, his clients—the repeaters, anyway—slept well at night, because they cared for nothing but themselves, their own desires, needs, whims and appetites. As long as *they* were satisfied, humanity at large could go to hell. It was the classic robber-baron attitude, and while some moralists might find it reprehensible, it bothered Adam Phelan not at all.

He might not be a captain of industry, but he stood at the top of his own self-created profession, and he recognized the sense of screw-you power that went along with it. What his clients failed to realize, in their arrogance, was that, at least for the moment, *they* were completely in his power, no less so than the man they would be hunting in about twelve hours.

Power and money, thought Phelan. Together, they were better than sex.

BOLAN WOKE to a riot of sensations, none of them pleasant. There was a dull ache in his skull, mostly behind the eyes, and a sharp medicinal taste in the back of his throat. He felt a chill, and rough concrete against his skin that told him he was wearing nothing but a pair of undershorts. His shoulders ached, to complement the sharp pain from the cuffs that bit into his wrists and kept his arms immobilized behind his back. His ankles were secured with narrow strands of something—plastic, wire, he couldn't tell—and lying on his left side as he was, he felt a fresh bruise where the tranquilizer dart had pierced his thigh.

The final moments of his unsuccessful flight from the hotel were coming back to him, when someone close behind him asked, "Are you awake, or what?" It was a woman's voice, familiar. Chelsea Rawlings.

"Right now," he said, "smart money's riding on 'or what.'"

Rolling over to face her was more difficult than Bolan had anticipated. Without the use of hands or elbows, he opted for a wormlike, wriggling motion. It required the stiffening of every muscle in his body, followed by a squirming, rocking motion that awoke a whole new panoply of aches and pains. When he was finally successful, flopping over on his right side, Bolan found that he was six or seven feet away from Rawlings, the young woman sitting on a narrow bed or cot and watching him with evident concern. She wore a T-shirt, maybe panties, though he could have been mistaken on the latter point, considering his worm's-eye view. Her legs were long and tan and very bare.

"I would have helped you," she told him, with a rueful smile, "but as you see..." She raised one hand and shook it, jangling the pair of handcuffs that secured her to the bed.

"No sweat," Bolan said. "Rolling over was one of the first tricks I learned."

"For a while there, I thought you were dead," Rawlings said, the sparkle gone from her voice. "Oh, they said you were doped, but I thought, well, you know, an OD, maybe something like that. Then I thought you were breathing, but couldn't be sure. I've been sitting here, watching you, wishing you'd twitch or do something."

"I'm alive," he said unnecessarily.

"I guess you are," she said, and found the smile again. "Is that a bratwurst in your pocket, or are you just glad to see me?"

"It's a physical reaction to the drugs," he told her flatly, "coupled with a need to use the toilet."

"Uh-huh. Well, you'll have to wait on potty time. We haven't got a toilet of our own, and there's no way you'd manage anyhow, trussed up like that."

"How long have I been here?" he asked her, to divert their conversation from the pressure in his loins.

"They brought you in sometime last night, I

think,'' she said. ''No watch, no window. Sorry. Anyway, I was asleep. The German and a couple of the locals brought you in and put you on the floor.''

''German?'' Bolan asked.

''Karl, the other guy my father mentioned on his tape,'' she said. ''He has to be. I mean, same name, and he's the only other Anglo on the island, that I've seen. He's obviously Phelan's right-hand man.''

Her words sank in. ''The island?''

''Oh, that's right. You missed the trip. We're on some kind of jungle island, off the coast of Baja. I'm no judge of distance, but it looked like ten or fifteen miles, out in the gulf. They've got a landing strip, but since I didn't hear the plane before they brought you in, I'm guessing there's a boat that takes them to the mainland, too.''

An island, Bolan thought. That wasn't good.

''So, have they told you what comes next?'' he asked.

She shrugged, breasts wobbling underneath the T-shirt. ''Don't ask me. I'm just the bait, you know? It's you they really wanted, but it's got me wondering. No offense, I mean, but if Phelan just wanted to kill you, he could've done it by now and moved on.''

The same thought had crossed Bolan's mind. One obvious reason for keeping him alive would be to facilitate interrogation, let Phelan find out who was tracking him, how far the knowledge of his hunt club had spread in official circles. If that was his game, Bolan was prepared to stall his captors for as long as possible, keep hoping for a chance to turn the tables. On the other hand…

"They haven't hurt you?" he asked Rawlings.

"Well, um, only what you saw on the videotape," she said, blushing. "Some cuts here and there. I'd show you," she added impishly, "but I don't want to aggravate your not-so-little problem."

"Thanks so much," he said sarcastically. And then he asked, "How mobile are you?"

"What you see," she told him, rattling the cuffs again. "The bed's not bolted down or anything, but it's no lightweight, either. I'm not going anywhere."

"Unless they want you to," he said.

"How's that?"

"Nothing." He had been talking to himself, trying to work out why the two of them were still alive. Rawlings had spilled the beans already, told her captors everything she knew, and she had clearly outlived her usefulness as bait. Still, she was breathing, and he knew that fact wasn't occasioned by any squeamishness on the part of Adam Phelan or his sidekick, Karl. One murder, more or less, would mean no more to them than spitting on the sidewalk.

The voice inside him cautioned him to wait and see, stay alert for opportunities.

A soldier's creed. And in the meantime, while he waited, there was plenty to distract him: sundry aches and pains, the pressure on his bladder and a half-naked young woman seated six or seven feet away.

The one thing he could count on, absolutely, was that Phelan, Karl or someone on the former Army Ranger's payroll would be coming for them, sooner or later. When that happened, Bolan meant to be in fighting trim, despite his bonds and minor injuries.

The fuzzy aftermath of his narcotic sleep was fading, even though it left a nasty taste behind. So be it. He could live and work with that.

He was alive.

His enemies had made another critical mistake.

BREAKFAST WAS COOKING for his guests when Phelan sent Karl and two of his Mexican flunkies to fetch the prisoners. They made an interesting couple: Chelsea Rawlings in a T-shirt and bikini briefs, with Mike Belasko wearing only undershorts. His ankles had been freed to let him walk, although the cuffs were still in place around his wrists. The man was rugged-looking, muscular, with scars that testified to battles he had walked away from. Shuker's clients studied him intently, all but Fiske, who concentrated on the woman with a leer that made his filthy mind an open book.

''My friends,'' Phelan addressed his clientele, although he didn't think of them as friends in any sense, ''I'd like to introduce your quarry for the hunt today. He calls himself Mike Belasko, which may or may not be his name, and he works for...which federal agency was it, again?''

His clients muttered to themselves, while Bolan offered no response. ''Oh, well,'' Phelan said. ''What's the difference, anyway? Long story short,'' he told his paying guests, ''this man has been assigned to penetrate, expose and prosecute our hunt club, meaning each and every one of you. He may or may not have reported his location back to others when he came to Baja, but they have no way on earth of finding us. His clothes were dumped in

Santa Rosalia, and a thorough body search revealed no transmitters of any kind. He's clean."

That seemed to mollify the clients slightly, though a couple of them still looked nervous. "I could grill him for the details of his mission," Phelan said, "but I've decided not to bother. He's already filed his last report, and that's an end to it. Removing him removes the problem."

He could see the fat cats starting to relax.

Turning to face his captives, Phelan told Bolan, "In just a few minutes, you will be released. Approximately ninety minutes later, when they've finished breakfast, my friends here will be along to hunt you down. There's no way off the island for you, short of swimming, and we're thirteen miles from the mainland, with hungry sharks and riptides all the way. Guards will be posted on the house, but otherwise, you're free to go where you like, use any little tricks you can think of to avoid pursuit. Any questions?"

"Suppose I refuse?" the stranger asked.

"Participation is mandatory, I'm afraid," Phelan replied. "If you won't provide my friends with sport, you and the lady will provide them with an interesting hour or two of target practice. Take your pick."

Bolan thought about it for a moment, then glanced at the undershorts, his only garment. "Clothing?" he inquired.

"You're right," Phelan said, with a glance at Shuker. "Karl?"

Shuker stepped up behind the prisoner, a knife appearing in his hand as if by magic. Acting with dispatch, before Bolan could react, he slipped the blade inside the waistband of the shorts and ran it down the cleft of the prisoner's buttocks, letting the ruined shorts fall around Bolan's ankles.

"There, that's better," Phelan said. "You're Nature Boy."

"It's gonna be like hunting Tarzan," Vernon Blake remarked, evoking laughter from Estcott and Fiske.

"We'll leave the cuffs on until you're well outside," Phelan explained. "You can go, now. Time's a-wasting."

Bolan's three-man escort led him from the room, Phelan noting the flush that had crept into Chelsea Rawlings's cheeks, the way she kept her eyes averted from the naked man. He stepped in close beside her and slipped an arm around her shoulders, tightening his grip as she tried to squirm away.

"I promised you a bonus to the victor, gentlemen," he said, "and here she is. The well-fed, very healthy daughter of a former client, who, I'm sad to say, was less a man than those I see before me. This one's daddy harbored a peculiar sense of guilt, until he killed himself. Along the way he tried to rat us out. You're cleaning up his mess today, as luck would have it, and it's only fitting that his little girl should help to make amends for Daddy's spineless treachery. A little taste of what awaits the winner at the end of his successful hunt."

As Phelan spoke, he hooked the fingers of his left hand in the collar of the T-shirt Rawlings wore and ripped it down the front. Her hands were cuffed behind her back, and there was nothing she could do to stop him, though he warded off a knee that jabbed in the direction of his groin, backhanding her with casual disdain.

"She's spirited, as you can see...and worth a bit of extra effort, as I'm sure you will agree."

"What's with the Band-Aids?" Melbourne asked.

"Some minor damage during acquisition," Phelan said. "It will require a man to tame this one."

"That's me," Fiske said, leering.

"Don't hold your breath, old man," Vernon Blake retorted.

"Asshole!"

"Please, gentlemen!" They quieted as Phelan spoke, though Blake and Fiske still glared at each other from across the room. "You have your target and your prize. You're sportsmen, right? Let's act that way."

Blake smiled, a smaller version of the grin he sometimes flashed on-screen, while Fiske wore the expression of a sullen child. There could be trouble there, but Phelan wasn't overly concerned. The usual precautions had been taken to avoid a trace of where his clients really were, right now. If one or two of them should suffer fatal accidents, so what? He had their money, and there would be no refund to the loser's estate.

He snapped his fingers at the remaining Mexican and nodded for the man to take Rawlings back to her cell. All four of his clients watched her go, each man considering the possibilities.

"That concludes our briefing," he told them, satisfied with the double motivation he had provided.

"And now, if I'm not mistaken, breakfast is served."

BOLAN'S CAPTORS took no chances with him at the point of his release. One walked in front of him to open doors, and kept a semiautomatic pistol ready in his free hand, while the other two—another Mexican and Phelan's second in command—brought up the rear. The number two carried a submachine gun, an Italian Spectre with a 50-round box magazine, and his companions never stepped in front of him to block his field of fire.

They were too damned professional for Bolan's taste, but there was nothing he could do about it at the moment. Phelan had already told him what was coming. If he had a chance at all, it lay in knowing that the four men who would track him after breakfast were civilian amateurs.

"What are my chances of getting some food?" he asked Shuker.

"Nonexistent," the German replied. "You can live off the land, I suppose...if you live." That made him chuckle, an ugly, predatory sound.

No food, no clothes, no tools or weapons. "Can I ask the rules?" Bolan said.

"You already heard them. Run and hide. The others come to find you in a little while, and someone shoots you dead. A simple little game."

"What I was wondering," the Executioner pressed on, "was *how* they're coming. I mean, is it four-on-one? Do they split up? Will you be coming with them? What's the deal? It can't hurt, telling me. Might make the game more sporting for your clients, if you think about it."

"Ah, I see." The German smiled. "You worry *I'll* be hunting you. In that case, you would not survive an hour. No—" Shuker shook his head "—each of the clients wants you for himself. Because they do not know the island, each will have a guide, from one of these." He fairly sneered while nodding toward the Mexicans who stood off to one side. "The winner gets a partial refund of his fee...and access to the woman. Not a bad incentive, yes?"

Bolan made no reply to that. The very last thing that he needed at the moment was distraction from the main goal of survival. He couldn't afford to think about what might be happening to Chelsea Rawlings, even now, while he stood naked in the yard, with guns trained on his chest.

"Take the cuffs off," Shuker ordered, tossing a key to one of the Mexicans and stepping farther to his right, keeping Bolan covered with his SMG. The second Mexican remained where he was, positioned so that any cross fire that erupted in the next few seconds wouldn't place either shooter at a risk from friendly fire. It was a simple, well-executed move that told Bolan he was dealing with professionals.

Bad news, but nothing he hadn't already figured out.

The Mexican who had received the handcuff key from Shuker first tucked his pistol in the waistband of his jeans, in back, before approaching Bolan. He kept his eyes on the soldier's hands and feet, recognizing where the danger lay, refusing to be caught up in a macho staring contest. He unlocked the cuffs, removed them and immediately stepped back out of range, the cuffs and key clutched in his left hand, while he drew the pistol with his right and made it three guns trained on Bolan, for triangulated fire.

"What now?" the Executioner inquired.

"You're free to go—run, hide, whatever," Shuker replied. "The others will be coming after you at 0730. That's eighty-two minutes from now, if they aren't running late. You come back to the house and we shoot you on sight. Otherwise, best of luck."

He was grinning, enjoying the moment. Bolan could have asked him further questions—on the layout of the island, for example—but he sensed that it would be a waste of precious time. He had an hour and a half, essentially, to put some ground between himself and the hunters, see if he could find some kind of makeshift weapon in the process.

Without a backward glance, he turned and jogged off toward the tree line, half expecting Karl to change his mind and cut him down. It didn't happen, though, and after he had traveled some two hundred yards, he knew he was alone.

So far.

The ground was alternately soft and rough beneath his feet. He had to watch his step, avoiding stones and other sharp-edged hazards that would gash his soles, potentially disabling him, while leaving blood trails for his pursuers to follow. Shoes and clothing were beyond his grasp for now, unless he managed to lay hands on one of his intended killers. Concentrating on the urgent need to arm himself, he scanned the earth around him, checked the trees, alert for any object that could be converted into weaponry.

It would be like hunting Tarzan, one of Phelan's clients had remarked. So what would Tarzan do?

There were no jungle vines on hand, to use in making snares or nooses, fashioning garrotes or stringing bows. He had no time to make a bow, in any case—no blade or flint with which to whittle arrows.

Still...

The first true weapons used by humankind were sticks and stones, employed as striking implements. He could certainly find stones to lob, but they would be a poor defense against high-powered rifles. He could probably pick up a club or two of sorts, but that meant fighting hand-to-hand with men who would prefer to shoot him from a distance and be done with it. Their modern weapons gave them an advantage that seemed insurmountable.

Unless he took them by surprise.

"Each of the clients wants you for himself," Karl had explained, and each would have an armed guide in attendance, to prevent his getting lost or walking off a cliff. With any luck, then, Bolan would be facing only two men at a time. Two men with rifles, more than likely, but the odds weren't entirely hopeless. Not if Bolan used the time remaining to prepare himself.

Unarmed and naked, Bolan pushed on through the virgin forest, searching for the tools that would allow him to survive.

CHAPTER FOURTEEN

"You're sure about the bow?"

Arthur Estcott smiled at Phelan's tone of skepticism. "Positive," he said. "It works all right on moose and grizzly bear. I see no reason why it shouldn't drop a man."

"Of course not, Arthur," Phelan said. "But *this* man—"

"Is a creature made of flesh and blood, like any other," Estcott said, cutting him off. "You sink a broadhead arrow where it needs to go, he'll bleed out just like any other prey."

"As you like," Phelan said. "If you don't mind Luis being armed with a rifle—"

"What for?" Estcott asked. "You have jaguars or boar on the island?"

"No, Arthur, we don't'"

"Then a side arm should do him just fine," Estcott said. "This hunt is mine. I didn't pay to have some wetback do the killing for me, Adam."

"Suit yourself."

"I always do. Can we get started now?"

"Enjoy," Phelan said as he turned back toward the house.

The bow was light, six pounds and change, but powerful, with complex pulleys, like the one Stallone had used when he was playing Rambo. The broadhead arrows were razor-sharp killers with slate-gray aluminum shafts. On his hip, just in case, Estcott carried a two-inch Colt Lawman Mk V, chambered in .357 Magnum. It was all the gun he ever carried when bow hunting, just in case he met a snake along the way or had to give some dying animal a mercy shot behind the ear.

Estcott had brought a rifle with him to the island, an imported Husqvarna 9000 Crown Grade, chambered in 7 mm Remington Magnum, but he had decided to go with the bow after meeting his quarry at Phelan's little briefing. The man was unarmed and naked, after all. How dangerous could he be?

That was the critical question, of course. It was the question he had asked himself each time he went hunting big game on four continents, the same question that had occupied his mind each time he faced a business competitor over the past thirty-odd years. And thus far, his judgment had always been correct. He had never been beaten in business, never injured or outwitted in the wild.

On his first safari with Phelan, in Angola, Arthur Estcott had bowed to his guide's expertise, aware that they were stalking guerrillas with long years of combat behind them, equipped with modern weapons from the former Soviet bloc. Estcott had armed himself accordingly, and he had nailed both targets from a range of eighty yards or so, with no help from Phelan or his German sidekick, even when the second target started shooting back.

It was a job well-done, but nothing like the present case. He didn't need assault rifles and body armor to confront a naked man, for heaven's sake.

Of course, he didn't underestimate his quarry, either. From his physical development, his attitude, his scars, it was apparent that the man had seen his share of combat, whether in the military or in some clandestine service. Estcott didn't care about the details. He didn't intend to let the man lay hands on him. At his age, Estcott knew, a hand-to-hand engagement with his quarry would be tantamount to suicide.

The bow was his concession to chivalry, a recognition of his quarry's disadvantage. It was also a challenge to himself, his own nerve and ability. The moose he had dropped with this very same bow, in Alaska, had carried an impressive rack, but it had been no threat to Estcott in terms of personal danger. The grizzly in Alberta was another story altogether, and he had nearly wet himself when the first arrow failed to stop its charge, praying he would have a chance to get the second off before his guide was forced to use the .460 Weatherby rifle. Before the grizzly had them both for lunch.

He had survived that hunt, but at a price. Though he had brought his trophy home, with skin and dignity intact, Estcott had come to doubt himself that afternoon in Canada. The first step toward his personal redemption was Angola, where he learned another, darker lesson—namely, that he had a taste for hunting men.

This time, the fifty-five-year-old millionaire had decided, he would shave the odds a bit. It wouldn't be an equal contest, granted, with his quarry naked and unarmed, but it was close enough for Estcott's taste. Next time—if he decided there should be a next time—maybe he would give his prey a little extra fighting chance.

Maybe.

This day, though, he was focused on the kill, his first glimpse of spoor that would lead him to his tanned, battle-scarred quarry. One arrow should do it, at least bring him down, and then Estcott could finish the game at his leisure. When he was done, and Pedro or whoever had snapped the Polaroid photos for his private collection, then Estcott could begin to think about the woman.

A special treat for the mighty hunter. Dessert, to climax a feast. To the victor, the spoils.

He felt himself begin to stiffen, thinking of the woman, and forced the image of her naked body from his mind. He had to make the kill first, and his so-called guide had still found nothing to suggest that they were even headed in the right direction. Christ, for all he knew, one of the others could be lining up a shot right now, prepared to bring the target down.

My target, Estcott told himself. My trophy.

"Here!" the Mexican blurted, speaking for the first time since they'd left the house, one brown finger pointing to a scuff mark in a bed of moss. It could have been a human footprint, Estcott thought. He wasn't sure.

"What is it?" he demanded of the guide.

"Man go this way," the Mexican replied.

"All right," Escott said. "What are we waiting for?"

BOLAN HAD FINALLY been forced to compromise on weapons. The projectiles were no problem, stones that ranged in size from golf balls to grenades, but even if his adversary only had a pistol—most unlikely, Bolan thought—the hunter would have better accuracy, range and striking power. Give the enemy a rifle, the most likely tool of choice, and even a mediocre marksman could drop Bolan well beyond the range of any stone's throw he could manage.

The only clear response to that threat was an ambush that would place Bolan closer to his enemies, perhaps within arm's reach. But that scenario posed special problems of its own.

For starters, any decent trap that he could think of, from deadfalls to pits lined with pungi stakes, required at least some basic cutting or digging tools for their construction. They also took time to construct—hours, at the very least, with helping hands—and time, for Bolan, was almost as scarce as clothing. Still, the heavily forested island *did* provide a range of vantage points from which to strike. He had discovered several by the end of his first hour in the woods, moving more or less due north, and Bolan had no doubt that others would present themselves as time went by.

Assuming he survived that long, of course.

For close-in weapons, Bolan fashioned a club from a fallen tree branch—minus twigs and withered leaves, still clinging to the larger shaft—and found a second, smaller branch to serve him as a stabbing tool. The latter was forked near its tip, a smaller branch jutting out at a seventy-five or eighty-degree angle. With some sweat and strain, Bolan snapped off the last six inches or so of the branch and roughened up the three exposed ends, until they were suitably jagged. When he curled his fist around the branch, its offshoot protruded as a spike between his second and third fingers, while a sharp-pronged inch or more of splintered wood was clear on each side of his fist, allowing him to strike with damaging effect in all directions. He knew it wasn't much against the modern hardware his assailants would be packing, but it was the best that he could do.

He also had to deal with fighting naked, if he wanted to survive.

There was an aversion among modern human beings to confronting adversaries in the nude. Ingrained modesty contributed to the problem in some cases, but Bolan had divested himself of that inhibition in high school and boot camp. More pressing concerns at the moment included potential discomfort and distraction—jock straps were standard features of the male athletic costume for a reason, after all—and the risk of unnecessary injury. A naked man in combat worried first about his dangling genitals, but he also had to be concerned about his feet. A stubbed toe in the heat of battle could disable the most hearty warrior, or at least provide his adversary with an opening, a chance to strike. Proper footwear protected not only the feet, but also helped with traction on treacherous surfaces. Clothing, meanwhile, provided camouflage, while helping protect a warrior's skin from all manner of abrasions, cuts and gouges while he fought for his life.

The Executioner had none of those conveniences. He was stark naked, being hunted in his birthday suit.

His first concession to the situation came when Bolan found a small creek with muddy banks. He scooped up handfuls of the sticky mud and smeared it over face, chest, belly, arms, legs, buttocks. Bolan couldn't reach the middle of his back, so he was forced to lie down in the mud and wallow like a hog until he satisfied himself that he was fairly camouflaged. The mud would itch like crazy as it dried, but he could live with that. It would begin to flake as well but he had no options at the moment. If he caught a break, he might be wearing someone else's clothes before he shed his second skin of brown and gray.

Selection of the ambush site was critical. He had no fear of being overlooked; the island was too small for that, his trackers too well motivated. They would find him if it took a week, but Bolan didn't have that kind of time to spare. For one thing, hunger would begin to sap his strength, even if he discovered nuts and berries that had so far managed to elude him. First and foremost in his mind, however, was the threat of injury—of violation—hanging over Chelsea Rawlings in the custody of Phelan and his cronies as time dragged on.

Her fault, thought Bolan, as he sought his ambush site. The whole damned thing. If she had kept her promise and stayed out of it—

He stopped himself, unwilling to pursue remembrance of things past when his survival in the here and now demanded total concentration. If he didn't find the proper setting for his ambush, didn't time his move precisely right, he would be killed. And who would fight for Chelsea then?

No one.

He concentrated on the stand, looking for someplace, something, that would let him hide without the cover being too damned obvious.

Bolan began to check his watch from force of habit, then remembered it was gone. He reckoned that he had already used more than an hour of his ninety minutes, and there was no way of telling whether Phelan had insisted that his clients wait an hour and a half. If one or more of them had jumped the gun, it might already be too late for him to find a decent killing ground. Still, there was nothing he could do but try.

He knew the layout when he saw it, felt the rightness of it, though it would have wasted precious, fleeting time to run down the mental checklist and put it into conscious thought or words. He saw the layout, recognized he was swiftly running out of time and knew that it was here he had to make his stand. His first stand, anyway.

Another point of critical uncertainty: he didn't know if Phelan's number two had told the truth when he said Bolan's trackers would be hunting individually, each man with a single guide. With what he had in terms of weapons, cover and experience, he thought that odds of two-to-one were manageable, even with his adversaries packing firearms. He might be killed, of course; there was no guarantee of victory, but it was possible.

So, wait and see, the warrior thought.

And started to prepare his stand.

ESTCOTT COULD FEEL the tension mounting as he crept along behind his guide. He felt a sudden urge to urinate, though he had used the toilet twice before he left the house. There was a tightness in his chest, the feeling he mistook for guilt until his teenage years, when he had learned that "conscience" was a myth imposed on him by other men who wanted to control his life. Guilt had no place in Arthur Estcott's world. A thing was either good for him, or it wasn't. He loathed uncertainty and valued tough decisions under fire.

He had decided they would forge ahead.

The trail had put him off, at first: too narrow, with the forest pressing close on either side; too many hiding places, where a man could lie in wait and spring to the attack. It was the rock pile that decided him, made Estcott tell the Mexican to go ahead, despite his own misgivings at the start.

He doubted that the rock pile would qualify as a hill. It struck him as too small for that—though large enough, perhaps, to grant at least some elevated view of the surrounding woods. Estcott had started to feel almost claustrophobic in the forest, wondering if they had passed their quarry, if he might be creeping up behind them, moving stealthily on naked feet. It would be good to catch a glimpse of the surrounding territory, get his bearings if he could.

And then, there were the tracks suggesting that his prey had passed this way.

Why not? His quarry—if, indeed, a man had left the tracks they followed—might have seen the same qualities Estcott noted in the rock pile: a potential lookout point, maybe a hiding place, even a makeshift fortress. The latter thought made Estcott uneasy, thinking of the naked man somewhere up above them, straining at a boulder that would soon come crashing down.

Go easy, then.

Estcott walked in a semicrouch, unconscious of his change in stance until his knees and lower back began to send out sharp alarms of pain. He had an arrow nocked, the bow half-drawn, preparing for a shot, although he had no target yet. A high-pitched buzzing in his ears told Estcott that his blood pressure was elevated, and he felt the sturdy thump-thump of his heart, reverberating in his skull.

Goddamn! he thought. He was making so much noise, the quarry would hear them coming from a quarter-mile away.

The notion made him smile. In fact, they were already much closer than that to the rock pile. Another fifty yards or so would see them there, and Estcott was alert to any sounds of thrashing in the undergrowth, suggesting that their prey had seen or heard them coming and was on the run. No such luck, though. The battle-scarred bastard wasn't about to make it that easy.

Good for him.

Estcott found himself wondering what the target had been in real life, before he stumbled into Phelan's web and became a clay pigeon. Some kind of ex-soldier, perhaps, or a lawman with a rugged history behind him. Arthur Estcott was no expert, but he had recognized scars left by bullets and blades on the stranger's muscular torso and limbs. Whatever he had been or done to earn his daily bread, the stranger introduced to them as Mike Belasko clearly hadn't led a sheltered life.

They reached the looming rock pile without incident, Estcott straightening from his half crouch, feeling an almost audible sigh of relief from his back and legs. He kept some tension on the bowstring, even now, prepared to draw and fire in one fluid motion if a target presented itself.

The rock pile—more an upthrust slab of bedrock, Estcott saw, with jagged bits around the base that had been broken off somehow, and tumbled down—was fifty feet or so in height. Without a walk-around, he had to guess at the perimeter dimension, estimating thirty, maybe forty yards. A strip of earth around the great slab's base was clear, as far as he could see in each direction, with the nearest trees fifteen or twenty feet away.

The trail—if trail it was—had led them here, and Estcott scanned the trees around him, ready with an arrow if he glimpsed a naked specter staring back at him. For all he knew, their quarry could be on the far side of the rock pile at that very moment, waiting, listening. It was conceivable that Estcott could pursue him endlessly in circles, like some old Three Stooges skit, unless he sent the Mexican around to head Belasko off.

In which case, Estcott thought, the guide might

feel compelled to use his pistol in self-defense, and that would mean a million dollars down the drain.

No, thank you.

"I go up," the Mexican told Estcott, pointing to the rocky face in front of him as if there were some other way of going up, without a rocket pack.

"You do that," Estcott said.

He thought of scrambling up the face himself, but then thought better of the exercise. He was in decent shape, for a man who had passed the half-century mark five years ago, but he was no great athlete, and rock climbing had its own special hazards, even for those who were deft at the sport. He had a dread of falling, maybe breaking bones, but there was more to his reticence than simple caution.

If he started up the rock pile, even if he made it to the top unscathed, Estcott would have to sling the bow across his back, return the broadhead arrow to its quiver. He would be effectively disarmed—and worse, he would be helpless, splayed across the cliff face like a lizard, clinging for dear life. Better to wait below, he thought, and stay on guard. The Mexican would signal if he spotted anything, and Estcott could respond accordingly. They were a team, of sorts, and while his million-dollar ante put him in the driver's seat, Estcott was wise enough to recognize his limitations here, on unfamiliar turf.

The Mexican was climbing swiftly, sure of foot. Estcott glanced up to check his progress now and then, but he was mainly focused on the trees surrounding him. There seemed to be no realistic prospect of their quarry waiting on the rock pile's pinnacle, now that he saw it for himself. The slab came to a ragged point, with barely room enough for one man to stand up and turn around. Belasko might be clinging to the other slope, Estcott supposed, but he would be in no position for a clean attack from there. The Mexican would see him coming, draw his gun and—

No!

Before he really thought about it, Arthur Estcott was off and running, circling to his left around the base of the rock pile, keeping tension on his bowstring as he made a circuit of the slab. His escort would be near the top by now, if not already there, in a position to alert him if the prey was visible and trying to elude him.

When the scream came, Estcott halted in his tracks so suddenly, he almost toppled onto his face. He didn't recognize the voice, per se, but reckoned it could only be his guide. A glance toward the pinnacle showed only vacant sky. No lookout on the summit, but it hadn't been a warning shout, he realized: more like a cry of mortal terror.

Suddenly afraid and shamed by the sensation, cursing his own weakness, Estcott spent a moment wondering if he should run ahead or double back. What fucking difference did it make? he asked himself, disgusted.

With a snarl that would have startled those who knew him at the office in Chicago, Estcott drew his bowstring even farther back and sprinted recklessly along the strip of clear ground at the rock pile's base.

BOLAN HAD BEEN surprised to see the hunter with a bow and arrow. It seemed like such an affectation, so much macho posturing that he had nearly laughed out loud. The bow was still a lethal weapon, though, and both men, white and brown, were wearing pistols on their hips.

No laughing, then. This game was deadly serious.

The bow could work in Bolan's favor if he played his cards correctly. If the first shot missed, there had to be at least a brief delay before the hunter nocked another arrow, aimed and let it fly. That lag time would belong to Bolan if he found a way to take the hunter's native escort out, assuming that the bowman didn't simply drop his bow and draw his pistol when he saw the arrow go astray.

Assuming that he missed his target.

An arrow wouldn't kill him instantly, unless it struck him in the heart or brain, but many other wounds could still prove mortal—or disable Bolan long enough to let his would-be killer nock another arrow, try his luck a second time. His weapons in the present contest were surprise, speed and experience in killing men beyond the gray-haired hunter's wildest dreams.

Bolan had done his best to leave a trail without being childishly obvious. He was staked out near the massive rock pile, watching from the trees when the hunter and his Mexican pointman arrived. It would be risky taking both of them at once, but he was hopeful when the Mexican began to climb, damned near ecstatic when the bowman took off on his own to scout around the rocky slab.

For distance work, he had collected half a dozen stones the size of hen's eggs, polished to a low gloss by millennia of exposure to the elements. Now, as the Mexican scrambled toward the peak of the rock pile, his companion nowhere in sight, Bolan stepped into the clearing, feeling warm wind on his naked body, lining up his shot.

The first pitch missed, but it was close. His missile struck the stony face a foot or so the left of the Mexican's head, rebounding with a crack. The climber tried to look around, but he was hampered by the need to keep a firm grip on the cliff face with both hands. The basic choice was up or down, and he decided to continue, maybe hoping he could find a mark and use his handgun from the pinnacle.

He never made it.

Bolan's second pitch was dead on target, striking home between the climber's shoulder blades. The pain sent him into some kind of spasm, clinging to the rock with one hand, while his other hand and both feet flailed at empty air. Half-turned toward Bolan, he was wide-eyed, mouthing curses the soldier couldn't hear from where he stood.

One more to finish it.

The third pitch missed, but it was close enough. The climber lost his grip and hurtled earthward, bouncing once on impact with a stony shelf that had provided aid and comfort halfway up the cliff. He came down screaming, one long, wordless shriek that cut the forest stillness like a razor slicing silk. The solid thud of impact left him crumpled, motionless, some twenty strides from Bolan's pitching mound.

"Paco! Paco! Are you all right?"

The hunter advanced, sprinting by the windy

sound of it, and Bolan had a choice to make. Any scenario that wound up with him breathing called for forward motion, in a hurry. Scooping up his makeshift club, he sprinted toward the fallen climber, straight into the path of his approaching nemesis.

The Mexican had fallen on his right side, covering the pistol with his body. He was still alive and moaning when Bolan reached him, a stiff-fingered jab to the larynx cutting off his wind for good, as the soldier rolled over his body. He could only guess how many bones were broken from the feel of it, but injuries made no more difference to this one.

Bolan found the guy's side arm and recognized the .32-caliber Harrington and Richardson revolver, one of your classic bargain-basement Saturday night specials. He was reaching for the weapon when the hunter found him, lurching around the last curve of the rock pile with his bow drawn and ready to fire.

The Executioner chose the only course of action he could think of, tossing his club at the bowman, its three-foot length turning through the air, end over end. The bowman ducked, but he also loosed his arrow prematurely, the broadhead striking sparks from stone a yard or so above his target.

"Shit!"

Before the bowman had a chance to choose between a second arrow and the pistol on his hip, Bolan drew the Mexican's revolver and shot him, one round to the center of mass. The H&R .32-caliber didn't pack much of a kick, but his target was already shaky, off balance, and Bolan's shot drilled him a hand's width below the heart, taking him down.

The guy was still alive when the soldier reached him, but his eyes were glazing over, telling Bolan that the slug had done some lethal damage going in. Most likely it had drilled his liver, maybe clipping the aorta, possibly colliding with his spine. Whatever, he was fading in the stretch, without the strength or will to reach the snubby Colt revolver on his hip.

Bolan didn't consider shooting him again. One shot would very probably alert his enemies; a second would have given them a halfway decent chance to work out his position.

He left the hunter breathing, bleeding, while he decided whose clothes fit the bill. Both men were smaller than Bolan, but the bowman was closer to his size, and that made the choice simple. He stripped the dying man, ignoring the occasional wheeze or whimper as he removed shirt, boots, socks and pants. The man had fouled himself when he was shot, so Bolan let him keep his boxer shorts.

The pants were snug, but he had room to move around in them if they were pushed down slightly on his hips. The hiking boots might blister him, but any shoes at all were preferable to running barefoot over unfamiliar ground. The borrowed shirt fit best of all, and Bolan managed to ignore the bloodstain on its front.

The hunter's Colt was fully loaded, and he stuck the Mexican's revolver through his belt to balance the other side. He also took the bow and quiver, with eleven broadhead hunting arrows. Turning out the dead guide's pockets, Bolan found a six-inch switchblade and appropriated that, as well.

When he was dressed and armed, he turned back to the hunter and found him still alive, if barely conscious. Bolan thought of leaving him that way, but mercy won out in the end. He found his club, came back and finished it with a well-placed blow to the skull.

Aside from ending the man's misery, he thought, the kill would also send a message to his other enemies, if any of them stumbled on the bodies. They would work out that the rules had changed; it was a very different game now, and the hunters had become the prey.

He hoped so, anyway.

Barring some fluke of personality, the others would be armed with rifles, but at least the Executioner was clothed and armed.

It was a start.

The rest was up to him—and Fate.

CHAPTER FIFTEEN

Wayne Melbourne thought that whoever said a rich man let himself get out of shape was full of shit.

Oh, sure, he had his share of servants down in Bayou Vista, eight or nine of them to keep his big plantation house and forty-acre grounds in line, but that was busywork, the kind you left for peons any time you had the chance. He was too busy making money and enjoying its rewards to waste time washing dishes, pushing vacuum cleaners, mowing lawns and washing cars.

Melbourne still worked out at least four days a week, though, in his private gym. And not some pussy workout, either, but an hour straight of pumping heavy iron and sweating on the stationary bicycle, as if he were training for some damned decathlon. He followed up the workouts with a shower and a swim, as many laps as he could manage of the indoor Olympic-sized pool.

And there was hunting, when he had the time.

Melbourne was filthy rich and loved every moment of it. Twenty-six years earlier, when he was barely twenty-one years old, he had invested every penny he could beg or borrow in a wildcat oil rig, planted in the middle of the godforsaken swamp land in St. Mary Parish, fifty miles southwest of Baton Rouge. The well was good. Better than good, in fact—it was the first strike on a vast new reservoir of crude, and Melbourne had been wise enough to keep his mouth shut, swearing his half-dozen roughnecks to silence with bloodcurdling threats and promises of fabulous stock options, while he mortgaged himself to the hilt, buying up a hundred square miles of snake-infested swamp at cut-rate prices. When the news broke, half a dozen major petrochemical conglomerates were knocking on his door, outbidding one another for the privilege of selling Melbourne's oil.

Within six months, Wayne Melbourne was a multimillionaire and looking forward to the day when he could spell that with a *B*. His sidekicks on the first well were delighted to retire on proceeds from their stock and leave the daily chores to Melbourne—which was just exactly how he wanted it. The rest was all gold-plated history, with no end to the gravy train in sight.

Melbourne worked hard, and he played hard. He had been hunting since his childhood, when it meant the difference between a meal with meat or nothing but a plate of grits and greens. Years later, when he dined on steak and lobster seven nights a week, he kept on hunting for the thrill it gave him, the last bit of power—life and death—that still eluded Melbourne in the world of business.

He had discovered Adam Phelan via word of mouth, the kind of locker-room talk rich men shared from time to time, like passing on the phone numbers of their favorite thousand-dollar whores. At first, he had been skeptical, but then he tracked down Phelan, listened to his spiel and finally decided why not?

A million dollars wasn't chump change, but he made that much every two or three days, and a fair piece of his earnings went directly to numbered accounts, overseas, to elude Uncle Sam and his IRS vampires. The trip to Chechnya had been a revelation for Melbourne, and he had been hoping to repeat the experience sometime soon, but word of mouth was a bitch, and Phelan had a waiting list that spanned the best part of twelve months.

The call to Baja, therefore, had been an especially pleasant surprise. Not only did he get another shot at human game, but if he scored, Melbourne would get a portion of his money back. *And* have a wild time with the target's little lady, in the bargain.

Perfect.

It had been an hour and a quarter since they heard what sounded like a pistol shot from somewhere north of Melbourne's patch. The four of them had each picked out a compass point when it came time to leave the house, Melbourne hiking eastward with his guide, while Arthur Estcott and his stupid bow went north. They weren't bound to stay in any special quarter of the island, and they didn't have a clue which way their quarry had been headed when the house staff turned him loose, which meant the hunters might cross trails or, if their luck ran sour, this Belasko guy might remain at large for days.

So be it. Melbourne was a self-made man, and he was punching no one's clock. He could check in by telephone and see how things were going at the office any time he wanted to. Meanwhile, he had a hard-on for the hunt, and for the prize that waited for him when the game was bagged and tagged.

The single gunshot could mean anything or nothing, he decided. Phelan was supposed to blow some kind of air horn from the ranch house when somebody nailed the trophy, but a pistol shot was meaningless. One of the others could've glimpsed a snake and gotten edgy; maybe it was some kind of a signal. Melbourne didn't know, but he remembered Estcott and his Mexican had carried only handguns, in addition to the bow and arrows. Now, he thought, *that* might mean something. At the very least, it seemed worth checking out.

"We're going north," he told his guide, who shrugged and nodded, veering to his left. It made no difference to the Mexican, since they had spotted nothing in the way of tracks or sign so far. One place was as good as another for looking when you had no idea where your quarry had gone.

Melbourne could only hope the man was still alive, that Estcott hadn't nailed him with the wicked broadheads, that the gunshot hadn't been a coup de grâce. Whatever, he would keep on looking for his man until somebody blew the horn and called it off.

No mercy, no concessions, no time-outs.

It was the only way he knew to play the game, and it had served Wayne Melbourne well enough, so far. With any luck at all, he just might score a kill, retrieve $330,000 on the deal, then get laid to boot.

Now that, he thought, would be a righteous triple play.

THE HIKING BOOTS weren't as bad as he expected, though they chafed his heels a bit. Still, they permitted Bolan to proceed with greater haste, while leaving tracks that would confuse a hunter looking for a barefoot man—at least, until the bodies of his first two kills were found.

He had no way of knowing when that might occur. If one or more of the remaining hunters homed in on the gunshot, he supposed the corpses could be found within an hour, maybe less. He didn't know where any of the other hunters were, whether all four had trailed him northward, or if they had scattered to the corners of the island, each man looking for some elbow room.

Whatever their technique, he knew the only certain method of protecting Chelsea Rawlings and escaping from the island was to kill them all, along with Phelan, his Germanic second in command and the assorted native members of his staff. That left seven men he had seen for himself—a minimum of eight, assuming each of the remaining hunters also had a guide to help him find his way around the island. Then, too, Phelan had spoken of guards on the house, while the hunt was in progress. That meant two or three extra guns to deal with, before he was home and dry. He would call it a dozen, to be on the safe side, and hope that his estimate was high.

Twelve men, against which Bolan had eleven broadhead arrows and eleven pistol rounds, as well as the switchblade knife. It ought to be enough, if he was careful, but the weapons had their limitations. He could strike from ambush with the arrows, silently, but there was no such thing as rapid fire when you were fighting with a bow. The .32-caliber H&R had fixed sights, making it a weapon of dubious accuracy and minimal stopping power at any range beyond fifteen or twenty yards. A sturdy human target, Bolan knew, could absorb all five of his remaining rounds and keep on coming, unless one slug found a vital mark. The Colt Lawman was a certified killer, chambered in .357 Magnum, but its runty two-inch barrel ruled out any trick shots from a distance. If he wanted to be sure of killing, even with the Colt, he knew that he would have to work in close.

For all their limitations, though, the weapons he had managed to acquire gave Bolan greater confidence, a sense that he had leveled out the playing field a bit. Role camouflage could help him, too, as it had served the Executioner in other life-and-death campaigns. His enemies were looking for a naked man so far, and were unlikely to cut loose on anyone they spotted wearing clothes. They knew the late archer by sight, if not from personal acquaintance, and while Bolan bore no great resemblance to the bowman he had killed, he counted on the archer's clothes and his distinctive weapon to confuse the other hunters for a crucial moment, if they chanced to glimpse him moving through the forest.

As for Bolan, if he saw them first, well, there would be no need for camouflage.

The island had a spine of rocky hills that seemed

to run along a north-south axis. Bolan's first engagement with the enemy had happened in the northeast quadrant of the island, and while he had no clear indication of the island's size, he calculated that his other enemies couldn't have traveled any farther north than he, considering his ninety-minute lead. With that in mind, he had been moving southward, on the east flank of the hills, since he had dressed and armed himself with liberated gear. He knew it might take hours to find another adversary, but Bolan had no choice. The one alternative, sitting still and waiting for the others to find him, could waste days instead of hours. This way, at least he would be covering ground, working back toward the house.

The terrain would have been easy going, for a midday stroll, but caution and the need to watch for adversaries slowed him considerably. Bolan moved as silently as possible, using the landscape for natural cover. It helped that the forest, while reasonably thick, wasn't the kind of jungle he had known in Southeast Asia. He wasn't required to hack a trail through clinging vines and chest-high ferns, with visibility so close to zero that a Vietcong patrol could wait and open fire from nearly point-blank range. He likewise had no fear of mines or other booby traps, since Phelan wouldn't send his million-dollar clients out into a slaughterhouse.

The trees thinned in places, but he didn't let it worry him. Whatever risk he ran of being spotted by his adversaries, from a distance, they were equally at risk. More so, in fact, since they were traveling in pairs, each hunter with his guide. If Bolan didn't hear them coming—and, he knew, there was a decent chance that he wouldn't—at least he had a reasonable hope of spotting them, before one of the trackers saw through his disguise and opened fire with something more effective than a bow.

It would be interesting, he thought, to see if he could nail them all. In other circumstances, Bolan could have treated the assignment almost as an academic exercise—a kind of live-fire war game—but the crucial difference here was Chelsea Rawlings. If she hadn't been a prisoner in Phelan's hands, he would have gone directly to the house, taken his chance with any guards and left the hunters wandering around in circles through the bush. Instead, he had to play the game, if not by Phelan's stated rules, at least within parameters that wouldn't increase the risk to Chelsea Rawlings's life.

He guessed that she was still alive, though he couldn't be certain of the fact. Phelan had let her live until that morning, when he could have made things easy on himself by killing her back in the States, and Bolan's instinct told him Phelan wasn't finished with the woman yet. If she had no part in the hunt, why had she been delivered to the briefing room with Bolan, placed out on display? There was an outside chance that she was being hunted in another quarter of the island even now, but Bolan didn't think so. Phelan hadn't mentioned anything about a second quarry while explaining details of the contest to his paying customers, but there was something.

Bolan didn't want to think about the details, hoping the woman's role in the festivities was meant to follow a successful hunt, once Bolan's head had been delivered on a plate. In which case, she would still be relatively safe while he worked his way around the island, thinning out the herd.

Her fault, the small, unwelcome voice repeated in his head. She wouldn't be here if she'd kept her word.

That didn't matter now, of course. The Executioner wasn't concerned with "could have, should have" arguments. He had perhaps a dozen lives to take, and one to save.

If he was lucky and didn't relax his guard, he thought he just might manage to come out of it alive.

BEFORE HE FLEW UP to New Iberia and caught the flight to Baja, Wayne Melbourne had spent the best part of an hour pondering his choice of weapons for the hunting trip. His final choice for long gun was a Remington Model 7600 SP, chambered for the classic .30-06 that had been dropping men and other game for nigh onto a century. The rifle was a smooth pump action, and the SP stood for "special purpose," meaning that its steel and wood alike were treated with a nonreflective finish, making it attractive to police and such, for SWAT teams. Melbourne was using open sights, in lieu of the ten-power Leupold scope that he had brought along for distance shooting, since the forest didn't offer him much hope of spotting any target more than seventy or eighty yards away.

His backup weapon, worn beneath his left arm in a shoulder rig, was a Beretta Model 96 Centurion, loading eleven rounds of the same Smith & Wesson

.40-caliber ammo that was now standard issue for FBI agents. Around his waist, a leather cartridge belt held twenty spare rounds for the Remington, two extra clips for the pistol and a bone-handled skinner with a six-inch, razor-edged blade.

The oilman's armament and camou outfit made him feel like something he had never been: a warrior. Even now, for all his daring in the world of petro business, all the wealth and fame he had accumulated, Melbourne still had moments when he wished that he had been a soldier like his father, and his grandfather before him. Not that either one of them had made careers of soldiering, but both had fought with valor in a world war, returning home with medals on their chests and scars that they could brag about while they were bumming beers from jealous friends.

Wayne Melbourne, meanwhile, had been lucky in the draft for Vietnam and missed the whole damned shooting match, ignoring imprecations from his father—a pathetic drunk by then—to take a chance and "do his part." Instead, Melbourne set his sights on oil and had become one of the richest men in the United States, perhaps the Western Hemisphere. His father had died of cirrhosis eight months before the first well in St. Mary Parish had come in. The old man shuffled off this mortal coil believing that his only son was both a coward and a failure, doomed to waste his life on dead-end dreams.

So fuck him anyhow.

Oswaldo, the Mexican guide, had been leading Melbourne steadily northward for close to an hour, since the gunshot had sounded from that general direction. There was still no signal from the house to indicate that anyone had bagged the trophy, and Melbourne was determined to continue with the hunt until he either scored or knew for sure that someone else had taken home the prize. It was a different kind of contest than the trip to Chechnya, but Melbourne didn't mind a little competition on the hunt. He had been dazzling competitors for years now, and if he lost out this time, so what? The experience alone was worth a million dollars, and if he succeeded, bagged the naked runner *and* the woman, it would absolutely make his week.

Although he kept it to himself, the gunshot they had heard was preying on his mind. He was convinced the sound had emanated from a handgun, and a small-to-medium-caliber weapon at that. None of the other three hunters carried a pistol as his primary weapon, though all—and their guides—packed handguns in addition to their other arms. What did the lone shot mean? Did it mean anything at all? Had he been duped into a vain excursion to the northern quarter of the island, while their prey was safely hidden elsewhere, to the west or south?

Melbourne had learned to trust his instincts through the years, and they were telling him to keep heading northward, regardless of his doubts and second thoughts. A gunshot on the island had to mean some kind of action going down, and since it wasn't rifle fire, his first reaction told him that it had to be something curious, perhaps significant.

Of course, he could be wrong. One of the hunters could have stumbled on a snake, for instance, and decided not to waste a rifle bullet. Adam Phelan had suggested that the island harbored no dangerous wildlife, but who could ever really tell about such things? It was ridiculous to think that he had scoured every square foot of the island, probed each nook and cranny to determine whether there were any creepy crawlers currently in residence.

Melbourne wasn't afraid of snakes. He had grown up with moccasins and rattlers in Louisiana, learned to watch for them while he was fishing on the bayou, later when they started sinking wells around St. Mary Parish. For the most part, vipers had no more use for a human being than Wayne Melbourne had for agents of the IRS. They kept their distance and let well enough alone, an attitude Melbourne was delighted to reciprocate. If an ill-tempered cottonmouth or canebrake rattler got in Melbourne's way, however, it was treated to the same reaction he applied to human pests: it was eradicated on the spot, by any means at hand.

Oswaldo had found a sort of game trail through the forest, picking up the pace, and Melbourne wondered just what sort of animals had blazed the trail in the beginning. He supposed there might be some kind of small deer about, though Phelan hadn't mentioned it. Why should he, though, when he was being paid to offer human targets, so much more exciting than a whitetail on the run?

His mind's eye pictured Mike Belasko dodging through the trees, stark naked, like some kind of jungle man from movies he had seen in childhood. It didn't occur to Melbourne that it might be wrong for him to track and kill this total stranger or to pay his host a million dollars for the privilege. What was the point of being filthy rich if he wasn't allowed to stand apart from common men and step outside their petty laws? What did it matter if Belasko was an agent of the state? What were the vast majority of government employees, anyway, but leeches who attached themselves to working men and tried to make life miserable with their silly rules invading every phase of modern life, micromanaging everything they could think of from cradle to grave?

Distracted for a moment by his personal antipathy toward Washington and all that issued from the nation's capital, Melbourne nearly missed the airy whisper of a sleek projectile in flight, barely noticed when Oswaldo stopped dead in his tracks up ahead. He was on full alert as his guide turned to face him, however, the shaft of an arrow still quivering, where it protruded from his sunken chest.

"Jesus Christ!"

His first thought was Estcott, the bowman, but how could the old man mistake Melbourne's Mexican guide for a tall, naked Anglo? Before he had time to puzzle it out, Oswaldo folded, dipping at the knees and slumping forward, arms outflung as if to catch himself. It didn't work, but the arrow's free end rammed into the loam and caught him, somehow supporting his weight on the narrow aluminum shaft. At first, Melbourne thought it would support the other's weight, but then he saw the man begin to slip and understood that he was inching down the shaft, his own weight pushing the razor-edged tip deeper into his flesh.

He heard the *sshh-sshh* of a second arrow coming,

this one meant for him, and threw himself behind the nearest tree.

THE SECOND SHOT WAS OFF, but Bolan had anticipated certain problems with the bow. It was an unfamiliar weapon, there had been no time to practice with it and it had been several years since he had tried his hand at stationary targets, on a range set up at Stony Man. That had been playtime, something to amuse himself, and Aaron Kurtzman took the honors from his wheelchair, nailing bull's-eyes eighteen times in twenty tries.

The hunting bow wasn't a weapon Bolan had anticipated using in a combat situation, and he told himself that he was fortunate to have scored with his first shot, dropping the Mexican guide in his tracks. That cut the odds by half, at least theoretically, but he couldn't forget that his adversary carried a repeating rifle, with a longer range, superior accuracy and a faster rate of fire than his own primary weapon.

Never mind.

He nocked another arrow—eight remaining, after this one flew—and started drifting through the trees to his right, taking advantage of his target's temporary blindness as he hid behind a sturdy tree trunk. Bolan wondered what was going through the hunter's mind, if he suspected that one of his fellows had turned on him, either from madness or spite. Did these pay-as-you-go thrill-killers know one another socially? Was there a history between them? Bolan didn't know or care, unless it helped confuse his enemy and further shave the odds.

When he had counted forty paces to his right, due west by Bolan's reckoning, he changed direction and began to advance slowly on his prey. He took great care to keep from making any noise, a quick glance to the earth before he took each step. Silence was possible in most environments, at least for a limited time, if you were moving slowly, every sense alert. He took his time, waiting for the enemy to show himself, hoping that jangled nerves would triumph over common sense.

When he was twenty-five or thirty yards from contact, Bolan got his wish. The hunter showed himself, just long enough to fire a rifle shot off to the north, across the crumpled body of his guide. The blast reverberated, battered back and forth among the trees, and Bolan wondered how far it would carry, who was listening and might respond. Instinct took over as he let another arrow fly, and it was another miss, grazing the trunk that hid his enemy before it glanced off into space and disappeared among the trees.

It was a clean miss, and he was surprised, therefore, when his opponent burst from cover, sprinting through the dappled shadows, squeezing off another wild shot as he ran. The bullet didn't come within a dozen yards of Bolan, and he concentrated on mechanics, reaching for another arrow, nocking it, drawing the bow and aiming, letting fly.

Another miss.

Too hasty, Bolan thought, and quickly added too slow to the judgment. Setting down the captured bow as quietly as possible, he drew both pistols, carrying the Colt .357 in his right hand, the H&R

.32 in his left. He thumbed both hammers back, to make his first shots quicker off the mark, and grimaced at the sharp metallic click-clack sounds as the pistols were cocked.

Eleven rounds, and if he needed even half that many shots to drop his target, once the hunter showed himself again, Bolan would judge that he was slipping. Even with a weapon like the snubby Colt, at forty feet or less, he should be able to take down a man-sized target on the run. It helped, furthermore, that the Colt was loaded with hollowpoints, for maximum stopping power once they found their mark.

When he was twenty yards from contact, Bolan judged that it was time to take a chance, risk something to flush his opponent from cover. Swiftly scanning the turf at his feet, he spied a fallen branch about two feet in length, off to his left. To reach it, he would have to sidestep, placing himself beyond the reach of immediate cover, but the rifleman's aim hadn't been impressive so far, and Bolan decided to risk it.

Shifting off course, he found the branch, stretched out one foot and brought his weight down squarely, deliberately on target. The crack seemed improbably loud in the stillness that had fallen behind the last rifle shot. It was immediately followed by a gasp and scuffling sound, the shooter moving—but which way?

Bolan was ready for him, pistols bracketing the tree that hid him, when the hunter burst out toward his right. It was the logical choice, continuing his run from the last time, though a more experienced jungle fighter might have reversed directions for the hell of it. Bolan led his target, ignoring the rifle as it swung his way, and the guns went off together with a swift bam-bam that echoed through the forest.

Bolan saw his bullet strike the runner low, off center, slamming home below his ribs and spinning him. He lost the rifle as he fell, with no chance to pump the slide and feed another round into the chamber. He was still alive, though, groping for the autoloader in his shoulder rig, when Bolan reached him, stooped to place the .32-caliber pistol at skin-touch range and drilled another hole between the hunter's eyes.

All done, but it had taken time and made more racket than the Executioner intended. Five shots from three distinct and separate weapons would alert anyone within a mile or more of the killing ground to a battle in progress, and he assumed the other hunters would be moving toward the spot even now, urging their guides to all deliberate speed.

No time to waste.

He stripped the dead man of his shoulder rig and cartridge belt, discarded the H&R .32 pistol after dumping its last four rounds and flinging them away. The Remington felt good in his hands, and he reloaded on the move, putting ground between himself and the corpses of his two most recent kills.

Four down, and he had cut the tracking force by half. It was a start, though he was still a long, hard fight away from free and clear.

But it was coming, right.

The Executioner was on his way.

CHAPTER SIXTEEN

When Vernon Blake went off to war, he was normally followed by a camera crew, stunt doubles, makeup artists, wardrobe specialists, special-effects technicians, publicists, caterers and assorted gofers hired specifically to insure that his war didn't, in fact, resemble anything approaching Hell. The blood he spilled was fake, most of the sound effects were dubbed in later, at the studio, and every combat scene was choreographed in advance, rehearsed to guarantee that Blake came out looking like a star. And when it was time to stop shooting, somebody yelled, "Cut!"

The public loved him—all except the drunken geeks who tried to call him out from time to time—and Blake had everything a thirty-something millionaire movie star could want, from plush digs and the occasional snort of Bolivian flake to hot and cold running groupies.

All except guts.

At some point, in the middle of the whole damned sideshow, Blake had started to doubt himself, question the image that had been so carefully crafted for him in Hollywood. Of course, he realized that it was just an image, not to be confused with flesh-and-blood reality, but it began to grow on him. How did you tell a babe, "I'm not a hero, but I play one in the movies"?

Screw that shit.

Vern Blake was larger than life, and proud of it. He wanted to feel that way offscreen, as well, and the first step in that direction, beyond some transparent studio hype, had been his reaching out to Adam Phelan. Their safari in Rwanda was a revelation to him. Blake learned more about himself inside four days than he would ever have thought possible.

And he had killed, damned right.

All right, so it wasn't the sort of thing he could advertise, but that made no difference. He felt the power reflected in a whole new attitude, and he could hint around the subject, now and then, relaxing in the hot tub with a couple of foxes and a snootful of blow. What harm could it do? Let the grapevine take over and handle the rest.

This second hunt was different, but he liked it. Blake appreciated checking out his target in advance, instead of taking potluck, and the competition galvanized him, made him feel a different kind of rush than what he had experienced in Africa, trolling for prey, when they basically had all the time in the world. Blake was between pictures, that time, with nowhere to go and all summer to get there, a leisurely kind of killing spree. This time around, with three other hunters involved, competing for the kill—and the woman, he couldn't forget *her*—he felt a greater sense of urgency, a fresh kick of adrenaline.

And it was great.

Right now, though, Blake was worried that one of the others had beaten him to the prize. He had counted five or six shots, from at least two different guns, maybe three, in the last flurry of firing. Before that, maybe ninety minutes earlier, a single shot, but that had to have been a clean miss, if the competition was still firing. If it was two guns, he figured that one of the others was blasting away at their target, along with his guide. If it was three guns, well, he didn't have a freaking clue what that could mean.

Blake, for his part, had ordered his guide not to fire under any circumstances, short of saving Blake's life from a clear and imminent danger. If and when he dropped his man, Blake wanted every bullet in the runner's carcass to come from his own Colt AR-15, or maybe the .45-caliber Browning Model BDA pistol he wore on his hip. Either way, it would be his kill, and nobody else's.

"How much farther?" he demanded. His guide glanced back at Blake and shrugged, his face blank, as if he either didn't know or didn't care how much ground they had covered. Phelan was probably paying them all by the hour, a flat rate in pesos, regardless of who bagged the prey. Why should this man care anything about a gringo he had never met before the previous night?

Blake felt a sudden urge to shoot his escort, punish him for disrespecting an honest-to-God celebrity, but he let it go. It would be bad enough if he missed his quarry, without getting lost in the bargain and having to face Adam Phelan with a dead guide on his hands.

No, thank you very much.

Win or lose at the game, Blake intended to go home alive, and riling Phelan on his own home turf was one surefire antidote for longevity.

The problem with this hunt, of course, was that he had no script, which meant the hero might be edged out at the finish line by someone else. There was no prize for second place in this event; Blake either took the brass ring, or he went home empty-handed, out a million dollars for a run around an island that was something short of paradise.

The million didn't matter, really. There was plenty more where that came from—another twenty, for example, when he started shooting his next feature in Manhattan, six weeks down the road. He also had the standard deal for points on that film, as with the last five, to guarantee himself a cut of any profits made in theaters.

But all he wanted, here and now, was one clean shot at a perfect stranger who called himself Mike Belasko. One shot, that was all. If Blake could see his target, he could make the kill.

No sweat.

So, why in the hell, he wondered, was he sweating so damned much?

IT WAS A TOSS-UP which way Bolan should go after dropping the second pair of trackers. He had no fix on the last two teams, but he *did* know where the house was, where the men behind the hunt had Chelsea Rawlings caged. It couldn't hurt to make his way in that direction, Bolan thought, as long as he did nothing to alarm the guards and jeopardize the lady's life.

Until, that is, he was ready to go for broke.

At some point, Bolan knew, he would have to take the risk—unless, of course, one of the two surviving hunters or their escorts nailed him first. Dealing with amateurs, he felt a certain confidence in his ability to triumph, but the Executioner had learned from grim experience that overconfidence was a surefire killer in combat. A fighting man could push his luck a hundred times, maybe a thousand, but it only took one slip, one faulty judgment, for the game to blow up in his face and put him in the ground.

Five hundred yards due west of the last kill, Bolan found another stream and slaked his thirst, wishing one of the hunters had been thoughtful enough to bring a canteen along. It was a curious omission, and it spoke to him of their confidence, a belief that someone would probably bag his naked prey before he got thirsty. If all else failed, of course, and some particular hunter failed to find a clear-water stream in his wanderings, he could always hike back to the house for a soda or beer, maybe whip up a sandwich if his stomach was grumbling.

If Bolan were to hate his enemies, that would have been the time, for their sheer arrogance, their stubborn belief that nothing—not even elemental thirst—could interfere with their blood sport. Hatred was a luxury the Executioner couldn't afford, however, since its passion would serve only to inflame his senses, cloud his judgment and propel him into rash behavior that could get him killed.

Cold steel, he thought, and willed himself to emulate the sharp blade of the skinner on his liberated cartridge belt. A knife had no more interest in the flesh it cut than rocks and sand had in the latest news of politics from Washington. A keen blade did its job, without elation or remorse, and then retired to wait until it was required again. Nothing was personal to keen, case-hardened steel.

Bolan resolved to execute the rest of his surviving enemies as cleanly and efficiently as possible. His twin goals of survival and releasing Chelsea Rawlings from captivity were all that mattered now. It made no difference if his enemies were evil men or simply self-indulgent fools; he didn't care if one of them was balding or another had bad breath. By stepping into the arena with an unknown force, each one of them had sealed his fate. Their judgment would be bloody, swift and irreversible.

But Bolan had to find them first…or else let them find him.

The second option brought a subtle change of plan to mind. Instead of making for the house at once, he thought it might be useful to assume that one or more of his adversaries would respond to the reports of gunfire generated by his latest confrontation. Bolan had already left the kill site, and he didn't fancy doubling back, but he could still improve his odds of contact with another team, he thought, by sketching out a rough perimeter around the spot and going on patrol, hoping his path would intersect the track of hunters homing on the sounds of battle. It was worth a try, in any case, and if he didn't score within the next three-quarters of an hour or so, Bolan could always change his mind again and chart another course toward Phelan's digs.

It would have helped to have a map or mental layout of the island, something to at least provide the basic scale, but he was guessing that the rock couldn't be all that large. For one thing, there were no huge islands in the southern Gulf of California—none that showed on current maps, at least—and Bolan doubted whether Adam Phelan could afford a massive island to himself, in any case. The huntsman wouldn't run his game on populated islands, such as Isla Tiburon or Isla Angel de la Guarda, in the northern part of the gulf, for fear of attracting unwanted attention and bringing the *federales* down on his head. That meant a smaller island—call it two or three miles in diameter, at most—and *that* meant Bolan's trackers could have heard the gunshots almost anywhere, from coast to coast. The full two or three miles could be covered, by someone in shape, in the space of an hour or two.

He could wait.

Bolan had checked and double-checked his weapons, releasing the pertinent safeties, reloading where possible. With the Remington, the Colt and the Beretta, plus the wicked skinning knife, he was as ready to confront his enemies as he would ever be.

Now, all the hunters had to do was show themselves. It wasn't much to ask, all things considered, and he hoped they wouldn't let him down.

He had paced off something like one-quarter of the arc he pictured in his mind, when something froze the warrior in his tracks. A sound of voices, maybe...or had he imagined it? The forest—any forest—could play tricks like that sometimes. A bird's call or the low hum of a passing insect could deceive a pair of hopeful ears into believing they had fixed on human sounds. Sometimes, the "words" were even audible, coherent conversations conjured up from thin air via wishful thinking.

Not this time.

He waited, rock still, breathless, for the sound to be repeated. When it came, he knew that he had found another of his enemies.

"So, how much farther, dammit?" someone asked. There was no answer he could hear, but Bolan didn't care. He had a rough fix on the voice and was already moving out to intercept. No racing through the woods to put his adversaries on alert—rather, a slow and steady pace, watching his step, alert and ready to adjust his course if he received another signal from his prey.

Hang on, Bolan willed his enemy. He was on his way.

IT SEEMED to Vernon Blake that he had been jogging for hours. A glance at his watch proved him wrong, but it did nothing to relieve the burning muscles in his thighs and calves. It didn't help the sharp stitch in his side, either, the pain reminding him that there was still a world of difference between hoisting free weights and running your ass off over rugged open ground.

Goddammit all! Where *were* they? Were they

making *any* progress whatsoever toward the shooting scene?

"So, how much farther, dammit?" he demanded of his guide.

The Mexican didn't even glance back at him this time, flapping one hand in a limp-wristed signal for Blake to keep trailing him. Shit! It seemed to Blake they had to have jogged at least a mile by now. How far could it be, for Christ's sake? If they didn't find something soon, he was going to call a rest stop, or the guide could run on by himself, and to hell with him. He could kiss his frigging tip goodbye, and Blake would have a word with Phelan about the quality of his hired help.

The Colt AR-15 felt heavy in his hands. It weighed seven pounds empty, maybe eight, with the 20-round box magazine in place, but it was starting to feel like double or triple its actual weight. His palms were clammy with sweat where they clutched the rifle's plastic grips, his knuckles blanched by tension. He was smart enough to keep his finger off the trigger, but it made him nervous, fearing that a microsecond's lapse might give his prey an edge somehow.

What fucking edge? The guy was naked and unarmed, for God's sake. Even if he jumped out of the bushes like a wild man, what was he supposed to do? Flash Vernon like the perverts who hung out in L.A.'s Griffith Park?

Still, when he thought about it, there had definitely been a hint of something in the quarry's eyes, his attitude, when Phelan showed him off before the hunt. The guy was built—not like a power lifter, granted, but more like someone who stayed automatically in shape, by working at a steady job that tested his strength. It was the eyes that Blake came back to, though, each time he pictured Belasko in his mind. The guy had killer's eyes, as if he'd seen and done most everything there was to see and do.

Like Adam Phelan's eyes.

Two of a kind, Blake thought, and drew no comfort from the notion, even if Belasko was unarmed, buck naked in the wilderness. A guy like that, you had the sneaking hunch that he could whip up weapons out of nothing, maybe rub two sticks together, if he felt like it, and start a forest fire.

Get real.

Whatever his experience and background, Belasko was a man of flesh and blood. Shoot him, and he would die like anybody else. Like the guerrillas in Rwanda, sure. And if Blake couldn't nail him with the twenty rounds of 5.56 mm ammo in his rifle, he would use the Browning. If he couldn't nail him with the Browning, he would let have at it, then reload and give the guy some more.

He wasn't a superhero, man. There were no frigging superheroes in the real world, right? Damned right!

If heroes lived up to their reputations, Vernon Blake wouldn't have been so nervous at the moment, clutching the AR-15 more tightly to prevent his hands from trembling.

He found himself wishing the air horn would sound from the cabin, announcing a kill, and just as quickly cursed himself for cowardice. The kill was his, by God! The woman would be his, as well. If someone else had tried to bag the quarry and had failed, so much the better. It would make his victory more satisfying, let him rub it in their faces when he brought Belasko in and went to claim his bonus from the dead man's lady.

The thought of her excited him, recalled the time in college when he was accused of date rape. He was playing football then, of course; the coach had smoothed it over, and the snooty bitch who blew the whistle on him wound up dropping out of school before the end of the semester. On the second time around, unfortunately, he had gone off campus, where the coach and dean couldn't protect him. Charges had been filed, then quietly dismissed a few weeks later, when the second bitch was made to understand that she had nothing but a life of grief in store if she made trouble for a bright young man on the rise. Because the charge was dropped, he had been able to go back and have the record of his bust expunged, nothing to pop up in the tabloids later and embarrass him.

By that time, Blake had seen enough of college, and thanked the coach for nothing when the old man turned on him after the second so-called rape. Blake's grade-point average was hovering around the cut line anyway, and Hollywood was calling. He could hear it in his dreams.

Since he had broken into movies, there had been no end of willing women, lining up to make his every fantasy come true. If he got rough with some of them, sometimes, there had been no complaints to anyone except his agent and the publicist they kept on staff. A monetary settlement would make most problems go away, and there had been no leaks so far, not even in the sleazy tabloid press.

And there would be no comebacks from the woman Phelan had locked up back at the house. This was the perfect opportunity, Blake saw, to let himself unwind and go for broke. Why not, for Christ's sake! He was paying for it, wasn't he? A million dollars of his hard-earned cash, up-front. Cash had its privileges.

Blake would have thought it was impossible to get a hard-on that way, jogging through the woods and sweating like a pig, but there it was. He pushed the woman out of mind, broke stride to grapple with his camou trousers for a moment, then resumed his pursuit of the Mexican guide.

The shot came out of nowhere, as loud as thunder, shocking him. Blake stopped abruptly, lost his balance, stumbled and went down on one knee before he caught himself. In front of him, some thirty feet away, his guide was twirling like a goofy dancer, arms outflung, his head thrown back. It took another beat for Blake to recognize the crimson spouting from his ruptured throat as blood, the bright arterial spray pumping rhythmically skyward.

He went down in a heap, and Blake scuttled for cover, hunkered down behind the nearest tree of any size. Sweet Jesus, what was happening?

The action hero felt a sudden dampness at his crotch, and realized that he had wet himself.

BOLAN WAS GLAD the shooter with the Remington had left him open sights instead of slapping on a scope. Most of his sniper work, both in Special

Forces and beyond, had called for telescopic sights, but they were often worse than useless in a firefight staged at normal combat range. With sniper scopes, you had to pick out a specific target, calculate the range, windage and elevation, zero in and hope to score a kill with your first shot. Close up, with moving, multiple targets, a telescopic sight would leave you dizzy, damned near cross-eyed, while your enemies closed in and cut you down.

He was already in position when the targets showed themselves, both jogging, one man trailing ten or fifteen yards behind the other. Bolan recognized the Anglo as another of the hunters he had met in Adam Phelan's briefing room. The face had been familiar, even then, from somewhere else, but Bolan couldn't place it at the moment and he didn't really care. It made no difference to him if the hunter was a congressman or had a sitcom on TV. Celebrity and status offered no protection whatsoever when he cast his lot against the Executioner.

The guy was bitching at his guide, for all the good it did him. Out in front, the Mexican would lift a hand to wave the hunter onward or ignore him all together, make the gringo think he didn't speak English. It was clear the pointman had a fix on something, though, for he was jogging on a beeline toward the spot where Bolan's last two kills reposed.

The thing he couldn't know was that he'd never get there.

Bolan led his moving target just enough to let the runner meet his bullet on the fly, instead of missing it by inches. The aught-six went in low—he had been aiming for the pointman's face and drilled him through the neck instead—but it was close enough. Explosive impact spun the guy and dumped him on his backside, while the man behind him stumbled, ducked, recovered and threw himself behind a tree.

Bolan pumped the Remington's slide to chamber a new round, regretting the noise that came with manual-action repeaters. His surviving adversary had an M-16, or maybe the civilian semiauto version, with what looked to be a 20-round magazine. That gave him five times Bolan's ammo capacity, on top of the semi- or full-auto weapon's superior rate of fire, but those advantages could easily be canceled out by inexperience and lack of guts. So far, the hunter hadn't fired a shot, and while his hasty duck-and-cover made good sense from a survival point of view, it also indicated hesitation to engage his enemy.

Bolan risked a glance around his own tree, ducking back again when he discovered that the coast was clear. His enemy hadn't emerged from hiding yet, and Bolan seized the opportunity to make his move. He rolled out to his left, having determined in advance that better cover lay in that direction, but he met no fire as he emerged. Indeed, Bolan was halfway to his second vantage point before he glimpsed a blur of movement downrange, to his right, and heard the pop-pop-pop of 5.56 mm semiauto fire.

The nearest of his adversary's tumblers missed him by a yard or more, the net result of hasty shooting, and he reached his destination in three more loping strides. Bolan's opponent cranked off half a dozen wasted rounds, the last one coming close enough to graze his tree, but Bolan could see no advantage in returning fire until he had a target. As for how that goal might be achieved, he was already working on a plan of sorts.

It was a risky proposition, since the hunter had him spotted now, but Bolan would be gambling his experience, his list of kills, against what seemed to be a jumpy amateur. The hunter knew his prey was armed; the game had changed from simple killing to a contest for survival. And in that arena, Mack Bolan was second to no man.

For all its risk, the plan was relatively simple. A feint to one side of the tree, to get his enemy blasting away, while Bolan broke in the other direction and hoped for a shot. If it worked, he would be six-for-six. If it fell apart, he might not have a shot—or then again, he could be dead.

A gamble, sure. What else was new in Bolan's world?

He feinted to the left, hoping that his opponent would be forced to show more of himself, if he took the bait and fired in that direction. The immediate crackle of gunfire rewarded Bolan's move, and he backpedaled swiftly, came around the right-hand side of the tree with the Remington already shouldered, his index finger taking up the trigger slack.

He had a fair shot at his target, not the best, but Bolan didn't hesitate. He squeezed the trigger, pumped the rifle's slide and fired again before he registered the impact of his first round. The double tap from his aught-six slammed Bolan's target backward, into the clear, one arm flailing as he toppled, sprawling on his back. The other arm, his left, hung limp and useless below the crimson wreckage of his shoulder.

Bolan kept the Remington trained on his fallen opponent as he stepped from cover, closing the gap between them with long, steady strides. He was prepared to fire again, if need be, but the guy was finished, stretched out on his back and blowing bloody bubbles from mouth and nostrils. One of Bolan's shots, at least, had found a lung. The guy was bleeding internally, and Bolan doubted that a team of trauma surgeons could have saved him.

He could have spent another aught-six round to finish it, but Bolan judged that he had spent enough time on the scene as it was. Between the two firefights, any surviving gunmen on the island had to know approximately where he was, and if he meant to lay another trap for the remaining two-man team of hunters, he would have to get a move on.

He relieved the dying hunter of his Colt AR-15 and claimed a second belt, this one complete with spare mags for the rifle and a .45-caliber Browning autoloader. Bolan slung the belt over one shoulder, carried the AR-15 by its sling and set off through the woods with the Remington pump in his hands. It was a motley arsenal, but he was making progress. He had started out with nothing and had cut the home team by half—or so he hoped, at any rate.

If he was wrong about the numbers, Bolan thought, at least he had enough hardware to deal with any reasonable number of opponents who remained. And what was Adam Phelan thinking now about the little game he had arranged?

Bolan looked forward to asking that question in person, and the sooner the better.

CHAPTER SEVENTEEN

Standing on the front porch of his house, an AUG assault rifle in hand, Adam Phelan listened to the sounds of gunfire from the eastern quarter of his island and couldn't help thinking about what was going on out there.

He had expected shooting, granted. It had even crossed his mind that Mike Belasko might pick off one of the hunters, if his clients weren't extremely careful. He had cautioned each of them in turn, however, and attempted to forewarn them of the risk involved. Whatever happened afterward, from that point on, his hands were clean—at least, as far as *his* opinion was concerned.

And his opinion was the only one that mattered on the island. He was lord and master here, the alpha and omega of whatever happened while he was in residence.

Unless, of course, his best-laid plans went sour and blew up in his face.

More shooting, and he found that he had taken half a dozen steps in the direction of the sounds before he caught himself. It was instinctive, the initial impulse to respond, but he wasn't about to traipse off through the woods alone and walk into the middle of a firefight when he didn't know the players.

For all he knew, a couple of his clients could have gotten nervous, maybe started shooting at each other. Serve them right if they were so damned jumpy that they couldn't tell a naked runner from another man, both dressed and armed, whom they had met the night before, shared breakfast and a briefing with. He had no patience for such foolishness, and almost hoped that they would kill each other off. He had their money, after all, and that was all that really mattered in the long run.

Still, the more he thought about it, Phelan knew his jumpy-hunter theory wouldn't fly. There had been too much shooting over too much time, for one thing. First, what sounded like a single pistol shot, followed some ninety minutes later by a flurry of handgun and rifle fire from another part of the island. Now, the latest exchange, with two rifles banging away, and the source of the gunfire had shifted again, though not as widely as the space between the first and second outbreaks.

Shit!

If he was willing to admit it, Phelan knew exactly what was going on. He didn't want to face it, but the longer he stood there and watched the newly silent tree line, he could reach no other logical conclusion.

Mike Belasko was alive, and he was picking off the men who had gone out to hunt him down. How many dead so far? If he dismissed the first shot as some kind of aberration, that left two distinct and separate firefights in the space of an hour or so. Belasko had to have won the first round, or his killer would have checked in to report and claim his bonus prize. Because no one had come back after the exchange, Phelan assumed that both the hunter and his guide were dead.

Which hunter? It was difficult to say, since two of them had left the house with rifles that would sound alike, or nearly so, to someone listening from distances of half a mile or more. Estcott had gone out carrying a bow, the idiot, and Vern Blake's Colt had clearly been the lighter weapon rapid firing in the later skirmish. Call it Fiske or Melbourne, then, and figure one of them was dead, for sure.

The second fight, though clearly finished now, was still too recent for survivors to have reached the house. There was a chance that Vernon Blake had bagged and tagged Belasko with a lucky shot. Phelan would wait and see, but he wasn't about to bet the farm on Blake. The movie star had carried his weight all right on their Rwandan safari, but he wasn't the soldier he played in his films. Not even close, in fact.

Belasko, on the other hand, just might be.

Phelan was developing a grudging new respect for the man his clients had set out to kill, and the feeling, forced as it was, only made him wish Belasko dead with greater zeal. He had contrived the present hunt to rid himself of problems, not to aggravate the situation and created an even greater hazard to himself.

He turned back toward the house and found Karl Shuker watching from the porch. Like Phelan, he was armed, not only with a pistol, but also with the Spectre SMG he favored, dangling from a shoulder strap. ''Something's gone wrong,'' the German said.

''Sounds like it,'' Phelan admitted grudgingly.

''You think he's gotten them.'' It wasn't posed as a question.

''Some of them, anyway,'' Phelan agreed. ''I think he must have, yeah.''

''When he is done with them, he will be coming here, to get the woman,'' Shuker said.

''He might not wait to finish off the others. It's not like they can match him, one-on-one.''

''We should go out and find him,'' Shuker suggested.

''No. He'll come to us. That's one thing we can still be sure of, while we have the woman.''

Shuker stepped down off the porch. ''I wish now I had killed him on the mainland, when I had the chance.''

Phelan wished so, too. ''Four million dollars, Karl. It's in the bank. We couldn't know they'd fuck it up this badly.''

''But they have,'' the German said. ''We must do something, soon.''

''One of them may get lucky yet,'' Phelan replied, not believing it. ''If nothing else, they'll slow him. Gives us a chance to get things squared away to meet him when he gets here.''

''It will be a pleasure,'' Shuker said.

''We'll see. Send me the others now. I want to talk to them, make sure they understand what's going on before you bring the woman out.''

And then, the hunter thought, They would see who had the stones to play the game out, to the end.

GREGORY FISKE HAD KNOWN he was "different" by the time he was eight or nine years old. The sense of power and excitement he experienced from causing pain—to animals, at first; then to his ever dwindling group of playmates; finally, to his younger siblings—might have been a sickness in the eyes of "civilized" society, but it was all Fiske knew. Of course, after a string of ugly incidents, complaints made to his parents by their neighbors, once or twice to the police, he had adapted to the so-called rules of living.

If you couldn't beat up your girlfriend, he learned, there was a class of prostitutes that suffered gladly, for a price. And if you couldn't rent a punching bag, why, you could always marry one. Breed little punching bags to keep yourself amused.

His natural ferocity found other, more acceptable outlets in Fiske's daily life, of course. As president and CEO of a vast media empire, he both reported and created the news, made stars and broke them, promoted bestsellers and sent other books down the tubes to oblivion and the remainder tables. Fiske was responsible, at least in part, for the outbreak of two border wars—one in Africa, the other in Southeast Asia—wherein his reporters, acting under their CEO's personal direction, had crafted stories to reflect a certain point of view, inflaming both sides while embracing neither.

Fiske was proud of that. He often saw himself as William Randolph Hearst with satellites, a TV network, record labels, a major movie studio and the Internet. If Hearst could touch off the Spanish-American War through yellow journalism, using nothing but his chain of newspapers, what might Gregory Fiske achieve, if he really, really tried?

The possibilities were endless.

At the moment, though, he had to concentrate on picking off one man, and it was looking rather grim. There had been all kinds of shooting in the past couple of hours, and still there was no air horn sounding from the house to indicate a kill. Fiske didn't know exactly what to make of that, under the circumstances, but it didn't strike him as encouraging.

His first trip out with Phelan, nine months earlier, had taken him from Venezuela, across the frontier into northern Colombia, the infamous Guajira Peninsula. At Fiske's suggestion they had lain in wait for a drug caravan, the target chosen not because Fiske had any grudge against cocaine—in fact, he liked a toot, from time to time—but rather because he thought that it would be exciting.

And it was.

Fiske killed four men that day, while Shuker and Phelan each dropped one. Of Fiske's quarter, one man—a peon from the mountains—might have survived his hip and shoulder wounds, except that Fiske compelled him, at knifepoint, to open a kilo of flake and gobble the contents until he collapsed and died in convulsions. Fiske had felt Phelan watching him with a newfound respect after that...or maybe it was simply caution.

Either one was fine.

This business on the island was a different story, though. Something told Fiske that it had gone to hell, or else was on its way, and while his better judgment urged him to quit, cut his losses and leave, Fiske couldn't bring himself to run away. If one of the others was first to bail out, maybe then, but how would he know?

Fuck it!

He trusted his Winchester, and more to the point, he trusted his own ability to kill on command. Fiske didn't care if his quarry had taken out one of the others, somehow armed himself with one gun or an armload of weapons. He was still just a man, still mortal, and Fiske saw himself as innately superior, a cut above the common herd.

The more Fiske thought about it now, the more he hoped his prey *was* armed. It made the contest more exciting, like the shootout in Colombia, instead of just an exercise in marksmanship. His guide looked troubled, but what could you expect from a peasant hired by the hour?

Who was left, he wondered, if their prey was fighting back? Fiske didn't know the others, although he had seen two or three of Blake's movies, surprised to find out the man was a hunter, since so many macho stars from Hollywood were closet queens. Blake's presence on the island meant that he had gone out hunting with Phelan and Karl at least once in the past. If he had folded in the crunch or failed to bag his man on that occasion, Fiske didn't believe Blake would have been invited back. Not this time.

So, you lived and learned.

Fiske snapped at his guide in Spanish, one of five languages he spoke fluently, demanding that the peasant hurry up and locate the source of the most recent gunshots. Answered with a shrug and frown, he almost lashed out at the smaller man, but stopped himself in time, remembering the Latin temperament. The Mexican might be a peon, living hand to mouth, but he would still resent an insult, possibly fight back, and Fiske would have to waste time killing him, then try to find his way around the island on his own.

"How far?" Fiske said, and tried to make it sound as if he didn't think the Mexican was shit beneath his custom hiking boots.

"Not far, I think," the guide replied.

"Then we should hurry," Fiske informed him in a voice that brooked no contradiction.

"Sí, señor."

With visible reluctance, then, the Mexican picked up his pace. Fiske had no trouble keeping up. If anything, he was in better shape than his guide, strength and stamina maintained by a daily regimen of exercise. He might not qualify for calendar shots, like Vernon Blake in his artfully shredded jungle fatigues from *Blood Law*, but Fiske would match his staying power against the younger man's any day, with no fear of coming off second best.

The Winchester Model 70 had a live round in its chamber, five more in the magazine, and Fiske wore a gleaming bandolier of thirty extra rounds across his chest, like some kind of *bandito*. He wouldn't need thirty rounds to make the kill, he told himself, nor even five. He only needed one clean shot to wrap it up, and then he could relax, prepare to celebrate.

With the woman.

Even hot and sweaty as he was, the thought of her, what they would do together, made him smile.

KARL SHUKER DIDN'T CARE much for the plan Phelan had devised. In fact, as far as Shuker was concerned, it hardly qualified as a plan. Sitting on your ass and waiting for the enemy to show himself, start shooting at you in his own good time, might be a species of defensive strategy, but the German had been trained in proactive aggression, taking the fight to his opponents and hunting them down instead of giving away the first move. Phelan's plan struck him as a fairly decent way of getting killed, but he wasn't in charge. The best that he could do, for now, was stay alert and watch his back.

He understood Phelan's choice, of course. They lacked the manpower to hunt Belasko as it should be done, sweeping from one end of the island to the other, driving their quarry before them until he ran out of room or found the guts to make a stand. The only other option, sending Shuker out into the bush alone or with one of the remaining Mexicans to keep him company, would be a joke, like playing blindman's buff. The island was approximately five square miles in area, and it would take a one- or two-man hunting party days to cover every inch of that terrain, their quarry free to duck and dodge ahead of them the whole damned time. It could drag on indefinitely, and the German understood that Phelan's method was the only way to go.

Still, he wasn't required to like it.

It ran against Shuker's grain to play the sitting duck and wait for someone else to take a shot at him. He was supposed to be the shooter, not the target; he had trained for years on end to make himself the hunter, not the bait.

The flip side of the problem, though, was that the home team did have some advantages. Five guns against Belasko's one, to start with, counting the three Mexicans who still remained. Despite his firmly rooted ethnic prejudice—and the regrettable snafu at the hotel in Santa Rosalia—Shuker found them sharp-eyed and alert, swift to react in crisis situations, not at all the stupid, sluggish folk imagined by so many white Americans. Who better to defend a little piece of Mexico against a gringo from El Norte?

They had well-constructed shelter, in the form of Phelan's house, and enough spare ammunition, food and water to withstand a siege if it should come to that. It was ridiculous to think in such terms, though. One man couldn't surround a hacienda. He couldn't watch all directions simultaneously, or defend himself against attacks from every side at once. If Belasko lived, it was because he had been able to defeat the hunters piecemeal, two by two. The first kills would have armed him, Shuker thought, and after that, a soldier in the forest stood a better chance of coming out alive than any fat cat playing great white hunter on his holiday.

Another bonus for the home team was that their opponent had been facing amateurs so far, and evidently using up a portion of his limited ammunition reserve to destroy them. If and when he reached the house, he would be squaring off against professionals—well, two professionals, at any rate, plus three more proved killers—and a minimal effort wouldn't do the trick. It would be all or nothing, with the home team rated as the odds-on favorite to win.

And finally, they had the woman. Belasko obviously cared for her, if not romantically, at least enough to risk his life on learning she was taken prisoner. That quaint protective urge had brought him to his present pass, and it would get him killed before another sunrise kissed the island treetops. Shuker had no doubt of that at all.

He had deployed the Mexicans as Phelan ordered: one atop the house, positioned on a kind of widow's walk with a high-powered rifle, to survey the property while daylight still remained; one hidden on the front porch, waiting for Belasko with an automatic rifle; number three out back, in the garage-cum-workshop, covering the rear approach. Shuker could easily have found positions for another six or seven guns, but they would have to work with what they had.

Which left the woman.

Shuker didn't like to deal with her. It wasn't that he found her unattractive—quite the opposite, in fact. In other circumstances, he might well have paid to share an hour of her time. Nor was it that he shrank from female tears and suffering, a weakness that had never troubled him at any point throughout his life. He had killed women, more than once—two female terrorists in Germany, and a young guerrilla fighter in Sudan—and lost no sleep over the deeds.

If necessary, he could murder Chelsea Rawlings in cold blood, and not think twice about it.

Examining the problem in his mind, Shuker decided that what he disliked about the present situation, dealing with the woman, was her lack of fear, her sheer refusal to be terrorized. Oh, Phelan had found ways to make her scream and weep from pain, but that was no great victory. She had resisted being stripped in front of strangers, hard eyes bleeding bright tears of embarrassment, but that meant nothing. She was still unbroken, and if Phelan thought he had subdued her, vanquished her, then he was very much mistaken.

Shuker could have told him that, but it wasn't what Phelan wished to hear, and so he kept the message to himself. Better to do his job and try to keep himself alive at any cost, instead of feuding with the man in charge. When they were done with this, if both of them were still alive and he still questioned Phelan's judgment, then it would be time to seek another situation for himself.

Right now, the German had no choice but to remain and fight.

He finished checking on the Mexicans and walked back to the house. Inside, he spotted Phelan at the broad front windows, staring toward the trees.

"No sign of Belasko, then?" he asked, already knowing the response.

"Not yet," Phelan replied. "You'd better fetch the woman."

Fetch, Shuker thought with distaste. The same command a person gave a dog. If Phelan wasn't careful, this dog just might turn and bite him, when he least expected it.

But not this day. With Belasko on the loose and coming for them, surely armed by now, Shuker and Phelan still needed each other. Divided and alone, their chances of survival were reduced, and Shuker didn't plan on dying here for no good reason.

And so, he went to fetch the woman, hoping she could make the difference, throw their opponent off his guard and make him vulnerable. It would only take one shot to do the job, and Shuker hoped he would have the honor of pulling that trigger himself. With luck, the trophy from this hunt might be his.

THE ADAGE CAUTIONED, "If it ain't broke, don't fix it." Bolan's plan to take the hunters down piecemeal had worked all right so far, and with a single pair of trackers left to go, he saw no good reason to give up a proved technique. The hunters were vulnerable. In order to find him, they had to keep moving, searching, and the racket from his latest firefight was the best lure Bolan could have devised.

His problem now lay in not missing the last pair of hunters when they arrived. Waiting at the kill site was too obvious; indeed, there was no guarantee his enemies would even find it, in the absence of gunshots to guide them. This time tomorrow, the smell would be enough for them to follow, but he didn't have a night and day to spare.

Neither did they.

Bolan kept moving, as before, his eyes and ears alert to warning signs of any hostile presence in the woods. He took for granted that the men he sought would come, that they would try for stealth, and hoped that they wouldn't succeed in slipping past him, much less stop and lay an ambush of their own. Bolan had no illusions of his own invincibility, but it would be embarrassing to go this way, picked off by amateurs.

Not that it mattered when you were dead.

The grim thought kept him going, and another ten or fifteen minutes passed before he heard his quarry up ahead—at least two men, one of them making noise enough for both. He changed his course to intercept them before they reached the spot where he had dealt with the familiar-looking hunter and his guide.

His first glimpse of the hunters was a shadow flicker through the trees. At first, he thought his eyes were playing tricks on him, but then he heard the noisy runner cursing as he stumbled over something in his path. It didn't stop him, didn't even seem to slow him that much, but Bolan had them marked now, homing in. Another hundred yards or so, and they would reach the general vicinity where he had killed his last two enemies. It wasn't quite what he had planned, but seemed to make no difference in the long run. He could take them there as well as anywhere.

And dead was dead.

He trailed them through the forest, actually slowing a bit and watching as they neared the killing ground. This hunter's guide was slick and obviously knew the territory. Some five minutes had elapsed before he found the dead man who had donated his Colt AR-15 to Bolan's cause.

"My God!" the older Anglo said, standing above the corpse. "It's Blake."

The name meant nothing to Bolan, connected no dots in his mind. He ignored it, gliding into position some twenty yards from his targets, stooping to set the Remington on the turf, easing the Colt off his shoulder and raising it to aim, his thumb releasing the safety catch. The rifle felt familiar in his hands, from long nights on jungle patrol in Southeast Asia, from the many times that he had used an M-16 since then against a varied range of enemies.

The guide was drifting off, seeking another body, and it didn't take him long to find it. Bolan wondered if the Mexicans had been close friends, if there was any rage or sense of loss behind the dark, impassive face. Had this one's culture or his childhood training taught him to disguise his feelings in the presence of a gringo? When he said *"Aquí,"* and pointed to the second corpse, he might have been directing his companion's attention to a toadstool or an odd-shaped rock for all the passion he displayed.

"Both dead?" the hunter asked. His guide didn't reply, but there was no need for an answer when he saw the second body. Bolan watched him glance around, a superficial search for danger, and he asked, "What should we do?"

The Mexican responded with a shrug, unaccustomed to advising gringos on what course of action they should follow. He was studying the hunter's face when Bolan lined him up and shot him through the forehead, one round, quick but not so clean.

The 5.56 mm bullet left a tidy entry wound before it started tumbling, churning through the target's brain and punching a two-inch-square exit wound in the back of his skull. Dead before he ever knew what hit him, the Mexican flopped backward, sprawled beside his late associate, head to foot.

The hunter freaked. He spun and fired once from the hip with a bolt-action rifle, in Bolan's general direction. He was working the bolt for a second shot, still without spotting his target, when Bolan shot him in the chest and took him down.

The guy was dead when the soldier reached him, lying with his rifle—a vintage Winchester Model 70—across his stomach, still clutched firmly in his lifeless hands. Bolan let him keep it, since the weapon would add nothing to his present cache. At a second glance, however, he decided that the dead man's boots would fit him better than the pair he wore, and made the switch.

Eight up, eight down. The men who had shelled out at least a million dollars each to hunt him had seen the tables turned, and they were dead. That part of Bolan's job was finished, but he still had work to do. The worst of it, he realized, lay ahead.

Resigned to do or die, he turned and left the dead behind him, almost casual as he resumed his westward journey toward the island's one and only residence.

Toward Chelsea Rawlings.

Toward the hunters who were now the hunted, even if they didn't know it yet.

CHAPTER EIGHTEEN

The final burst of fire, another aught-six trading shots with Blake's AR-15, told Phelan all that he could hope to know about the action in the woods without going to see for himself. Blake would have reached the house by now, or sent his guide back at the very least, if he had killed Belasko in the first engagement where the Colt was heard. But he hadn't come back, and neither had his guide—which meant, at least to Phelan's mind, that Belasko now had the 5.56 mm and was using it against the other men who hunted him.

How many left?

There was no reason to assume that any of his clients were alive. The bowman, Estcott, might be out there somewhere, but if so, then he could damned well make his way back to the house on his own, without Phelan's help. At this point, it would be a blessing in disguise if none of them survived, no witnesses to carry tales about the superhunt that went to hell and wound up with the naked, unarmed quarry killing everything in sight.

Belasko hadn't made it yet, however. He was still light-years away from being home and dry. To leave the island, he would have to reach the motor launch tied up at Phelan's dock, and that meant he would have to fight his way through Shuker, through the three surviving Mexicans and through Adam Phelan himself.

Phelan was somewhat startled to discover that the thought appealed to him. He didn't mind the loss of clients who had paid him in advance, and who were now prevented from maligning him, disrupting any future business ventures he might organize. The Mexicans were nothing to him, hired help, outcasts in their own society and totally expendable. He didn't even mind if repercussions from the hunt forced him to leave the island and secure another hideaway in some other accommodating foreign land.

Phelan had never meant to spend his life here, on this rock, in any case. It was a hideaway and nothing more. Once it outlived its usefulness, as all things did, he would move on.

Before he started making travel plans, however, he would have to deal with Mike Belasko, and the prospect actually made him smile. It had been years since Phelan tried his skills against a truly worthy opponent. The hunts had been amusing, and immensely profitable, but they rarely challenged him.

Except, that was, within the past few days.

He thought back to Peru and Clifford Wix, the first time he had ever lost a client in the field. Now, within barely a week of that first calamity, it seemed that he had lost four more, and this time in his own backyard, on private turf. He blamed the run of sour luck on Belasko, stretching it to cover the Peruvian debacle, and convinced himself that he would never rest until he paid Belasko back in kind. In blood.

It was routine for superstitious peasants, like the Mexicans who served him here, to ward off curses and the "evil eye" with magic charms. When someone cast an evil eye on Adam Phelan, though, he had a very different cure. First, you gouged out the bastard's eyes, and then you ripped his head off, just to make sure that he got the point. It was a crude technique, but perfectly effective, and it never failed to satisfy.

He took his Steyr AUG and stepped onto the porch. "Be ready," he advised the shooter hiding there, and then proceeded into the yard, turning to face the sniper on the widow's walk. "Be ready!" Phelan called again, raising his voice, and waited for the Mexican to wave acknowledgment.

He didn't know exactly where Belasko was, how fast the man would travel, or how much time would elapse before he reached the house. All Phelan knew for sure was that his enemy would be there, probably sooner rather than later. It was guaranteed. A lead-pipe cinch.

Belasko would come looking for the woman. Never mind his martial skills, the fact that he had taken out six or eight men in the past four hours. He was still hog-tied by chivalry, committed to the rescue of a lovely damsel in distress.

And it would ultimately get him killed.

Phelan was counting on it. In fact, he was betting his life.

BOLAN APPROACHED the house with caution, wishing he could wait for nightfall, but he didn't feel that he could spare the time, dreaded the thought of Phelan and his sidekick getting bored or restless, maybe taking it out on Rawlings just for spite.

She was the chink in Bolan's armor, but at least he knew that going in. Sometimes, in combat, moral strength could be a weakness from the viewpoint of strategic planning. If a soldier fought for something personal then he could never truly be aloof, dispassionate. He placed himself at double risk, both physical and mental, never certain if his judgment had been clouded by a private need to win. His options were determined by the cause and not by common sense. He was committed to proceed, defying any risk, and might not even have the option of retreat.

Still, knowing that about himself was something. Once he recognized the problem, understood his danger, there were still a number of precautions he could take. And he could count on fury to sustain him, where a more detached combatant might be forced to wait and catch his second wind.

If Adam Phelan had the hostage and the odds, he still had no idea whom he was dealing with. Assuming that he guessed his paying guests were dead, Phelan would still assume that Mike Belasko had been lucky, dealing with a scattered string of amateurs. Despite interrogating Rawlings back in Stafford, Phelan still knew nothing of his adversary's background or experience.

If he had known, would it have made a difference? Bolan didn't think so. Adam Phelan struck him as a man who would be most reluctant to evacuate and leave loose ends—much less a living witness—unaccounted for. He would demand an ultimate solution that, if not exactly squeaky-clean, would still eliminate most of the danger to himself.

Although he had no wristwatch, Bolan judged, that it was coming up on three o'clock. He stopped as soon as he glimpsed the house, through the trees, and didn't move again until he had examined everything that could be seen. It wasn't much, but he made out a spotter on the roof, and took for granted that there would be other guards around, although he couldn't see them yet.

He could have tagged the rooftop gunner with his Remington, though it would be a dicey shot with open sights. Still possible, but Bolan didn't want to fire and thus alert the whole defensive force, unless he could be certain of a kill. There would be time enough for that when he was closer, when he knew more of the layout and had counted heads.

Bolan had been unconscious when they brought him to the house, sometime the previous night, and he had only seen the front of it when he was turned out for the hunt that morning. There had been no time to waste running around the property, stark naked and within an easy pistol shot of those who meant to kill him. He would now have to make up for that shortage of intelligence by recon before he moved against the soldiers in the house.

And he would have to pull it off without being seen, much less shot, in the process.

The forest served him well on his approach. He guessed that Phelan didn't have the manpower available to station roving sentries in the woods, but he remained alert, in case his guess was wrong. The rooftop lookout was a threat, of course, as long as he and Bolan shared a common line of sight, but he was handicapped by shadows in among the trees, and by the fact that he was forced to scan a full circle around the house from his elevated perch. At any given moment, he could only spare a glance in Bolan's general direction, and it would require some truly dramatic display in order for him to pinpoint Bolan's approach.

Instead of providing that signal, the soldier circled the house at an average distance of forty feet back in the woods. He moved erratically, waiting for the rooftop spotter to turn away before he proceeded, always keeping an eye out for other troops on the ground. The fact that he saw none didn't mean Phelan's house had been left undefended, though, except for one man on the roof. Instead, he marked the broad front porch, where one or several shooters could have been concealed behind a solid waist-high railing. Bolan noted the detached garage or workshop, with the large propane tank just behind it. Deliveries would be a bitch out here on the island, but if the tank was even partly full, he reckoned it could work to his advantage.

As he made his circuit, Bolan checked the windows, but saw only darkness or drawn blinds. He had a rough fix on the portion of the house where he and Chelsea Rawlings had been caged before he was released. Unfortunately, there had been no window, making it an inside room, and he would have to penetrate the house to know if she was still sequestered there, if she was even still alive.

Unless, of course, someone should bring her out.

It was a thought, and Bolan kept it in mind as he completed his circuit of the dwelling. His first move was obvious—the only move he could think of, in fact—and since he could make it from any angle, any side of the house, he decided to place himself at the northeast corner, where he could cover both the front porch and garage in back.

When he was in position, Bolan dropped his backup cartridge belt and propped the AR-15 against the tree he used for cover, close enough that he could reach it easily, without a major shift in position. If he needed it at all, then he would need it swiftly. A delay or any fumbling could prove fatal, once the shooting started.

Ready.

Bolan raised the pump gun to his shoulder, took his time in lining up the shot and gently squeezed the trigger, taking up the last three pounds of slack.

THE FIRST SHOT, when it came, made Shuker jump. He might have been embarrassed at his own reaction, but there was no time to think about it, just a loud crack from the woods, somewhere around the front side of the house, immediately followed by a loud thump on the roof.

Before Shuker had time to wonder what the second noise could mean, before he had a chance to recognize that he already knew, the thump was followed by a rumbling sound, as of some weighty object rolling down the near side of the gently sloping roof. Shuker was frozen at the window, staring outward, when the Mexican he had assigned to lookout duty on the widow's walk fell past him and collided with the ground. The dead man didn't bounce, but struck the earth as if his body were a boneless sack of meal or dirty clothes, somehow ejected from an airplane passing overhead.

The German bit off a curse, already turning from the window, scooping up his submachine gun from a nearby chair and moving toward the nearest exit from the house. He planned to go out through the kitchen, thereby saving time, instead of going twice as far to exit through the living room and thus emerge onto the front porch. He told himself his choice was a strategic one, allowing prompt access to what had now become a battleground. It had nothing to do with any fear of walking through the front door and emerging into hostile gunsights.

He wasn't a coward, after all.

An automatic weapon stuttered, firing from the same side of the house as the initial rifle shot. Shuker imagined it had to be the Mexican assigned to guard the porch, since none of Phelan's clients had gone out to hunt Belasko with full-auto weapons. It had to therefore be impossible for their intended quarry to have captured an assault rifle or SMG without intruding on the house itself.

Encouraged by the racket of defensive fire, whether it found the mark or not, Shuker reached the kitchen moments later, hesitating at the door while he decided whether he should exit cautiously or in a rush. The first approach was preferable if his enemy was still engaged out front, but it could get him killed if Belasko had a clear view of the kitchen door.

The hell of it, from Shuker's point of view, was

that the rooftop gunner could have been picked off from anywhere, from any distance that allowed a rifleman to aim and fire his weapon. It was difficult to place a single gunshot by its sound, particularly if the listener was indoors, while the shot was fired outside from some point yet unknown. The fact that Shuker's gunman on the porch was firing toward the trees could simply mean the Mexican was spooked, firing at shadows rather than at a solid target he could see.

Infuriated by his own delay, as if his very caution were a badge of cowardice, he flung the kitchen door open and leaped outside, running in a crouch toward the southeast corner of the house and the garage-workshop beyond. He needed cover, even if it put him farther from the battle for a moment. Once he reached the secondary building, he could roust the guard out, and the two of them could hunt down Belasko together. One of them could move in each direction, say, around the house, and meet in front if neither one of them encountered Belasko on the way.

It was a plan of sorts, but Shuker never had a chance to see it through. A few yards from the corner of the house, he veered off course and toward the detached structure, some thirty feet away. He didn't *see* the second rifle shot, of course, but Shuker heard it plain enough, and witnessed its result.

In front of him, the thousand-gallon propane tank was hit and detonated with a roar that deafened him. A blast of superheated air swept Shuker off his feet and slammed him backward, hard, against the house. He imagined that he knew how trousers felt inside a steam press as the breath was driven from his lungs and he collapsed into a gasping, gagging heap.

When he could see again, through singed eyelashes, Shuker found that roughly half of the garage was gone, either caved in or simply blown away, the rest of it engulfed by flames. The propane blast had sent a fireball lofting skyward, scorching trees that overhung the tank and outbuilding, while grass was charred and blackened almost to the point where Shuker lay, gasping for breath.

He was about to catch his breath, then lost it as a numbing shriek erupted from the heart of the inferno, followed shortly by a leaping scarecrow figure, all on fire from head to foot. The burning man cavorted briefly, falling twice and leaping up again, before he finally collapsed and moved no more, charred bits and pieces of his flesh or clothing dancing in the flames that hastily devoured him.

The grisly image forced Shuker to his feet, still short of breath. There was a panicky moment when he feared that he had lost his submachine gun in the blast, but then he found it, lying several feet away, and grabbed it on his way back to the kitchen door.

He needed time to think before he made another move outside. Before he wound up getting killed. Perhaps salvation lay with Phelan and the woman, after all.

Perhaps there was a chance to save himself.

THE PROPANE-TANK explosion did a better job than Bolan could have hoped. He had expected something in the nature of a slow leak, maybe dribbling flames that would amount to an explosion later, but the whole thing blew at once, taking much of the adjacent outbuilding along for the ride. He glimpsed a human figure lurching through the flames, devoured even as it stumbled clear, but there was no time for a mercy round to help the poor bastard.

By that time, he was under fire himself, an automatic weapon spitting from behind the waist-high wooden railing on the broad front porch. It might be incorrect to say the shooter had any specific target in mind, since he was raking the tree line in a full 180-degree arc, from left to right and back again. When he used up one magazine, the gunner dropped out of sight for a moment, reloaded, then came up firing again. One of his bullets came within a foot or so of Bolan, but the Executioner suspected it was more by accident than any grand design.

He could have left the shooter where he was, happily blazing away at the forest, but why take the chance? If this was truly Phelan's final soldier, next to Karl—and there had been no sign of any other gunmen yet—it would be foolish and potentially disastrous to let him live. Case closed.

He had two rounds left in the Remington, one in the chamber, and one in the magazine. Stepping from behind the tree that had sheltered him from the last spray of incoming fire, Bolan shouldered the rifle and made rapid target acquisition, framing the gunner's profile in his open sights. It was an easy shot from sixty feet away, but Bolan took the time to do it right, no rushing at the final instant that would spoil his aim.

The rifle bucked against his shoulder, and by that time death had raced downrange to find his adversary. The slug slammed through the shooter's starboard side, churning through vital organs on its way to exit from the left armpit. The Mexican went down as if someone had clubbed him with a sledgehammer, his submachine gun tumbling from lifeless fingers, clattering into the yard.

Three down, and if Phelan had any other native troops on his payroll, he was keeping them out of sight for reasons best known to himself. It seemed unlikely, after the exchange of gunfire, the explosion, the destruction of what looked like a detached garage. If there had ever been a time to field an army, it was now, but Bolan guessed that Phelan kept his house staff to a minimum. If anything, he reckoned, this was probably an unusual number of gunners to find on the island at any one time, their services hired for the hunt.

If he was right, that still left Karl and Phelan unaccounted for, plus Chelsea Rawlings. There was a possibility, he realized, that Phelan and his sidekick could have worked out from the gunfire that their clients weren't coming back and might have fled the island, leaving native troops to take the heat and buy some time. It didn't fit with what he knew of Phelan, though, not even if he killed the woman first. Phelan would want to see his adversary dead, might need to join the hunt himself before his craving for security was satisfied.

In which case, Bolan reasoned, he should be at home.

The house was still undamaged, from where the soldier stood. It could be scorched from the propane explosion, in back, but he saw no signs that the flames had spread to jeopardize the larger house. He also noted that the only vehicles in sight appeared to be two golf carts, painted olive drab, parked at the west end of the porch. From what he had observed, there were no roads of any consequence on Phelan's island, though a one-lane track of sorts led off westward, on a course that Bolan guessed had to ultimately lead to some point on the island's western shore.

It would be something to check out, if Bolan lived that long, but in the meantime he had work to do.

He propped the Remington against a tree and left its cartridge belt behind, buckling on the belt he had taken from the hunter named Blake, with its .45-caliber Browning autoloader, plus spare magazines for the pistol and AR-15. He still wore the captured shoulder rig, with the Beretta Model 96 Centurion beneath his left arm, two spare mags of .40-caliber beneath his right. When he picked up the Colt AR-15, he was as well armed as for most raids he had time to plan out in advance—except, perhaps, for want of hand grenades.

He had to check the house; that much was obvious. If it meant going room-to-room until he found his enemies, found Rawlings, that was what the Executioner would do. But first, of course, he had to find a way inside.

The front door beckoned him, and Bolan was aware of yet another entrance, to the rear. If he avoided both doors, there were still the windows, any one of which could easily accommodate a prowler, once the sash was raised. All Bolan had to do was choose an angle of attack and follow through.

He thought to hell with it, and started for the porch, hoping that the propane explosion would draw Karl and Phelan to south end of the house to check for any damage or potential spreading fires. Bolan had covered barely half the distance when he realized his hope had been in vain.

Instead of smashing out the window glass before he opened fire, as gunmen always seemed to do in Hollywood productions, Bolan's would-be killer fired directly through the windowpane, without a hint of warning. Bullets swarmed around him, several of them close enough for him to feel their heat, as Bolan hit the deck and started to return the gunner's fire.

And saw the problem right away. The waist-high railing that had sheltered Phelan's gunner on the porch now blocked his shot at the assassin in the window. On the up side, his assailant clearly had no view of Bolan, either, though he pumped a few rounds through the wooden barrier to try his luck.

No go.

It was a contest, now, to see which one of them could beat the clock. Digging in with knees and elbows, Bolan started lizard-crawling toward the front porch steps, holding the AR-15 ready, more or less, as he advanced.

And he was almost there, when he heard heavy footsteps clomping on the porch.

PHELAN KNEW he was dead if he tried to conceal himself inside the house. He didn't think the flames had spread from the propane explosion, though he wasn't sure, but any goddamned fool could set the house on fire and smoke him out. Would Belasko try it, knowing that the girl was still inside there with him?

He wasn't sure. His view of what the stranger would or wouldn't do, what he was capable of doing, had already undergone some radical revisions in the past few hours. Four clients and no less than half a dozen of his people dead, a total write-off on the workshop and garage. What would be next?

His answer came with yet another burst of automatic fire, this one accompanied by breaking glass. It sounded as if someone in the living room was firing outside, through the windows, and he knew it had to be Shuker. There was simply no one else remaining to defend the place.

And it was time to leave. He saw that now, regretting that he hadn't made the move an hour earlier, when he had first convinced himself none of his four clients would be coming back. The motor launch was waiting for him, some three-quarters of a mile due west. He simply had to grab one of the golf carts, motor through the woods along a fairly well-kept track and gun it for the mainland. If Belasko thought that he could make the swim, then let him try. Between the riptides and the sharks, Phelan could scratch another name off his enemies list.

He would be forced to take the girl along, at least halfway. She was insurance, just in case he met Belasko on the short run to the dock and had to bargain for his life. He didn't think Belasko would deliberately harm the girl to reach him—though, again, he couldn't be entirely sure. If Phelan gave the man a choice, watch Chelsea Rawlings die or let her tag along with Phelan for a drop-off on the mainland, how would he respond?

There would be no drop-off, of course. As long as Chelsea Rawlings lived, she was a prosecutor's wet-dream witness. Once he had her in the launch, a few miles out from shore, Phelan would shoot her and dump her overboard to feed the fish. No fuss, no muss. As for Belasko, on the island, it would be a simple thing to cancel any scheduled shipment of supplies and leave him there to die. It would take time for him to starve, with the supplies that Phelan kept on hand, and while he had no time or means to get rid of the food, Phelan could guarantee that anyone he left behind would have no contact with the outside world.

There were no phone lines from the mainland to the island, so he had relied on CB radio and mobile telephones for rare occasions when he felt the need to reach out and touch someone. Three telephones, one radio. It was a simple thing, five minutes' work for Phelan to retrieve them and reduce them to a pile of shattered scrap.

Well-done.

When Phelan entered Rawlings's room, he found her standing in the corner, back against the wall, dressed as he had brought her from the morning's briefing, in handcuffs and panties. Under very different circumstances, Phelan might have been aroused, excited by the vision she presented. As it was, she meant no more to him than walking Kevlar, a peculiar but effective life-insurance policy.

"Come on," he said, and stood aside to let her pass in front of him.

"Where to?" she asked defiantly.

"We're going for a boat ride," Phelan said.

"Like this?" She fairly sneered at him, and glanced down at her naked breasts. "I need some clothes, you know?"

"You *need* to understand that you have one shot at survival, and you'll blow it if you give me any lip at all." He raised the AUG and sighted on her sternum, just above her cleavage. "Are we clear on that?"

"I hear you," she acknowledged.

"Right. Then move your ass!"

She stepped in front of him, with no attempt to break and run. He prodded her along the hallway, letting her feel the Steyr's muzzle at her back, directing her to turn left, through the entry to his den.

"Okay," she said as she surveyed the room. "What now?"

"We're going out the window."

"Are you for real?"

"Believe it, babe," he said. "You do exactly as you're told, and you survive. One slipup, one false move, and I'll have no choice but to leave you where you fall. I hope we're clear on that."

"Crystal," she said, and somehow managed to make the word sound like a curse.

Phelan let it go, advanced to the window and swiftly unlocked it, hoisting the sash. When it was open, there was room for a large man to shimmy through.

"All right," he said. "You first."

"And how am I supposed to do this?" she asked him, rattling the handcuffs in a way that set her breasts to wobbling.

"Suit yourself," said Phelan. "Headfirst, feetfirst, pick your poison. If you need a boot, I'll help you out."

"No, thanks."

She stood and looked the window over for another moment, then ducked her head through, both hands braced on the sill, and tried to ease herself outside. It worked at first, but then the pull of gravity took over, dragging Rawlings forward, causing her to lose her grip. She scraped her legs and gave a little squeal before she hit the grass outside, her panties down around her knees.

"Goddammit!"

She was on her feet, with the bikini bottoms back in place, when Phelan cleared the window, pausing long enough to lower it behind him. There was no point leaving clues if it could be avoided. He cocked a thumb in the direction of the golf carts, some fifty feet away, and said, "Move out."

"You want to play a round before we go?" she asked.

He slammed an open palm between her shoulder blades and nearly made her stumble, driving her in front of him. Another burst of gunfire clattered from the porch, and Phelan wondered if they should just take off on foot, forget about the cart and hike to the pier. It wasn't all that far, and—

"Hey, they're shooting here!"

He slapped her hard across the back of her head. "Shut your mouth and keep it shut!" For emphasis, he jabbed the muzzle of his AUG against her spine and prodded her in the direction of the porch.

The carts were faster, he decided. All he needed was a fair head start. If they could only make it that far...

They were still some six or seven paces from the porch when Phelan saw a body tumble awkwardly across the railing, sprawling faceup on the grass beside the golf carts. Even with a bullet hole between the eyes, he recognized Karl Shuker.

And there was nothing he could do to stop it when the woman screamed.

THE SOUND OF BOOT HEELS on the porch was Bolan's final warning. He was up and on his knees a heartbeat later, blasting with his rifle, wishing that the AR-15 had a capability of automatic fire—or 3-round bursts, at least. The semiauto version was a leg up on the pump gun he had left behind, but his opponent's SMG still had a higher cyclic rate of fire, and that could sometimes make the difference in a pinch.

As Karl's face with its crown of ice-blond, crew-cut hair came into view, Bolan used it as a point of reference, firing through the porch rail's wooden face, aiming his rounds at where the German's legs and groin should be. He didn't know how many hits he scored, but Karl recoiled immediately, staggering, his face etched in a mask of sudden pain, and when he fired his SMG again, the rounds went high and wide, the weapon kicking back on him, out of control.

It was the moment Bolan had been waiting for.

A fluid surge of motion brought him to his knees, then to his feet, the rifle tracking as he followed Karl across the porch. This time, he only fired one shot, but it was all he needed, coring in between the German's cold blue eyes, slamming him backward in an awkward somersault across the rail.

Bolan had one foot on the porch steps when he heard a woman scream. It froze him where he stood for one heartbeat, then took him off in the direction of the sound. As far as Bolan knew, there was only one woman on the island. If she was close enough to watch Karl die and to react so volubly, she might be close enough to save.

He came around the corner in a crouch and saw Phelan at the golf carts, clutching Chelsea Rawlings by the hair, the muzzle of his Steyr AUG pressed tight against her cheek. The lady wore a pair of panties and familiar handcuffs on her wrists. The grim expression on her face was frozen somewhere between outrage and panic; there was no room left for anything so minor as embarrassment.

"You made it back," Phelan said. "That's a first."

"Your clients didn't."

"Small loss, if you stop and think about it," the hunter replied. "Can you think of anyone who'll miss them?"

"I don't know. We didn't get to know one another all that well."

"I guess that's right." Phelan was smiling as if he had all the time there was to make small talk with Bolan. "So," he asked, "how many people did you kill today?"

"Thirteen," said Bolan, "counting you."

"I'm not dead yet," Phelan reminded him, "but that's okay. I like a killer with a sense of humor."

"No one's laughing," Bolan said.

"In fact," the hunter continued, ignoring Bolan's last remark, "I'm so impressed, I've got a proposition for you." When the Executioner didn't respond, he forged ahead. "It would appear I'm short one business partner." He nodded toward Shuker's corpse. "I don't suppose you'd like to think about a change in your career path?"

"No, I don't suppose I would."

"We're left with a dilemma, then," Phelan said.

"I don't see it," Bolan challenged him.

"All right, I'll clarify. I have no plans for dying on this rock today. You want your bouncy little playmate back, but I'm the one who's got her. If you want her back alive, we need to talk about a deal."

"No deals," Bolan replied.

"See? You didn't think about it any longer than it takes for—oh, let's say, for any longer than it takes to pull a trigger. I suspect you wouldn't like it if I splattered little Chelsea's brains across the yard now. Am I right?"

"You'll never live to see her fall," Bolan replied.

"The question isn't whether you can kill me," Phelan said. "You've proved your skill on that score. No. The question is, my friend, if you can kill me quick enough to save your girlfriend's life."

"You're working from a false assumption," Bolan said. "I came for you, not her. It ends right here."

The hunter frowned. "Hear that?" he said to Rawlings, giving her head a shake. "Sounds like your white knight's got some rust spots on his armor. Looks like I'm wasting everybody's time, if this guy doesn't care what happens to you, either way. Say bye-bye, Chel—"

The echo of a gunshot cut him off, the hunter's right eye spilling blood, the other rolling up and back, as if to check the damage in his skull by peering backward through its socket. Phelan folded at the knees, his unfired rifle clattering beside him, but the fingers of his left hand kept their grip on Rawlings's tangled hair and pulled her down on top of him.

Three strides took Bolan to her, and although she fought him for a moment, cursing through her tears, she finally relaxed enough to let him pry the dead man's fingers free and help her to her feet.

"You would have let him shoot me, damn you!"

"You're alive," Bolan reminded her.

"Was that the plan? I mean, because you almost took my head off, when you shot—"

"It wasn't even close."

"You're pretty smug," she said, but with a tone that told him she was running out of steam.

"You need some clothes," he said, distracting her and bringing color to her cheeks.

Rawlings half turned away from him and folded her arms across her breasts. "I didn't pack for this," she said. "There aren't... I mean, I don't have any... Jesus! This is all I have, okay?"

"There must be shirts and pants inside. Let's check it out," he said.

"Go back in there? No, thank you, very much."

"Okay," he said. "You wait out here while I go check. I'll have to guess your sizes, but it should be fairly close."

"Like hell I'll wait! God knows who's wandering around this island, playing Daniel Boone."

He shrugged and said, "I honestly don't mind you going as you are, but it could cause some problems when we hit the mainland, don't you think?"

"What did you have in mind?" she asked suspiciously.

"I thought we'd take a little boat ride," Bolan said.

And watched her eyes light up as she replied, "You should have said so in the first place. Let's go find some clothes!"

EPILOGUE

The launch was waiting, unattended, when they reached the wooden pier and Bolan switched off the golf cart's motor. He wore a suit from Adam Phelan's closet, with a dress shirt from the dead man's wardrobe and a pair of new shoes on his feet. All things considered, Bolan would have said the fit wasn't half bad.

Rawlings had come up short on wardrobe, literally, given her stature. Both Phelan and Karl wore sizes that made her look small, almost dwarfish, when she tried them on before a full-length mirror in the hunter's private quarters. Finally, she had to settle for a denim shirt and blue jeans Bolan liberated from a duffel bag in the servants' quarters, apparently belonging to one of the housemen or guides. Bolan thought she looked fetching, like a sexy tomboy, but he kept the observation to himself.

The launch responded to his touch on the second attempt, and that was good enough for Bolan. He could see the rugged mainland to the west, and while the flat expanse of water made it difficult for him to judge the distance, their fuel tank was three-quarters full, more than enough to make the distant shore and back again, by Bolan's reckoning.

But he wouldn't be coming back. That part of it was settled well before they left the house of death behind.

"What will you do about the bodies?" Rawlings asked after they had finished dressing in their separate rooms and walked back to the golf carts, parked outside.

"I'll have somebody call the *federales* in a day or two," he told her. "They can sort it out and notify the next of kin."

"It's strange to think of all the families Phelan shattered with his little hunt club," Rawlings said. "I mean, on both sides of the game."

The only line that came to mind was a cliché about the chickens coming home to roost, and Bolan let it slide.

It felt good piloting the launch, the sea breeze in his face and blowing through his hair. It was still warm out on the water, but it felt as if the temperature had dropped some five or six degrees since they cast off.

"Will you be going back across the border right away, tonight?" she asked, when they were several miles from shore, the island fading in the dusk.

"I don't see any reason left to hang around," he told her honestly. "The more space we can put between ourselves and that—" he cocked a thumb behind him, toward the rock they'd fled "—the better off we'll be."

"That wasn't what I meant to ask, I guess," Rawlings said, lowering her voice until her words were barely audible above the engine noises of the launch.

"Okay," he said. "What's on your mind."

"I was just wondering... I mean, now that it's over, well, I don't suppose there's any reason we should ever see each other again.... I mean, forever."

"Forever's a long time," he told her, smiling.

"So, why does it feel like it starts the minute we hit land?"

"Could be you're still on eastern time," he said. "Some kind of jet lag kicking in. You need to cut your self some slack. Kick back and grab some R and R."

"Is that like FUBAR?" Rawlings asked.

"Not if you do it right," Bolan said.

"See, the problem is, I'm not much good at picking up new things. I'd need a coach or something, just to talk me through it, like."

"A coach," he said.

"Uh-huh. I wouldn't want to mess it up, you know?"

He made a show of frowning. "Well, I don't know how much downtime I've got coming. We might have to cram those lessons in," he said.

"Hey, cramming's good." Her smile was almost ear to ear. "I also like hands-on instruction."

It was Bolan's turn to smile. "Okay. One hands-on course in R and R," he told her, "coming up."